THE HUNT

Book 7 in the Lord Edward's Archer series

By Griff Hosker

The Hunt

Published by Sword Books Ltd 2023

Copyright ©Griff Hosker First Edition

A CIP catalogue record for this title is available from the British Library.

Contents

Real characters who are mentioned in the novel.

King Edward- King of England and Lord of Aquitaine and Gascony

Queen Eleanor of England

King Alexander of Scotland

Edmund Crouchback- 1st Earl of Lancaster and King Edward's brother

Thomas- 2nd Earl of Lancaster, son of Edmund Crouchback

Henry Lacy- Earl of Lincoln and Constable of Chester

Earl Marshal Roger Bigod- 5th Earl of Norfolk

Humphrey de Bohun- 3rd Earl of Hereford

Sir Reginald Grey- 1st Baron Grey of Wilton, Lord of Castell Rhuthun (Ruthin)

William de Beauchamp- 9th Earl of Warwick

Robert de Brus- 6th Lord of Annandale and Earl of Carrick

John Balliol- Lord of Galloway and Barnard Castle and, latterly, King of Scotland

John Comyn- claimant to the Scottish throne, supporter of Balliol and enemy to de Brus

Antony Bek- Bishop of Durham

Sir John de Warenne- 6th Earl of Surrey and John Balliol's father-in-law

Andrew Murray (Moray)- one of the Scottish leaders of the rebellion against King Edward

William Wallace- one of the Scottish leaders of the rebellion against King Edward

William Heselrig- Sheriff of Lanark

Robert of Béthune- Flemish leader of the attack on Damme

Henry Percy- 1st Baron Percy

Captal de Buch- Gascon mercenary leader

Henry de Beaumont- French Mercenary

Sir John Stewart- Commander of the Scottish bowmen at the Battle of Falkirk

Sir John de Graham- Wallace's second in command at the Battle of Falkirk

Sir John Menteith of Ruskie and Knapdale- Sheriff of Lennox

Arnaud de Gabaston- the father of Piers Gaveston

Piers Gaveston- a favourite of Prince Edward

Dedication

To Doctor Bob and Deri. Thank you for your hospitality. I hope to return it one day.

England in 1300

Prologue

It was ironic that the wound which affected me more than any other came from an arrow for I am an archer, an archer of some renown. I know that I was lucky that it hit my left and not my right arm but although the wound had healed, afterwards I had never felt confident about using it. When I practised with my son and my men at the meadow where we had permanent marks set up, I no longer felt happy when drawing the bow. It was stupid really as the left arm merely had to hold the bow in place while my hugely powerful right arm did the hard work. The arm had healed but it was in my mind that my left arm might fail me. Whatever the reason, from that first day back at the mark my son was able to send an arrow further than I could. I was proud, of course, but it was also a warning that I was ageing.

I had served King Edward since he had been The Lord Edward. I had been knighted and made a baron in thanks for my service. So far as I knew I was the only archer to have been thus honoured. I had followed my king on crusade and I had fought for him in every important battle. The ones in Flanders I regretted for they had not been of any purpose. I never fell out with the king but he knew that I was unhappy that he had taken his army into Flanders. It was the flexing of royal muscles. He still saw France as a land to which he had a right. I was more concerned with the borders. My wound had come about as a result of raids on my lands from Wales. The new Baron Mortimer had been impotent to save the lands from privations and it had been my archers and my handful of men at arms who had exacted revenge on the Welshmen.

The king and I had also disagreed about William Wallace. We had soundly defeated the man who had helped to humiliate the Earl of Surrey but instead of making his capture our priority, King Edward had dismissed him as a jumped-up brigand. That he may well have been, but he was a beacon of hope for the undefeated men who wished Scotland to be independent. The man I had hunted in the forests of Galloway was now, it was rumoured, in hiding and King Edward was doing as his father had done, and was fighting Parliament for the funds to pay his army.

I think the other reason I was in low spirits was that my most trusted men and leaders now lived far from me. Mordaf had married and was the master of my manor of Coldingham in Scotland. Others had either fallen in battle or hung up their hauberks. It added to my feeling of ageing. Increasingly, I was handing over power to my son, Hamo. That was no bad thing for he was everything a son should be. He had enjoyed

7

privileges denied to me growing up in the Clwyd Valley, and now married with children of his own, he would, in the fullness of time, become the Lord of Yarpole. Jack too, the orphan I had adopted and who was my squire, would also have a better life than he might have expected. He was becoming a good swordsman and my son and foster son complimented each other well.

My wife, Mary, was my rock, and it was she who would gently berate me, at night, when I grumbled my way to bed, "You have healthy children who are married and married well, at that. You have healthy grandchildren, and our manor is prosperous. We are both lucky and God has smiled on us. The wound to your arm does not stop you from being Baron Gerald of Yarpole and you are still Lord Edward's archer. It is a reminder that you are lucky and the arrow that struck your forearm could have ended your life. These words I now speak might be done, otherwise, to your effigy in our church. Think on that, Gerald Warbow and stop feeling sorry for yourself."

I kissed her and snuggled down. I was lucky and my greatest luck had come when I had stumbled upon Mary in the land of the Mongols. We had enjoyed an adventurous journey since that crusade. King Edward's touchstone, Queen Eleanor, had been taken from him. I thanked God that mine still lay in my arms.

Chapter 1

It was the loss of a castle in Galloway that prompted King Edward to march north once more and make war on the Scots. Lochmaben Castle was in Annandale and had fallen to the supporters of the Maxwell family. Sir Herbert had died at Falkirk and, so far as I knew, there was no lord in the castle of Caerlaverock. As we had learned with William Wallace, the loss of a lord was not important. Someone was making mischief. I had spent many years fighting both the Scottish and the Welsh and one thing I had learned was that while their leaders might not be the best, their ordinary fighting men were courageous and tough. They had stood in their circular schiltrons at Falkirk and fought until the end. The Scots were independent-minded and as the memory of the failure at Falkirk faded so the sparks of rebellion were kindled.

I did not know the pursuivant who rode into my yard with the message from the king but he knew me. "I am Richard of Craven and I served King Edward, my lord, at Falkirk. I witnessed the unleashing of your arrows." He handed me the sealed parchment. "The king has need of you again."

I handed the parchment to Jack. I would read it later. "And is your work here done? Will you stay the night? We have quarters."

He shook his head, "My lord, nothing would give me greater pleasure for I would love to hear of the battles you fought for King Henry and his son but I have been commissioned to visit Baron Mortimer and deliver his orders and then I ride to Chester where the muster will take place."

I knew that all would become clear when I opened the parchment but I also knew that Richard of Craven would be able to give me information that was not contained in the missive. "We go to the west coast of Scotland then?"

He looked at me with a surprised look on his face. Many men saw me as a hulking brute of a man, for the deformed body of an archer made monsters of men, but I also had a mind and that often came as a shock to men who met me. "Aye, my lord, but how did you know?"

I smiled, "Chester either means war against the Welsh or a war in the west of Scotland. I live in the borders and I know that the Welsh, for the moment, are quiet. We have caused them enough hurt to make the Welsh plot for the future."

He nodded, "Yes, my lord, you are right. The king's castle at Lochmaben has fallen. He goes to punish the Scots."

I closed my eyes as I pictured the area. I had been there when I had hunted brigands. It was Wallace's favoured ground. "Caerlaverock Castle then?"

He beamed, "You are right again, my lord." He glanced up at the sun. It was far to the west. "And now, my lord, I must ride before night. I shall see you, no doubt, at Chester." He mounted.

"No doubt."

After he had clattered over the cobbles I went inside the house. Mary had sent some wine, bread and cheese for she was a good hostess. "Sarah, tell Lady Mary that our visitor could not stay." I knew that she would have prepared a room and food for a small feast."

"Yes, my lord."

"Jack, fetch Hamo. This will concern him. I will open it when you return."

He bowed and hurried off. I poured some wine and using the knife in my belt cut off a hunk of bread and a piece of cheese. I poured the wine, not into the goblets that lay on the table, but into the wooden beaker. It suited me. I was on my second such cup when my son and foster son returned. There had been a time when I would have also invited a senior man at arms and the captain of my archers. This time it would be more of a family affair.

Hamo sat and poured himself a goblet. Jack, as usual, hovered, "Sit Jack, you are part of this family now and no longer serve the Lord of Malton."

"Sorry."

"And stop apologising." I knew I was becoming a grumpy old man.

As he poured his own wine, I sliced through the wax seal on the summons of service. The hand was not the king's. He had used a scribe but the signature at the bottom of the parchment and the seal were the king's. I read it aloud.

My Lord Warbow,

Know you that the rebellious Scots have taken Lochmaben Castle in Annandale. You are summoned to the muster at Chester Castle on the twenty-first of June, the year of our lord 1300. You are commanded to provide, as well as yourself and Sir Ralph of Wooferton, ten sergeants, each with at least two horses and forty archers, each of whom is to be a mounted man. Your service will be as long as is needed. There will be no scutage. You shall be paid three shillings a day, Sir Ralph the same, your

captain of archers two shillings, your sergeants a shilling and your archers the same amount.

My respects to your wife,

Edward

I put it down and smiled, "The letter would not read the same as that sent to Baron Mortimer."

Jack asked, "How so, my lord?"

"He asked after Lady Mary and we are to be paid more than is expected."

Hamo had been listening closely when I read the letter. He was clever and he was quick, "And it is more than the forty days we are required to give."

"Aye, but we are to be paid and as Captain of Archers you will be well rewarded."

He drank some wine, "Yet we have, thanks to the Welsh, just nine sergeants. Will we hire one?"

I shook my head, "I will not pay for mercenaries. Besides, you miscount." I smiled as I saw my son using his fingers. I gestured with my beaker, "Jack here can be a sergeant. We have mail for him and horses enough."

"Am I ready?"

"Only you can truly know that but I think you are. When we spar you can hold your own against me. You may not be of the standard of my other sergeants but this will be a siege. You will have time to learn. Your body still has growing to do but you are ready."

"You have no squire, Father."

"I need no squire and besides your wife's brothers, James and John, will come to war with us. They will be needed to keep the archers supplied with arrows but they can also tend to my horses."

The two boys had grown since coming to live with us. They both had muscular bodies and could draw a bow, but not yet a warbow. Taking them to Caerlaverock would be another part of their apprenticeship.

"Hamo, speak to the archers and let them know when they will be leaving. Their families need to be prepared. Jack, see the horse master and let him know the horses we shall need. I will speak to the sergeants."

My archers and sergeants were all yeomen too. Each had a plot of land or trade. Oswald the Bowyer and Ralph the Fletcher were two such. Ralph the Fletcher was too old to go to war. I had much to do before the muster. I would also have to ride to Wooferton and see my son-in-law Sir Ralph. That was no hardship as I would be able to see my granddaughter, Mary. The sergeants were all philosophical about the campaign. There would be no battle for it was merely a siege and that meant their horses would not be placed in danger. His mail apart, a sergeant's horse was his most valuable asset. We were lucky in that we had captured many coursers and my sergeants often rode horses that were the equal of any knight's. The drawback, as they saw it, would be the lack of loot. There would be few men in the castle to be ransomed and it was unlikely that they would profit. The shilling a day, however, was something. At the very least they would each earn forty shillings. None of them was badly off but, like me, had learned to make as much as they could while they were able. We had all seen too many archers discarded and abandoned when a wound took them or they became too weak to draw a bow. I rubbed my own scar unconsciously.

Wooferton was not far away and I had Scout saddled. Scout was not a warhorse but a good hackney. She was a mare and had produced good foals. She was easy to ride and her golden colour and shining mane drew approving glances from all. I would not take her to war. Ralph had been a landless warrior until King Edward sent him to me. Now he was a knight with two manors, one in Scotland and this, his most recent acquisition, close to mine. His stewards in Scotland, Stephen and Luke were local men and ran the manor well. Mordaf the archer had Coldingham which was mine and those two manors were a source of income for us. Ralph was in his yard with his squire, William. They were sparring and Joan was playing, in the shade of the hall, with Mary. Mary was three and since she could toddle and then walk had become a handful for my daughter Joan. However, I could forgive all that she did for I was her favourite. That was not a surprise as Ralph had no family to speak of and the only grandfather she had was me.

Squealing, "Anddad," she often missed the start of words, she hurled herself towards me and Scout. She was fearless but Scout was a well-trained and gentle horse. She stopped and Mary held up her arms for me to pick her up.

I dismounted and lifted her into my arms, "And aren't you the big girl?"

She giggled and threw her arms around my neck. She recognised my horse and shouted, "Cout!"

I knew that meant she wanted to ride on Scout's back. I sat her on the saddle and, keeping my arm around her back, put the reins in her hands. Once more she squealed with delight and I said, quietly, "Walk on."

Scout seemed to know that she had a precious passenger and placed her hooves gently on the ground. We walked over to her mother and father. All the time Mary was bouncing up and down on the saddle such was her excitement.

"More, more!"

Lifting her from the saddle I said, "Scout is tired and you are such a big girl. Next time you come to Granddad's I will let you ride with me."

That seemed to satisfy her and I placed her on the ground.

Joan came and standing on tiptoe, kissed my cheek, "How are you, Father? Is the wound healing?"

"It is." I nodded to Ralph and William. I was a blunt man and while I could waste words with my daughter and granddaughter, plainness was needed for Ralph. "Ralph, the king needs us in Scotland. We are mustered at the end of June."

Joan's hand went to her mouth and Ralph nodded, "Where to?"

"Annandale. It will be, I think, a siege and not a battle."

Ralph had no sergeants yet and only a couple of archers. "Do you need my men with you?"

I shook my head, "I have enough. Jack shall serve as a man at arms."

Joan looked shocked, "But he is just a boy."

"He shaves and he can fight. He is happy about it and there will be pay. You will receive three shillings a day. Perhaps that will enable you to hire men at arms. You need them, you know." I was criticising Ralph but I was trying to be gentle. Perhaps I was mellowing.

He nodded, acutely aware of how perilous life on the Welsh border could be. "I know it is remiss of me but there was much to do to make Wooferton a working manor. I hired yeomen."

"Then train them to be spearmen. If any show potential they can become men at arms. As I have learned farmers who can fight will survive. Those that cannot have an early grave."

We went indoors out of the early summer sun and I amused Mary until it was time for me to return to Yarpole.

That evening at the table we spoke of the manor of Wooferton. Margaret lived in Ludlow and her husband would not be called to war. He was a prosperous merchant and if my grandson, Gerald, was to become a soldier then it would be me who made him so.

"Should I invite Joan and Mary to come here to Yarpole whilst Ralph is away?" My wife always enjoyed having her children and grandchildren around the house.

"You could, my love, but as they have just begun to make the manor a working one she might not appreciate being away from it."

"But there are few men to guard the manor and the Welsh…"

"I will ask Ralph the Fletcher to go and stay there with a couple of our men. He can make arrows anywhere and he is fond of Joan."

Mollified Mary nodded. I looked at Alice, "And you, Alice, are you happy that your brothers go to war?"

She gave me a wry smile, "I would not use the word happy, Sir Gerald, but I am resigned to it. If their big sister stopped them from going to war then I would become a wicked witch in their eyes and besides I know that you and Hamo, not to mention Jack here, will keep a close eye on them."

I did not like secrets and brooding silences. I was a blunt man and expected others to be as honest with me as I was with them. Alice was a good wife to Hamo and he had made a wise choice.

Preparing for a campaign of more than forty days meant that we had much work to do. Panniers had to be made for the sumpters. We would need spare bows and sheaves of arrows. Mail would have to be repaired. I had no weaponsmith but my blacksmith, Bob Strongarm, knew how to repair armour and keep a good edge on swords. My mail had been damaged and I had yet to have it mended. Jack's hauberk would have to be adjusted so that it fitted. We had spare helmets and they were brought from the storage shed that passed as an armoury. Every man who went to war would have one. Some of my archers chose not to wear one but they all had the choice. Old buskins were replaced by new ones. Blankets were cleaned and cloaks oiled. My archers, with my permission, went into the woods of Yarpole and Luston to hunt deer. Much of the meat would be dried. When we were on campaign the dried meat would keep us going and it could be placed in a pot with greens to make a hot meal. We knew how to campaign. My men would not desert because of hunger and lack of food. We planned ahead. Horses were shod and horse furniture renewed. The last thing we needed was for a stirrup to break at the wrong time. None of our horses would wear armour. We would not need it. The winter oats and barley were bagged and would be on the new panniers to augment whatever grazing we could find. Water, ale and wineskins were checked and, if necessary, replaced. The time to the muster passed all too quickly.

Chester was two days from us and we left just after dawn when the air was cooler. This was England and not the hot lands of the east where I had ridden with the Mongols, but the lessons learned there persisted and we would rest when the sun was at its zenith to save the horses from fatigue. The night before we left we all dined at my house. Only Margaret and her family were absent. It was a joyous occasion for with the two grandchildren playing and laughing how could it have been otherwise? The boar that had been hunted gave us plenty of food and a haunch to take with us for the road.

The last night at home Mary cuddled in close to me, as we lay in the last comfortable bed I would have for the foreseeable future, "Watch over Jack, Ralph and Hamo, husband, but also yourself. The arrow that struck you was a warning. Heed it."

I sighed, "Men who fear that death will come are the ones who die. I was unlucky. I know that I could be unlucky again but I have had a good life, have I not?"

I heard the intake of breath and felt the fingers tightening around my arm, "You could live another hundred years, Gerald Warbow, and it would not be enough for me. I did not meet you soon enough and I want to make the most of every day that we spend together. Come home and come home alive."

I laughed, "And in that, my sweet, we are in perfect agreement."

Mary never wept when I left to go to war. She would miss me and there might be tears but they would be at night when she lay alone in bed and prayed to God for my safe return. Standing in my yard she held my grandson, John, in her arms and they waved at his father and me as we led my column of men north. We made a fine sight. None of us wore mail but our bright, freshly washed livery was not yet faded by the sun. My banner and the banneret of Sir Ralph fluttered in the slight breeze. The horses had been groomed and their coats shone. Our boots and buskins gleamed as did our scabbards and leatherwork. That would change. A campaign took its toll but as we rode through Yarpole we were cheered by the villagers. For the next twenty miles or so we would be welcomed by villages who knew the worth of Gerald Warbow and his men. Once we left the land that I protected, we would receive smiles and questioning looks. The land would not know of the muster. Most of the men who would be coming to fight for King Edward would be from the north. The great lords from the south and the west who followed King Edward would ride up the great road from London, the one built to take the Romans to Wales. We would cross that road closer to Chester.

For James and John, Alice's brothers, this was exciting beyond words. They had carried our banners back from the battle of Luston but this was different. They had leather brigandines and small pot helmets hung from their saddles. They were riding to war. They were youths and although they were big boys, they both rode small horses. They each had a saddle and while it did not have the high cantle of a warrior's saddle, they were able to ride with the archers. For my archers and men at arms, this was familiar territory. They were, until we reached the borders, in a land that was free from ambush and danger. They joked and bantered. Each saw the others when we practised at the mark each Sunday or sparred with swords but that was always a time to hone their martial skills. The ride north was the time to gossip, to talk of their families and to remember the dead. William of Ware's brother had died when the Welsh had raided and it was still a painful memory. However, the men spoke of him for his courage had saved the villages of Luston and Yarpole. Warriors died but those who fought with them never forgot.

Jack carried my banner and rode with Ralph's squire. I rode flanked by Ralph and Hamo. They spoke across me and I listened. I had never been the garrulous type.

"This castle that was lost, it must be important for the king to take an army to punish the Scots." Ralph was the one who was the newcomer.

Hamo knew the king better than Ralph and he shook his head, "It is pride, Ralph. The fall of any Scottish castle tells the king that the Scots are not yet ready to be subjugated by England."

"Will there be a battle?"

I snorted, "The Scots won the Battle of Stirling Bridge because of an accident. Had King Edward or I been there then Murray and Wallace would not have won. The Scots will not risk another Falkirk. The Maxwell clan see themselves as possible kings of Scotland although they have no claim to the throne. They took what was probably a weakly defended castle and when we reach Galloway will either take to the forests or hide behind the moated walls of Caerlaverock Castle."

Hamo nodded, "We fought Wallace in those woods and their winkling out took time. I would rather it was a siege for then we do not waste horseflesh seeking out an enemy."

"Caerlaverock is a mighty castle, Hamo."

He nodded and seeing Ralph's questioning look explained, "It is a three-sided castle and is surrounded by water. The only entrance is across the water and through a well-made barbican. It cannot be mined. We will need to use trebuchets to take it."

I added, "And they will need to be constructed. We will earn at least thirty days' pay even if the castle falls quickly. Remember, Ralph, to use your pay to hire sergeants. I am still an archer but even I have sergeants. When King Edward demands service from you he will expect sergeants. You have two manors. For the moment my presence takes some of the burden from your shoulders but one day you will be expected either to hire sergeants or supply them. Ones trained by you are better than mercenaries you do not know."

16

The Hunt

That first day we rode just thirty miles and using my name obtained accommodation in Shrewsbury Castle. The castle had been important. Stephen had besieged it and Llewelyn the Great had occupied it eighty-five years earlier. King Edward's new castles had made it largely irrelevant. There was a castellan and just six men at arms. My men had to clean out the quarters we took. The walls had not been maintained and, in places, had fallen into disrepair. Only the donjon was fit for purpose. The old castellan, who was almost sixty years of age, took the opportunity to plead with me to ask King Edward to attend to its repair. I said I would do so but I knew that the reality was the king did not have the funds to do so. Parliament had tied his hands. The wars with Scotland had been expensive and the rewards poor. We had not taken the loot we might have done had it been a French war. The Stone of Scone was a trophy, that was all.

We reached Chester and the muster in the late afternoon. We had not pushed our horses for we still had many miles to travel. The king's banner flying from the tower told me that he had arrived, but we were directed to a campsite outside the walls of the city by the river. It was the place the Romans had raced their chariots. A boggy place, it already stank of horses and excrement as we pitched our tents and made our hovels. The sooner we left the better.

Chapter 2

It was Richard of Craven who fetched me just after we had arrived. The king had been informed that my banner was close. Hamo and Ralph looked to see if they were needed too. I said, "Richard, do I go alone or shall I bring my son and son-in-law?"

Richard of Craven looked uncomfortable, "The king just asked for you, my lord."

"That means a feast with the high and the mighty." I shook my head, "You two will have the better of it. Do not save food for me."

As Richard had walked to fetch me, I walked back to the city walls with him. Our horses had ridden enough, and the walk was not a long one. King Edward had improved his royal castle. The moat was well maintained and there was a barbican with portcullis. I saw that the two new drum towers were well made. It was a bastion and King Edward was making a statement. If the Welsh decided to rebel again they would find it harder to take than the last time.

The other lords were already seated and the feast was well under way. Richard took me to speak to the king. I saw that there was no place for me to sit close to him and I would not be having a conversation with him. As I passed, I identified the other lords. They included Henry de Lacy, Earl of Lincoln; Robert FitzWalter; Humphrey de Bohun, Earl of Hereford; John, Baron Segrave; Guy de Beauchamp, Earl of Warwick; John of Brittany, Earl of Richmond; Patrick, Earl of March and his son, Prince Edward, Thomas, Earl of Lancaster, and his brother Henry; Richard Fitzalan, Earl of Arundel; and Antony Bek, Bishop of Durham. Many of them nodded as I passed and I acknowledged them. The man I did not see was Baron Mortimer. Had he hired another to take his place or were his orders to protect the border in my absence? I suspected the latter.

The king was seated between his son, the young Prince Edward and Bishop Bek. King Edward dismissed Richard and gestured for me to bend my head to allow him to speak to me, "I am glad that you are here, Warbow. I shall need your archers. I will send Richard of Craven to your camp at Prime. I need to speak privately to you. For this night get to know some of those with whom you will be campaigning. There is a place for you yonder." He pointed to a table which was as far from the important nobles as it was possible to be. I was still the archer who had made the unlikely rise to knight.

"Yes, King Edward."

18

The king did nothing without thought and I found myself at the end of a table with two Breton knights and two Scotsmen. The Bretons assiduously avoided speaking with me and as I tried to work out how soon I might excuse myself and rejoin my men one of the Scotsmen spoke to me, "You are Sir Gerald Warbow?"

"I am and by your accent, you are a Scotsman. There is a tale here, I am sure."

He smiled, "I am Sir John Menteith and I fought against you at Dunbar."

"That was some time ago, Sir John."

More food was brought and as I sliced some of the wild boar he nodded, "Aye, I was held for ransom for a year and when I was released, I served in Flanders with the king."

"I was there too but I do not remember you."

He laughed, "And I was at Falkirk with the king but I was keen not to be noticed too much. My countrymen, misguided though they are, do not take kindly to turncoats. I saw you and admired what you did both in Flanders and at Falkirk."

I began to see how King Edward was spinning webs. My seat at this end of the table was deliberate. "And will you fight in this campaign, my lord?"

He shook his head, "I am to be Constable of Lennox. The king wants a tame Scotsman to keep his subjects in order."

I wondered then if the reason I had not noticed the knight was that he was avoiding fighting against his countrymen. There was something about him that I did not trust. Many Scottish nobles had signed the infamous Ragman's Roll after King Edward had defeated the Scots. They had sworn allegiance to King Edward. This one, Sir John, had gone one step further. As Constable of Lennox, he controlled the land north of Glasgow and the road to Stirling. I would have expected it to be given to a loyal English noble.

I was curious about the other man and I said, "And you, sir, did I fight against you also?"

"I am Simon Fraser and the son of the Sherriff of Peebles. Aye, Baron, I fought at Dunbar. Now released and penniless I have taken the king's shilling to fight against my countrymen." He shrugged, "I am a warrior and I need the pay. Scotland has lost its leaders."

The words of the two renegade Scotsmen did not fill me with confidence. I knew that King Edward liked to use former enemies as a means of demonstrating his power but it seemed to me to be a mistake. For the rest of the feast, I listened rather than spoke for I knew that the king had put me here for a reason. As soon as the king left so I departed and after bidding farewell to the Bretons and Sir John I headed back to my camp. There were others who had been allocated the bog for a bed and we walked together, through the gates of the city to our camps.

"I have eaten better food." The Breton next to me had been seated at another table.

"It will be much worse on a campaign."

He nodded, "I will stay close to your archers, Sir Gerald, for I hear they are fine hunters."

"They are that but I fear we will be hunting the Scots rather than the deer."

He shrugged as we neared the tents and the smell of woodsmoke, "These are Scots, and, as such, easy to defeat. There will not be much treasure but as I will not be risking my horse the pay will be useful."

He was, like many of the Bretons, here because of scutage. He had been paid by another to fight in his place.

We parted as we neared my camp. Hamo had set guards and they stiffened until I waved a farewell to the Breton. "Did you eat well, boys?"

"That we did, Sir Gerald. The haunch of ham made a fine stew. And you?"

"The food was adequate but…"

Tom laughed, "Aye, Frenchmen for company."

Hamo and Jack had made my bed and after disrobing, I rolled into my blankets. The campaign had started.

I had the night watch wake me early and I dressed quickly. King Edward wanted to see me at Prime and he was not a man to brook delays. I thought there might be food but I had a drink of ale and a bite of the stale bread we had brought from Shrewsbury. Richard of Craven arrived just as I was about to leave. He smiled, "You are prompt, my lord."

I grunted, "I know the king of old. Come." As we headed towards the town I asked, "Will there be breakfast?"

"I believe so, my lord."

"Good."

We were waved through the town gates and the barbican. Richard took me not to the Great Hall, but a solar in one of the new drum towers. There was food and a beaker of ale for me. "Thank you, Richard. See that we are not disturbed." Richard would have to wait for his provender. "Sit, Warbow. You and I have endured enough together without waiting upon rank. Eat."

"Thank you, my lord."

We were both warriors and we ate before speaking. When the king had eaten enough, he wiped his fingers on his napkin, downed some ale and then put his fingers together almost as though at prayer. I knew he did this when he was thinking. "So, Warbow, what did you think of the Scotsman?" I raised an eyebrow. "I want honesty as always. Do not try to read my mind. Give me your opinion."

I wiped my mouth and my fingers to give me thinking time, "Well, my lord, he knew me but I could not recall him either from Flanders of Falkirk. That means he was not at the forefront of either fight. He was ransomed but I cannot see why your majesty favoured him with Lennox."

"You do not trust him."

"I trust no Scotsman, my lord. I have yet to meet one that I could trust."

He smiled, "You make a bad enemy, Warbow."

I nodded, "It is in my nature and you cannot change your nature, can you, my lord?"

"And that is why I keep you close. I do not trust him either. He followed me to Flanders and yet, as you say, did nothing. I watched him at Falkirk and he was always just a few paces further away from the pikes of his countrymen. Had I examined his sword at the end of the battle it would have been without blood and razor sharp."

"Then, why, King Edward, do you keep him close? Is it because you do not trust him?"

He shook his head, "The man is a friend of Wallace as well as Robert de Brus and William Wallace is still the biggest threat to our rule in Scotland. I hope that he will lead me to Wallace."

"And that is why he is constable of Lennox." He nodded and sipped some wine. "Excuse me, my lord, but why tell me? I am flattered but..."

"I am coming to that. When we have dealt with these rebels in Annandale, I want you to take a small group of men and hunt down Wallace." My mouth must have dropped open for the king smiled. "It is rare that I can surprise you, Warbow, I am pleased to have done so."

"King Edward, the world is wide and we know not where he is."

"He is not in Scotland, that much we know. There are rumours that he is in Rome or perhaps France."

"That hardly helps, my lord."

He sighed, "Warbow, you found Wallace in a forest and his size and shape have not changed. He is a giant of a man and he likes himself. He will not be hidden. He will be trying to drum up support for Scotland. The French are always keen to interfere in England."

21

I could see that I was getting nowhere. I would have to accept the Herculean task but I still had questions, "And when I find him, what then?"

"Bring him back so that he can stand trial and then I can hang, draw and quarter him."

That meant he would be given a traitor's death. I was silent for I knew I would need to choose my men carefully for this. I dared not take too many yet the ones I did take would have to be the best.

I was silent for so long that the king spoke before I had time to voice more concerns, "You will, of course, be paid and there are other considerations. I will make Yarpole and Luston both hereditary titles. Your son and grandsons will inherit in both Yarpole and Luston."

I had not thought of that but it would not make much difference to the task. "First, we end the rebellion, my lord?"

"That is vital. I want prisoners who will provide information about Wallace's whereabouts. When that is done return to Yarpole, put your affairs in order and disappear. I will have a warrant written for you. It may help in those parts of France that are still loyal to the crown but if you are found in France or hostile land then you will be on your own."

"That is understood, my lord."

He beamed, "Good, then all is well."

I decided to be blunt with him, "Not really, my lord, for it seems to me that I am either doomed to failure or, more likely, death. I have enemies abroad while Wallace has friends."

"Warbow, you do this for England."

I nodded. I also knew that I could tell no one what I was about until I had chosen the men who would go with me.

"When do we leave for Scotland, my lord?"

"On the morrow."

I stood, "Then we have preparations to make."

He also stood and towered over me, "The Queen always thought of you as her favourite, you know?"

It was an olive branch, of sorts and I nodded my acceptance, "And I thought her the finest of ladies, and that includes my wife, my lord."

"Aye, we were both lucky in the loves of our lives." He paused, "Do you need Richard?"

I shook my head, "I can find my own way back to the camp, my lord."

I needed time to think and I also needed my men to concentrate on one task at a time. I forced my face to mask my mind. "We leave tomorrow. Use the local market to buy anything you think that they have that we might need."

William of Ware nodded. Since his brother's death, he had grown into the role of leader. I did not doubt that he still brooded about arriving too late to save him but it had not affected his work. "The cheeses here are good and keep a long time."

Hamo, Ralph and Jack joined me, "Well, Father? What did the king want?"

I decided on a version of the truth which would explain why I had been seen alone, "He said that as we caught Wallace in the forests close to where we will be campaigning, he wants us to look for signs of him."

Hamo laughed, "And the last place that William Wallace will hide will be close to where Warbow and his archers hunt."

I nodded, "But we can look for signs. Remember that was where he had great support. Even if he is not there, we might find others who are part of the rebellion. The sparks need to be snuffed out sooner rather than later. At the moment there is no real heir to the Scottish throne and the king would keep it that way."

The answer seemed plausible and they accepted it but I did not like the lie on my lips.

I spent the rest of the day finding old comrades who were also going to be on campaign. Few were nobles but there were many archers and men at arms alongside whom I had served. We sought each other out and shared what we knew. Our leaders would come up with the grand strategies but they would be made to work by men like me. I learned that less than half of the men with us had fought in Scotland before and that was worrying. I also learned that King Edward had brought eighty-seven English barons with him. He was making a bold statement to both the Scots and English. The taking of Lochmaben Castle might have appeared to be insignificant but King Edward was letting all of Scotland know that any rebellion would be dealt with by a hammer and a mighty one at that. The nobles I had seen at the feast, Bishop Bek of Durham apart did not impress me. Prince Edward was just sixteen and yet I had heard his voice carry across the Great Hall boasting of what he would do to the Scots. Some of the other barons who had travelled with King Edward spoke of how he was gathering about him young men who seemed eager to impress the future King of England. As I recalled King Edward had never been like that. True, at Lewes, he had been reckless but that was because he was trying to win the battle and impress his father. Prince Edward would require some watching.

The meal with my men was of plainer fare than the rich sauces served in Chester Castle but the company of my men was more preferable. We did not carouse late and the sun had barely set when we retired. Richard of Craven had brought the details of the order of march and I had seen that we were to be the vanguard. For the journey to Lancaster that would mean little and even the ride to Carlisle would be without threat but once we crossed the river at Carlisle we were in the borderlands. As a result, I determined that we would ride at the start as we would at the end. As Bishop Bek was to command the vanguard I knew that I could impress upon the bishop the need for my men to be the ones who were at the fore.

By the time the king and his retinue emerged from the castle my men and I were already mounted. The men with the sumpters would wait until the rest of the vanguard had formed up and join the small baggage train that would follow them. Bishop Bek had already emerged and he had his knights rouse the rest of the van. I saw his wry smile when he saw us leading our horses to the road, "No matter how organised I think I am, Sir Gerald, there is always much to learn from you. Did you and your men sleep?"

"Of course, my lord, but we retired early. This is war." I waved a hand at the castle, "The feasts within those walls should be kept for the days after the victory."

"Do not let the king hear that, Sir Gerald."

"I am no fool, my lord, but the king knows me as well as any and he knows that I do not approve of feasting before the fight."

Some of those clustered around Prince Edward had the sorry look of young men who have tried to keep up with trenchermen. King Edward, in contrast, looked to be as bright-eyed as any. He turned to Henry de Lacy, the Earl of Lincoln and pointed to me, "There is a professional soldier, my lord. While the rest of the army rouses itself Sir Gerald Warbow and his men are ready for the day. My hunting dogs are ready to ride. I would that the rest of our men were as keen."

The earl said, "We can try to emulate him, my lord, but he has forgotten more about war than we shall ever know."

The king nodded, "Warbow, take your men four miles up the road and await the bishop there."

"And our first bivouac, King Edward?"

"Burscough Hall. The thirty odd miles there might sober up the young men who cannot hold their wine." He smiled at me, "You and your men will do better. As ever the men led by Warbow know how to fight and how to behave."

"They know they would suffer the sharp edge of my tongue if they did not."

Almost as an afterthought, he said, "We shall not have to build siege engines. I have my fleet ready to carry the preprepared pieces to the Solway Firth. Just give me an idea of where the opposition will be and I shall do the rest." The king made no allusion to my secret mission and to the army it would appear that we were just being used, as he said, as hunting dogs.

I nodded. The hall had belonged to the de Ferrers family. When King Edward's father had stripped the title of Earl of Derby from de Ferrers the hall was taken by the crown. As I recalled it was not a large hall and men would need to camp. As we would be the first to arrive it mattered not to us. We would have the first choice of good grazing, water and wood for hovels.

We headed for the crossing of the Mersey at Wallintun. The crossing would slow the progress of the huge metal snake that was King Edward's army and explained why he only planned for a thirty-mile ride this first day. We would be the first across and whatever was in Wallintun to be bought, we would have. I would not be with the baggage or the rearguard; there you rode in men's dust and picked your way through their animals' excrement. The vanguard was more dangerous but we preferred the danger.

Burscough was a small hall but there was plenty of grazing. The men who worked the land, for the king, had already gathered the crops harvested in spring and the land was fallow. They would not object to our horses fertilising the fields with their dung and we found a wood-lined stream where we could camp. Bishop Bek went into the hall. I knew that the nobles when they arrived, would seek out a roof over their heads. By the time the king arrived, with the mainward, our food was already cooking. He was in deep conversation with his senior lords. I knew that messengers had arrived the previous day from Scotland. They would, no doubt, bring the latest intelligence.

The sun set late at the end of June and it was still dusk when Richard of Craven sought me out, "My lord, King Edward has need of you. He will meet you at the horse lines." He saw my surprised look and shrugged, "He wanted privacy and the hall is packed to the rafters. A man cannot hear himself think within the walls."

The king was alone but four of his household knights stood close by, "Give the baron and I some space." They dutifully moved away and the king continued, "Warbow, I have conflicting intelligence from the borders. I know not what to believe. There are some Scottish lords who obfuscate and deceive me and the English knights seem to be confused. I want you to ride to Annandale and give me an accurate opinion. We will reach it in four days. You should be there in two. When we reach Carlisle, I will await your news."

"Yes, my lord."

With that, he turned and headed back to the hall. I suppose I should have been flattered that he knew me so well that he gave so little information, trusting me to complete my task.

He turned and said, as an afterthought, "Take the pursuivant with you. I shall not need him and as Craven is close by you can use him as a messenger should that be necessary."

Richard of Craven stopped and headed back to me. He gave me a big smile, "This shall be an adventure, my lord."

I shook my head, "Not dressed like a popinjay." I gestured at his brightly coloured livery. It was useful on a battlefield but we would be hiding. "You have plainer clothes?" He nodded. "Then wear them and find an old brown cloak. We need to escape notice. This may be an adventure to you but my men will not thank you if you cause them to be seen. Watch, stay hidden and learn."

We reached my camp and I said, "We leave before dawn. We are no longer the vanguard, we are King Edward's eyes."

The news made all of them happy. Being tethered to the army was not something that they enjoyed.

Chapter 3

We rode hard and reached Carlisle the next day after stopping at Kendal. The horses were still fresh but once we reached the borders they would need to be coddled. We frequently changed them. Richard of Craven was forced to buy a remount at Kendal for he alone had just one horse. He used his warrant from the king to do so. Once we reached Carlisle I met with the High Sheriff of Cumberland, John de Lucy. "Is there more news of the Scots, my lord?"

The knight shook his head, "Not since the survivors from Lochmaben arrived."

"You have not sent men to spy out the enemy?"

He gave me a stern look, "Of course I have. None of them have returned. I have lost eight good men and I will lose no more."

Now I understood the lack of usable intelligence, "I am sorry, my lord, I did not know. King Edward just said that he had little information."

"I know that he will be unhappy with the situation but we have a small garrison here and this is a most dangerous border. The east coast has many bastions to defend England from the rapacious Scots: Bamburgh, Norham, Alnwick, Warkworth, Morpeth and Prudhoe. Here, there are just two, Carlisle and Brougham. Dumfries still holds out but unless they are relieved soon then that castle will fall also."

I nodded. He was not quite right about there being just two castles, for Bowes was also a protection but I understood his fears. In the east, there were layers of protection and here they were vulnerable.

"We will stay for one night, with your permission, my lord. We would also like to leave the sumpters with our spare horses, tents, mail and arrows. We want to be able to move fast."

He nodded, "Of course, but then what?"

"The king and the army will be here in a day or two and as the last part of the journey will be through land devoid of accommodation, he will be looking forward to a bed chamber and good food."

"I know that Baron, I meant you."

"We will do as the king has ordered and scout out the border so that he has intelligence that will enable him to put down this rebellion quickly."

"You do not fear the brigands and the rebels?"

"When I was last here, before your time, my lord, we scoured the forests of Wallace and his bandits. It is we who will be feared and not the other way around."

"I see. I fear that if King Edward wishes to stamp out all rebellion, then he had best use the forests to hang every Scotsman. In my experience, none of them will bend the knee."

I did not use any local men this time. I had enough men who had grown up around here and both James and John had local knowledge. We left before dawn, the Sherriff himself seeing that we slipped silently from the castle to head across the river and into what was still a rebellious Scotland. We had arranged the formation as we saddled our mounts. Gwillim and Dick would be the scouts. Half of my archers would follow them led by Hamo. I would lead William of Ware and the sergeants. Jack would ride next to me, along with Ralph and his squire. Behind us would ride Richard of Craven and then the last of my archers as well as John and James. Richard had been useful in the land north of Lancaster and we had eaten well there, but once we had passed Kendal then he knew nothing of the land through which we passed. I began to realise that the king had sent him as a spy so that, if he survived, he could tell the king what I had done. Richard was an innocent and knew nothing of this. He was just honoured to be chosen to ride in such an elite company. It was my knowledge of the king that led me to that conclusion. It was not that he mistrusted me, it was in his nature to control things. I did not mind but now that we were close to danger, I wanted the pursuivant to be as safe as possible.

We first crossed the Eden, which was as nothing and then headed north and east towards the Esk. We went to the ford east of the place where the Lyne joined the Esk. Lochmaben lay to the north and west. As soon as we had crossed the Esk I set sentries and we dismounted. We were travelling light and that meant we moved quickly. We would be eating cold rations and sleeping in hovels but I did not anticipate spending longer than a day or two in the area. We tightened girths and with just arming caps and coifs for the sergeants we rode to cross the shallow Kirtle Water and then headed for Annan Water. We had a good twenty-mile ride from the ford to the castle and as we used the rivers and woods it was not a quick journey. This far north the nights were hardly deserving of the name and we stopped frequently. About an hour before the sunset, I halted in some woods. The old motte and bailey castle of Lochmaben lay just two miles north of us.

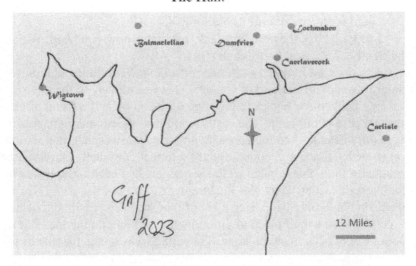

I sent two men to spy out the castle while the rest of us rubbed down our horses and laid our blankets on the ground. We would not need hovels but a fire would have helped to keep the flying, biting insects from plaguing us. The scouts returned to tell us that the castle was occupied and the gates barred but there was no one betwixt us.

"The walls and the donjon are made of wood, my lord. It is an old castle and I can see why it fell so easily." Gwillim was a wise old warrior.

I held a council of war.

"We need sleep and the horses need rest. Caerlaverock is less than twelve miles from us and that is where the enemy lies in strength. The men sent from Carlisle were all taken or killed before they could report back and that means there are watchers. I intend to scout out the castle and, if we can, take prisoners."

The two scouts had been Gwillim and Dick. Gwillim said, "We could take the castle, my lord. I can see why the Scots took it so easily. It must date from the time of the Conqueror."

I shook my head, "I do not rule that out but let us be cautious. The last thing we need is to alert the rebels to our presence."

Jack asked, "Sir Gerald, how is it that the Sherriff's scouts were found and we were not?"

"How many roads did we travel this day?" Hamo answered for me.

"The one to the river."

Hamo tousled his hair, "And the other men would have ridden along the road, clattering and making so much noise that they could have been heard five miles away. Our scouts kept us clear of danger."

"I am sorry, my questions are foolish."

I smiled, "No, they are not, Jack, for that is how you learn. We will be flexible for we all know each other."

The ones who looked most uncomfortable were Ralph and his squire along with Richard of Craven. This was all new to them.

We walked our horses to the edge of the wood and were in place as the sun rose to our right. The castle stood just three hundred paces from us. In my heyday, I could have sent an arrow and struck a man standing on its walls. Since my wound, I was no longer confident. The sun's rays gradually lit up the wooden walls. My scouts had been right, it was the simplest of castles. Why was the king worried about its loss? The garrison could only have been a handful of men. The castle did occupy a good site on a high piece of ground which jutted into the loch but it should have been made of stone. The village was on the far side of the loch. I could see the smoke rising as the villagers rekindled their fires. I thought, at first, that there were no sentries but then I saw movement. They had a man on the top of the donjon on top of the mound.

Ralph was both nervous and eager to do something and he said, filling the silence that was the way of my men and me, "We can get close and rush the gates. They look flimsy."

Hamo answered, "They are, Ralph, but we need a prisoner. We may well attack but where is the rush? The king is three days or more behind us. The men sent by de Lucy galloped in and were taken." He waved an arm, "We are hunters. The hunter that rushes often loses the prey. The sun is barely up and we have a long day ahead of us. Be patient."

I smiled and it was the smile of a man who is proud of his son. I had trained Hamo as well as any archer. He would be just like me when I handed over the reins of power. As I took out a piece of dried venison to chew, I realised he would be a better leader than I had been for he had his mother's blood in him too. He was kinder than I was. He had enjoyed an easier upbringing than me and that also made him a better man. He would never be as tough or as hard as I was, but he did not need to be.

"Ralph, if you are eager to do something then go and see that the horses are still tethered. Your presence might stop them from making a noise. Noise carries in the quiet of morning."

Keen to be doing something, he nodded and led his squire off. Richard said, "I will go and help them, my lord. I feel that I need to earn my place here. I am not a warrior and my skills are not needed."

I waved him away and said, "String your bows. Sergeants be ready to move on my command." I had no idea what we would be doing but I needed the men to be prepared.

The Hunt

The sun was rising. Had there been a church or abbey nearby then they would have sounded terce, but all was silent as the gates opened. The rough road to the village headed close to the woods before following the curve of the loch. It passed through the woods. Two men emerged and headed towards the village. I said, quietly, "Gwillim, take four men and bring them back."

They moved so silently that I heard nothing. I kept my eyes on the gates for they were open. There was another track, a better one and that led south. We had avoided it on our way to the castle for I wanted to leave no signs for the garrison that we were in the area. I guessed it went to Caerlaverock. I intended to head down it later that day when we had learned all that there was to learn. A rider emerged from the castle. The two men going to the village were on foot. Perhaps they only had a couple of horses, whatever the reason he took the road. The road passed within forty paces of our position. The two men heading to the village had disappeared. I could leave them to my archers. The horseman I would leave alone. If he was going to Caerlaverock then his news would just make them more confident. Lochmaben was still at peace. Perhaps this was a regular occurrence. If I was the Maxwell who ruled this land, then I would want confirmation that there were no enemies close by.

The problem was that it was Ralph, his squire and Richard who were at the right of our line, with the horses. I had placed them there to keep them from trouble. I now regretted my move for they were not as skilled as my men at arms and when one of the horses neighed the rider stopped. What happened next could not have been avoided. Ralph did the right thing. He ran to the rider to arrest the progress of his horse and to prevent him from shouting a warning to the castle. One of my men would have been able to do so quickly but Ralph and his two companions did not have the reactions my men did. The Scotsman wheeled his horse and, through the trees, I saw him turn his horse. He would escape and a warning would be given.

"Martin, take the man. The rest of you, take the castle." My men were well trained. I had not planned on taking the castle but the opportunity was too good to miss. The gates lay open and we were close enough to get within.

Thankfully the Scot had not shouted and he was still in the woods when the arrow plucked him from his saddle. The riderless horse was the warning to the castle that something had happened to the man but perhaps they thought he had just fallen from the saddle. I spied, as we emerged from the woods to cover the ground to the ditch and walls, two men pointing at the horse. They were on the top of the wooden hall atop

31

the mound. The gates were still open and appeared to be unmanned. My archers were faster than the mailed men at arms and they covered the ground quicker. Hamo had his bow and an arrow was nocked. When he spied the man, just one hundred and fifty paces from us trying to close the gates he stopped, drew and released an arrow in one motion. I had taught him well and a second arrow was drawn as the rest of the archers closed the gap to the gates. I forced my legs to run harder. My knees and calves complained but I endured it. I was the leader and the leader should be the first into danger.

Ned and Hob stopped close to the gates and drew back their bows. I could not see their targets but two cries told me that they had eliminated a danger. When Hamo and the others reached the gates, I breathed a sigh of relief. As we entered the outer bailey, I spied the inner curtain wall of wood and the second gate. Hamo shouted, "Archers, form a line and draw."

I drew my sword, "Sergeants, now we earn our shillings." Passing through the loose line of archers we headed towards the second gate which was also open. It was less than sixty paces from us. Even John and James could not miss at that range. Hamo and my men struck the two men attempting to close the gate and William and I used our metalled bodies to burst through to the small inner bailey. The route to the donjon wound up the mound and two men were racing up it. Arrows flew from behind and the two men were hit.

I knew that William was younger and fitter, "William, get into the donjon." He had, until then, been going slowly so as not to leave me alone. Now he sprinted and I said, "Jack, watch his back."

My foster son was like a hound released from a leash. He was on William's shoulder before my sergeant was halfway up the slope. Arrows still slammed into the top of the donjon and the gate. The hand that grasped the edge of the door to close it was pinned to the wood by a red fletched arrow. That was Ned's. It meant the door could not be closed and when William and Jack burst through then Lochmaben castle was, once more, in English hands. I stopped at the foot of the slope to catch my breath and to survey the castle.

Jack and John had been told before we left Carlisle, that they were not to put themselves in harm's way. They had obeyed and now ran to join me.

"Have we lost any men?"

John shook his head, "No, my lord."

I nodded, "Find Sir Ralph, his squire and the pursuivant. Fetch the horses."

"Yes, my lord."

William and my sergeants brought out the six men from the donjon. The one who had a hand pierced by an arrow was trying to stem the flow of blood with a piece of cloth. "This is it?"

William nodded, "By my reckoning, my lord, just twenty men were holding this place. We have disarmed them."

Hamo joined me and I said, "You did well today, my son, as did the other archers."

He shrugged, modestly, "It is what we do." He unstrung his bow and then waved a hand at the inner bailey, "And King Edward has his castle once more."

"I would burn it but that would tell whoever leads this rebellion that we are here. We will wait on Gwillim and then I will decide what to do. What is the interior like?"

Jack said, "A pigsty, Sir Gerald. Either these men or the former garrison lived like animals."

I said, "Leave the wounded man with me. Take the rest and have them clean up their mess."

"Yes, my lord." My sergeants prodded the men with their daggers and William said, "Let us hope that you are better at cleaning than you are at fighting."

"Hamo, have the archers clear the dead then return here. We will tend to this man's hurts."

The arrow had made a clean strike through the back of the man's left hand. He had managed to pull out the arrow and he had stemmed the bleeding. I was not being altruistic in helping the man. I wanted information and so I engaged him in conversation as Hamo fetched vinegar and honey from within the wooden donjon.

"What is your name?"

He glanced at my face for my words were gentle. My appearance and, probably, my reputation meant he expected something different. "Jack Short, my lord."

His accent was north country without being Scottish. That was not unusual. The land between the Tyne and the Forth and the Esk and the Clyde had once, so a priest had told me, been one kingdom. It was not until the Romans left this island that they became separate.

"Why do you support the Scots?"

His voice told me that he was fearful, "Who says I support the Scots, my lord?"

I laughed, "Do not take me for a fool. This castle was taken by the Scots from the English, and you are defending its walls."

"I had to, my lord, or Lord Maxwell would have locked me up."

The man was lying but I allowed him to continue to lie. Hamo returned with the vinegar and honey. I waited until he began to clean the wound with honey before I resumed my interrogation. His mind would be on the astringent pain of the vinegar, and he might blurt out other matters.

"Which Maxwell is that?"

"Ow." His eyes closed as Hamo pulled out a sliver of an arrow. "John Maxwell, the younger brother."

"Surely if he is a young man, he has no authority."

The wound was cleaned and Hamo began to smear the honey on the two open ends of the wound. It was soothing and I saw relief on the man's face. "He is obeying the commands of his elder brother David, who is in Edinburgh, my lord. Now that Lord Eustace is dead, he is the laird." Eustace Maxwell had died at Falkirk. I knew that there were brothers of the dead lord as well as sons. I now had names.

I pretended that I knew all, "Well they will not last long at Caerlaverock once the king comes north and he will come."

"Caerlaverock is a strong fortress, my lord," He frowned, "You are from Carlisle, my lord?"

"Aye, for your countrymen have slain too many of my comrades and I was sent to find out why."

He smiled, "That is because the roads are watched, and you Englishmen are noisy. My brother and I were watchers for a while."

"Your brother?"

He gestured with his good hand, as Hamo wound a bandage around the wound, towards the wooden donjon, "Robert Short, Bob, my lord, he is cleaning up the mess."

"So, Jack Short, we have healed your hand and in return we need information."

His eyes narrowed and the smile left his face, "I will not betray my comrades."

"You already have. The Sherriff could hang you and your brother for the murder of his men and you have told me that the rebels are in Caerlaverock and that John Maxwell commands."

His face fell, "But, my lord, if my comrades discover that I will have my throat cut."

I smiled, "Exactly, so, while we are alone speak, and I may let you and your brother go when we leave, so long as you swear not to join the rebels again."

I saw him debating. "What will you do with the others?"

"Have them taken to Carlisle and the king's pleasure."

"Hanging then."

I shrugged, "What do you think?"

He nodded. "I know little, my lord."

"Then tell me a little and I will see if that satiates my appetite for information."

"There were three hundred of us who took Lochmaben, and we lost not a man. Some are in the castle and others wait to ambush those who seek to find us."

"Knights?"

"A few but most are Wallace's men. I was one such man. I followed Wallace to Falkirk."

It was on the tip of my tongue to say, 'and then you ran' but I wanted him to speak further. "And is Wallace in Caerlaverock?"

I prayed that he was and then once this little game was over I could return home and not seek him, God knows where.

"No, my lord. He is in France seeking help from our friends over there."

He looked to have told me all but I tossed some names at him, "Balliol, Comyn, Brus, are any of those in the castle?"

I had learned to look for signs of lies and there were none on his face when he shook his head and said, "They do not like the Maxwell clan. They think the Maxwells also seek the crown."

Hamo asked, "Then why follow them?"

He shrugged and gave a sad smile, "When a man follows William Wallace he does so wholeheartedly or not at all. William Wallace asked me to help Lord Maxwell and William Wallace is my friend."

The men given the task of cleaning out the hall emerged and as they headed towards us, daggers still pricking them I said quietly, "We will bind you and your brother loosely. I will tell my men that when you slip away, on the other side of the Esk, that they are not to follow." He beamed. I wagged a finger at him, "You will cease to be a rebel. If I find you again, fighting against England, then I shall hang you myself. Do I make myself clear?"

His face became serious, "Yes, my lord."

I nodded to Hamo, "Robert Short?" A younger version of Jack Short raised his hand and looked nervously in our direction. "Is this your brother?"

"It is, my lord."

"You are all to be taken, bound, to Carlisle. As he only has one good hand, he will be bound to you." He nodded and looked relieved."

William bound the others and when he had done so I waved him over. "Take four archers and return these to Carlisle and tell the king, when he arrives, that we hold Lochmaben and that there are only three hundred rebels at the most in Caerlaverock. Tell him that we will rid the forest of the ambushers. Make sure you do not use the roads, they are watched."

"Yes, my lord."

I lowered my voice, "When you reach the Esk the wounded man and his brother will escape. Allow them to do so. Make a fuss and shout a lot, threaten dire retribution, but let them go."

He looked puzzled, "Why, my lord?"

"Because of the information I was given. I do not think the pair will be a threat to us."

We had to wait for the return of the horses before William could leave. Ralph, his squire and Richard all looked shamefaced. I waited until the prisoners and their escort were on their way before I addressed the men, "We will use this as a base. Gwillim, make a duty rota; include me and Sir Ralph. Tomorrow, we take a patrol and rid the forest of the watchers."

"And the dead bodies, my lord?"

"As much as I want to burn them that will only let the village know that the castle has been retaken. Bury them."

As the men set about their grisly task I turned to speak with Ralph, Richard and Hamo, "I do not blame you two or you, William, for the disaster we barely avoided. That was my fault. I should have used my archers or my men at arms for such a position. I am sorry. From now on I will keep you from harm's way. Watch and learn. Ralph, until William of Ware returns, you shall command the castle. Hamo and I will lead the patrols."

Ralph said, "I am sorry, Sir Gerald, I let you down."

"No, you did not for my men and I are the masters of this type of warfare. It is why King Edward uses this grizzled old warhorse. You will learn... or I will have to return to my daughter with a corpse slung over a saddle."

I knew, from Hamo's face, that I had used stronger words than he would have chosen. It was a lesson for him to learn. Honeyed words were best kept for women and children. Men deserved the truth.

The two men who had been sent around the loch were brought back before William of Ware left and they were bound and added to the prisoners heading for Carlisle. Taking them had been child's play for Gwillim and my men.

The castle had not been well maintained and I knew that the best thing to do would be to burn it to the ground. I could not do that for fear of alerting the countryside. We made the best of it. There was a kitchen outside the hall, and we could use it to cook hot food. The garrison was well supplied. The wooden donjon had stabling at the base and we secured our horses there. Half of the men slept in what would have been the lord's bedchamber while the rest moved the table from the hall and slept there. With a quarter of our men on watch at any one time, it was comfortable enough.

Word had spread about my apparent clemency and they were curious. Hamo was on watch when the question was asked. "Why did I let two rebels go? Gwillim, a good question. There is a simple answer, I gave my word that in return for information, I would allow it."

Ralph asked, "But what did we learn that we did not before?"

I had still to tell my men of my new task but there was no harm in giving them the real reason, "I know that William Wallace is in France. The men I let go were his men. He is in Paris. King Edward needs that information."

Jack had helped me to track Wallace and he shook his head, "Wallace is just a brigand, Sir Gerald."

I leaned forward, "He was a brigand, Jack, but now he is a symbol of victory and freedom. The Scots have forgotten the disaster that was Falkirk and, instead, remember the glory of Stirling Bridge and the way that Wallace rampaged through Carlisle, Bowes and Newcastle. He achieved nothing but they cling to that single victory. Until another rises to take the place of Sir Andrew Murray then it will be William Wallace that holds the smouldering flame of rebellion."

Gwillim used a chicken bone to prise some meat from between his teeth, "Then why does not the king send a killer to Paris? Slit the bastard's throat and there is an end to it."

There were nods and grunts of approval from around the table. My men were not liberal-minded priests. Wallace had rebelled and deserved death. The manner of his death was, to them, immaterial.

"King Edward will want a trial. He needs to show Scotland the price they pay for rebellion. A slit throat would suffice for me, Gwillim, but it might make Wallace a martyr and a dead symbol around which they could rally."

Chapter 4

Leaving the men at arms along with Ralph and Richard to guard our new and temporary home, Hamo and I led the remaining archers. Jack came with us. We would separate closer to the Scottish bastion. I would ride to Caerlaverock and Hamo and half of my archers would ambush those waiting to pick off riders heading to the Maxwell castle. We rode through heavily forested land and used hunter's trails. I had Gwillim and Dick with me. They rode ahead of the other archers, sniffing the air like hunting dogs. Their strung bows, like the other archers, hung from their cantles. Mine was at the castle, still in its case. I still feared trying to draw it in case I could not show the same skill I had before the wounding. The horses we had were well-trained. They would not neigh if they heard or smelled another animal but they would react and I knew that Gwillim's mount must have given him a sign when he held up his hand and, along with Dick, slipped from the saddle. The arrows were drawn and the two of them slipped silently into the forest. Without being told Jack nudged his horse forward and took the reins of the two archers' mounts. The horses would probably stay and graze but Jack had learned enough not to take chances. I was proud of my foster son. It was a little thing but neither Ralph nor his squire would have thought of it.

Waiting is always the hardest part of being a warrior. I trusted Gwillim and Dick but I wanted to be the eyes that saw what they were seeing. I knew I could not for, while I could still hide, the ease of movement was gone. My reactions were not what they were. I heard the two arrows, in the distance, as they were released. I had been waiting for the sound and whilst Richard of Craven might have thought it was wind, my archers and I knew that Gwillim and Dick had sent arrows at a target. When I heard the sound of something falling and there was no accompanying cry then I knew that whatever they hunted was dead.

Dick returned and after slipping easily into the saddle and taking Gwillim's horse's reins said, "We found two men. They are dead and there are no others."

He led us to Gwillim who had finished searching the bodies of the two dead men. I reflected that the two men could have had an innocent purpose but as we knew that Caerlaverock lay just a mile or two away Gwillim had made the right decision. He handed me two crossbows. "I think they were hunting men such as the ones the Sherriff lost." He shook his head, "If the Sherriff's men were taken by weapons and warriors like this then they were piss poor at their job."

He was right, of course, and showed that de Lucy was not up to the task the king had assigned him. "We cannot leave their bodies here. Sling one on the back of Jack's horse and the other on Robert's. Fetch the crossbows too."

Gwillim hated the weapon he called the 'devil's machine', "They will make kindling, I suppose."

I sighed and shook my head, "We will have few enough archers when we besiege Caerlaverock to dismiss two more weapons that could be used by men with bodies weaker than yours, Gwillim."

"Yes, my lord."

"Keep your bows ready and an arrow to hand." I drew my sword, "Jack, have a weapon ready."

He drew his own sword. It had been a gift from my wife last Christmas. She knew weapons, having lived in a Mongol encampment where prowess amongst the Mongols was measured both by skill with a bow and a sharpened sword. The sword had not been cheap and though it was not as long as mine, to Jack it was a most precious gift. He had almost wept when he had unwrapped it.

We stopped just four hundred paces from the edge of the water that surrounded the triangular castle. We dismounted and just Jack, Gwillim and Dick accompanied me to the tree line. The rest had loosely nocked arrows and waited with the horses. It was a well-made castle. The twin towers of the barbican afforded the only entrance to the castle. The drawbridge could be raised making the moat a complete defence. There was a tower at each end of the walls. The towers were the highest points of the castle and the barbican had to have at least four floors. The water looked to be the size of a loch but I knew that it was a moat. De Lucy had told me that and that meant it would not be too deep. I looked around and saw that the castle and its moat were slightly higher than the land around it. Trebuchets and siege engines could be used but having height was always an advantage.

I said, quietly, "You all have better eyes than me. How many men can you see?"

They were silent and finally, Gwillim shook his head and said, "'Twoud be a guess, my lord. They have hoardings and embrasures. There is movement, we can all see that, but it could be one man or ten."

I nodded, glumly. Only the defenders would know their true numbers. The Maxwell banner flew from the towers and not that of Scotland. Was the lord of this land giving himself a way out if his castle fell? As we mounted our horses to head back to Lochmaben I thought about his position. The men we had taken were evidence that Lord Maxwell had taken a castle of the king but, without the flying of a

Scottish standard, he could argue it was nothing to do with the overlordship of the English and he was not a rebel. The sooner the king came the better. As well positioned as the castle was, the army the king was bringing was so strong that even a castle like Rochester or Windsor would eventually fall. The trees that lay close to the moat could be made into rafts and men sent across the moat with ladders. I knew it would fall and the only question was how long that would take.

When we reached Lochmaben I spied half a dozen new horses grazing in the outer bailey. As we dismounted to walk our animals into the inner bailey Hamo came to join me, "We found six men waiting by the road ready for an ambush. I invited surrender but they chose death."

"Did any escape?"

He shook his head, "We were so close to them that even as they scorned our offer they died."

Jack took my horse and I headed with Hamo to the hall, "Tomorrow we will ride closer to Carlisle. The two men we killed will be missed and I think Maxwell will know that the foxes are sniffing around the fowl."

"Will he come here?"

I nodded, "I would expect so. Would you not want to know why the killers of his men were not spotted? We leave early so that we can get back here in case there is an attack. If the numbers are the same tomorrow as you discovered today then we can leave half of the archers here."

As we ate, I explained to Ralph and Richard what was happening. This was all new to them and I wanted them to be quite clear about their role. "It may be that Lord Maxwell sends men to scout out the castle. We will fly no banner and offer no defence until they are within the range of our bows. I will leave Gwillim to command the archers. We defend the outer wall with archers and the inner with men at arms. If, and it is a mighty if, the Scots take the outer walls then the archers are fleet of foot and will easily make the inner bailey."

"But you do not think that they will try to take the walls."

"No Ralph, I do not."

I led just eight archers and Jack as we rode towards the road from Carlisle. That the men ambushed by my son would be missed was clear but I knew we still held the advantage. They would be tied to the road to watch for their enemies and we were not. My men could move like wraiths and come from any direction; it gave us the advantage even though this was their homeland. We did not rush for, in rushing, noises would be made and we needed silence. Accordingly, neither Jack nor I wore any mail, not even a coif. Instead, we just wore our arming caps.

The Hunt

As an archer, I had grown up wearing soft rather than metallic headgear. It was noon when we made our way down the small stream to the road. My archers and I had agreed that any ambusher would choose somewhere close to water, and small streams often had simple bridges that would afford a good ambush site. We heard them chattering in the distance. I later deduced that they had to have a man on the road from Carlisle to warn them of an approaching enemy. What they would not know was that the next enemy they might encounter would be the vanguard of King Edward's ten thousand-strong army.

We dismounted and Jack and I acted as horse holders. The men each nocked an arrow and headed through the trees stepping carefully so as not to make a sound. I signalled to Jack to tether the horses to a tree and when that was done, we moved after our archers. I wanted to see the ambush and, if truth be told, to be a part of it. I stopped five paces behind the archers who were all drawing their arms back. They worked as a team and I know they would have each identified their target. Similarly, when they began to draw, it would have been as one and the release which followed a heartbeat after the full draw was also simultaneous. The six Scotsmen never knew what killed them. One moment they were enjoying a conversation and the next a war arrow slammed them into oblivion.

I drew my sword. It was a precaution in case any of them had survived. The range had been so short that the arrows protruded from the corpses, buried to the fletch. None were alive. I walked past their sorry-looking horses to the road. I could see nothing. I was about to return to my men when I heard the thunder of hooves. Looking up I saw a solitary rider galloping down the road. I did not think that he was an Englishman and so I stood my ground. The rider would have to leap into the stream to avoid me and as my archers were nocking an arrow and racing to the stream's banks, he could not avoid capture. As he neared me, he slowed and drew a short sword.

I took a twohanded grip on my sword as Hob shouted, "We can deal with him, my lord."

I ignored them. I was not too old to rid the world of a wild-eyed Scotsman. Just then, over the rise in the road, I saw a column of horsemen and they were not only English but they were also led by William of Ware. The man heard them as my archers rose from the banks of the stream and levelled arrows at him. He sheathed his sword and reined in.

Hob and my archers ran to him and pulled him unceremoniously from his horse and disarmed him. "Jack, fetch the horses." My foster son hurried off to obey me.

William had with him the archers I had sent as well as some hobilars, the local light horsemen. I guessed the Carlisle scouts who had been taken would have been similar to them. They rode hill ponies and wore a pot helmet, leather jack and carried a spear and small shield.

I smiled, "The king comes?"

"He is ranting and raving in Carlisle even as we speak. When he heard my news and of our success, he berated the Sherriff. I fear there will be a new lord of Carlisle soon." He gestured at the hobilars, "These are to take over the castle at Lochmaben and we are to meet the army at Caerlaverock."

Jack had returned with the horses. I pointed to the single prisoner, "Bind him and then burn the bodies of the others. There is no need for secrecy any longer."

My men had already taken the paltry purses from the Scots and the variety of weapons they had about them. The dirks were a particularly prized find as they could be hidden in a boot. The weapons would be taken with us on the ambushers' horses. What we did not need we would leave for the new garrison of Lochmaben.

I rode with Jack and William. I allowed Jack to regale William with the tale of our success and then I said, "And how many have reached Carlisle?" William cocked an eye and I shrugged, "The nobles and the horsemen have little choice about staying with the army. They are paid. Archers will stay as they are paid. The rest of the foot? If they do not get the food they like they are more than likely to desert."

He nodded, "You are right, my lord. We have the same seventeen hundred horsemen who mustered at Chester but some of the fyrd left on the road. There are just eight thousand who remain and some of those look ready to run."

"How many archers are there?"

Shaking his head he said, "There are none who are of the same quality as our men, Sir Gerald, and less than a hundred were at the muster. The king did not use the Welsh."

I had worried about the omission of the Welsh. I had fought against them, and I had Welsh blood in me. The Welsh archers were the best. Cheshire men were improving and that was because they were so close to Wales that they had been forced to learn to fight fire with fire. I was just glad that Caerlaverock was such a small castle. It would be tricky to take but it would fall.

We passed through a village on the way back. Recognising that we were English they hid. It allowed us to take a couple of sheep, beans, some bread and fresh cheese. That was the way of the world. Invaders always took. The sheep were slaughtered, and we would take their fleece and use it when we were back at Lochmaben. The meat would be butchered and, when we went to Caerlaverock, we would have the beginnings of a meal. Rabbits and squirrels, not to mention birds would be hunted as we headed to Caerlaverock, and we would enjoy a fine hunter's stew.

Hamo's patrol had enjoyed similar success to ours and we now had a string of animals that could be used to carry arrows, food, armour, weapons and loot. All the animals we had brought could now be used for riding. The captured prisoner was hobbled and used as a servant. He was forced to accept his new position for he was the sole survivor of the ambushers and he wanted to stay alive. He cooperated eagerly. Such men were braver when with companions. There was strength in numbers.

I let the hobilars stand the night watch. We had already done more than was asked and besides, there was a lack of space. We left the next morning and headed for the road to Caerlaverock. There was no need to hide. The king would be along soon enough, and we had seen little to make me fear the rebels. There were watchers and seeing and hearing us they fled back to the castle. When we reached it, the drawbridge was raised and the ramparts were manned. This time I did have my banner flying and the Scots knew Gerald Warbow well enough to respect it. There was no need to do anything other than set up a camp that was close to the barbican and the twin towers. We made it far enough from the walls to be safe and also where we could enjoy some privacy during the siege. We set the animals to graze, built hovels and erected the three tents we had brought. Gwillim and five archers mounted a guard within bow range. The Maxwell standard fluttered but they did not waste crossbow bolts on us. This was a siege and the defenders knew that, at some point, we would need to close with the walls and that was when the bolts, arrows and darts would do some damage.

We found some logs and used them for seats. We sat on them while a fire was lit and food was prepared. If nothing else the fire would deter the midges and flying insects that proliferated close to the moat. I pointed at the water, "That is their best defence. We might build rafts but even if we did we would still need ladders for an escalade. Until the fleet brings the trebuchets, we can do little." Hamo nodded his agreement. Ralph and Richard were like boys at school. Each time Hamo and I spoke it was like a lesson. "Tomorrow, Hamo, take the archers and hunt."

"Animals for food?"

"Aye, but we tell the king we seek enemies. There will be some enemies outside the castle and we want them to know that King Edward

43

is here. Your horses will let them know that King Edward's archers are now in Galloway."

Hamo grinned at William of Ware, "And that means, my friend, that you and the sergeants will be the ones who labour."

He shrugged, "Better that we are occupied than have idle hands and minds."

It was in the middle of the afternoon, and we were eagerly anticipating the food we had prepared when Bishop Bek and the vanguard rode in. The Bishop of Durham dismounted close to me and waved his lieutenant to make their camp, "Your food smells good, Sir Gerald."

"Hunter's stew. Join us, Bishop, but these are not loaves and fishes, we only have enough for you and not your men."

He nodded and handed his reins to his squire, "I will speak with Sir Gerald. Let me know when my tent has been erected."

"Yes, my lord."

Hamo whistled and waved. Gwillim raised his arm and he and his watchers headed back to the fire. Now that the vanguard was here our job was done. We had secured the castle and what happened next was up to the king.

As if he read my mind Bishop Bek said, "The king will be hard on our heels. He follows with the horsemen. The ones on foot and the baggage will take until midnight to reach us." He shook his head. "A sorrier mob of men I have not seen. They moan and complain the whole time." He nodded at his own men, "The men of Durham that I brought know the need to quash the Scots. The ones who come from the south think that we in the north exaggerate the dangers of a Scottish rebellion."

"Aye, it is ever thus and besides soldiers like a fight where there will be loot. The Scots are like the Welsh. They are hard to beat and when you do beat them the rewards are rarely worth the effort. Frenchmen fight with coins in their purses."

The arrival of the vanguard brought more men to the battlements, but it was still hard to gauge the number of defenders. As John and James spooned out stew into our wood bowls the bishop and I discussed the castle. "Good stew, Warbow."

"My men and I live as well as we can when we fight for the king."

"When the trebuchets arrive then this castle will fall quickly."

I nodded, "I know but I am guessing that the king has brought a mighty host to bring the Scots to battle."

"Aye, this spark is just that, the hint of a rebellion. He is giving the Scots the chance to bring their men to fight."

I shook my head, "Maxwell is no Wallace."

"De Brus is seen as more of a threat. De Brus has lands north of here. The king hopes to provoke the man who would be king into battle. He would defeat him and make him either an ally or keep him a prisoner. He still wishes to make war on France."

I remembered the words of Jack Short. William Wallace was trying to enlist the aid of the French. Was the former brigand working with Robert de Brus? That would be a harder combination to defeat. Wallace had the people behind him and de Brus the nobles.

We were mopping the last of the stew with some stale bread we had liberated on our patrol when the king rode in. He looked at the empty pot and shook his head, "And you left your king not a drop, Warbow."

I bowed apologetically, "It was a simple hunter's stew, King Edward."

He dismounted and laughed, "And I have served with you and your men and know that such food is the best preparation for war." He turned to look at the castle. "Have you asked them to surrender yet?"

The question was aimed at the bishop. He was the senior lord here. "No, King Edward. I thought such a request came better from their monarch rather than a Prince Bishop."

"Hmnn." He nodded to the empty pot, "We will let them stew overnight and when all our host is here by the morrow and the castle's three sides are surrounded, then they may be intimidated enough to surrender."

He was about to leave and I said, "King Edward, a word?" He cocked an eye and I said, quietly, "I have information about the task we discussed at Chester."

He led me away to the horse lines. Their noise would mask our words. "Wallace?"

I nodded, "The man I spoke to said that he was in France, and to be more specific Paris. He is trying to enlist the help of the King of France."

"And that is what I have heard too. When we have dealt with this annoyance and scoured the southwest of Scotland of rebels, you shall leave. I would not have you lose his spoor. Wherever he goes I would have you follow him and when you have the chance, you take him."

I sighed. I had thought about the problem when in Lochmaben, "The problem is that if I take enough men to guarantee taking Wallace then he and the French will know. I will be taken and if I take so few as to vanish into the crowd then I may not have enough men for the task."

"And that is why I have chosen you. When I chose you, Hamo L'Estrange and Sir John to go to the Mongols, you and everyone else

45

thought the mission was impossible. The three of you succeeded. I do not know how you will do it, but I know that you will."

Chapter 5

Although we slept, my men could sleep through a thunderstorm, the king's slumbers were disturbed as the men on foot arrived, grumbling and with rumbling carts. The result was that he awoke in a foul mood. We were awake and preparing food as we heard him ordering men who had barely enjoyed two hours of sleep, to surround the castle. I knew that it was a mistake and would simply result in more desertions, but King Edward was his own man and did things his way. I sent Hamo and my archers off to forage for food. They would not be needed yet.

It was terces by the time the castle was surrounded. He ordered his senior lords, me included, to dress for war and fetch our banners. He wished to make a statement. Richard of Craven donned his brightly coloured garb once more as he joined the heralds and pursuivants. The trumpets sounded and we marched, bare-headed, to the edge of the moat. The ten thousand men who followed King Edward surrounded the moat on all three sides and silence fell.

King Edward had a powerful voice and even as the last echoes of the trumpets rolled across the water he spoke, "Know you, the rebels in Caerlaverock, that we have retaken Lochmaben and that I intend to take Caerlaverock. Surrender now and save both hurt and damage for I have a mighty host. What say you?"

The voice when it spoke from the walls sounded reedy and thin in comparison to that of King Edward. I later learned that Lord John Maxwell was relatively young. "I am Lord Maxwell and I have never yielded to King Edward. I dispute your right to rule this land. You are not the King of Scotland and so far as I am aware this is still Scotland. Lochmaben was ours by right. It is you who are in the wrong and we will hold out here until our allies arrive to drive you hence."

Until that moment I had thought this was just an isolated rebellion but now I saw a plan. The Scots had intended to draw the king north. This land was ripe for an ambush. I doubted that they would fight a battle but they could whittle down both our numbers and our willingness to fight.

The king must have realised that too for he shouted, "Then know that I will destroy Caerlaverock and any Scotsman foolish enough to fight against me."

He turned his back and strode off. We followed. I would take off my mail as soon as I could. There would be no fighting. We had to await the trebuchets and as they were coming by sea we were bound by wind and tide. The men would be commanded to build rafts and make ladders, but the lords would be mere spectators.

With Hamo and my archers gone, the construction of the ladders and scaling equipment was left to William and my sergeants. They were all hardworking and that was in direct contrast to some of the companies from the south of the land. They had to be badgered and supervised. King Edward became so angry that he ordered two men to be flogged. Needless to say, they deserted that very night. By the time Hamo and my archers returned from their chevauchée, a dozen rafts that could be joined together to make a pair of bridges were ready as were two dozen ladders. We would need more, of course, but until the parts for the trebuchets arrived there was little rush. It would take a day to construct the war machines, and, in my experience, it would take another day for the engineers to be satisfied with them. Each day saw more desertions. The floggings had not done as the king had hoped.

It was as we watched the men building the rafts that I saw Prince Edward for the first time in warrior garb. He had been a boy at the time of Falkirk but now he was a young warrior. He had with him young men who knew that their stars would rise if they were part of the retinue of the young prince. I had joined his father not as a noble but as an archer who could do the tasks for him that were seen to be beneath a noble. It was as I saw them sparring that I first encountered Piers Gaveston. He was a personable young man and he had good sword skills but I did not like him from the first for he was arrogant. He was better than those around him and he showed it. I had always been a good archer but I had never flaunted my skill. I accepted that others were not as strong or as skilled as I was but I knew that one archer would not win a battle; it would take massed ranks. I do not think that King Edward liked him either. There was something almost effeminate about him and that was strange for he had the physique of a warrior and, as I said, he had skills. King Edward liked warriors to be scarred and rugged. It was one reason he liked me. I was not a pretty man, Piers Gaveston was.

I had Hamo take one of the deer he had hunted and present it as a gift to the king. It was a calculated move on my part as it meant we would avoid censure for not having worked on the ladders. The king was grateful and spent some time talking to Hamo about the hunt. King Edward liked to hunt although his preferred choice was the hunting of wild boars. A man did not use a bow for such a hunt.

The ships arrived just before dusk on the next day. The king was unhappy that it had taken so long to bring them. The engineer in command tried to explain that navigating the twisting river was not easy but the king was in no mood to listen. It took the combined voices of his senior leaders to persuade him to let the engineers have a night of sleep before assembling the mighty stone-throwing weapons. I could not understand the king's impatience. He knew that the castle could not last long and I finally worked out that it was the defender's decision to refuse surrender that had galled him. We were awoken by the banging and clattering of hammers as the engineers obeyed the king's command. The rafts and ladders were finally finished and, as the trebuchets rose like some primaeval creature from the piles of timber, he had had the army don armour and stand along the three sides of the castle. He was giving the defenders one last opportunity to surrender but they decided not to. At least they did not bare their backsides at him. They had learned what a mistake that was.

I met the Scotsman next to whom I had been seated, Sir John Menteith. He and Simon Fraser were dressed for war. They came to speak to me, "Sir Gerald, we will get to see your archers at work," Sir John gave me a wry smile, "this time from behind them. The last time we saw them we were cowering beneath shields."

"That will not be until the war machines are ready, Sir John. It is a pity more archers were not brought. I think that King Edward has brought too few to make an effective show but, then again, I believe there are few defenders within Caerlaverock."

"What makes you say that, my lord?"

Simon Fraser was older than Sir John. As I had not heard a title I guessed he was just a gentleman or, perhaps, a younger brother of a noble. "The castle is strong, but it is not big. Warkworth is much bigger. The jewel of the north, Norham, is larger and has a better position. Bamburgh would laugh away such a siege. No, I am not certain what Lord Maxwell plans, unless," I studied their faces as I chose my words carefully, "this is a plan to draw King Edward north. Are your countrymen ready for another battle, Sir John?"

I saw no lie in his eyes as he answered, "We have learned that King Edward is the master of a formal battle. Scotland is not yet ready to stand toe to toe with England."

His words told me much. He was a diplomatic ally. He would not, in all likelihood, be at the fore of any fighting. He was here because of the promise made by the king to give him a position. He was an enemy hiding in plain sight. The king did not trust him and I believed he was wrong to use such a man but the king was the king and knew his own mind. I was still a simple archer. The two men gave a slight bow and left.

Ralph had never seen a trebuchet in action and he and his squire were fixated on the strange-looking machines. I had seen them at work in the Holy Land. There they had been less than successful but the strongholds there were more substantial than Caerlaverock. "How do they work, Sir Gerald?"

I pointed to one that was further along the assembly process, "The stones are loaded in those bags and men haul on ropes. When that lever is pulled then the counterweight falls and that hurls the stone at the walls. Smaller ones with wheels can also be made but their range is shorter and they take more time to build. They are however mobile. These trebuchets will be placed in one position and remain there until the walls are breached."

His squire, William, said, "Where will they be used, my lord?"

"Not at the towers that is for sure. They will probably aim them at a section of the wall between the towers. The king could attack on three walls at the same time but I think he will choose either one or, perhaps, two walls." He nodded. "And when they have breached then we go in. The archers will clear the defenders and then we shall cross the moat and use ladders to scale the walls."

Ralph asked, "Will men not cross where the walls are breached?"

"Some will but not my men. Fallen masonry can be treacherous. A broken leg can end the career of a man at arms. The breaches are there to prevent the defenders from using their fighting platform effectively. It is why I think that the king will, on the morrow, attack one wall."

I was proved right although I was not senior enough to be involved in the discussions. We were woken before dawn and that meant little sleep for any of us. My night watch had hot food for us and after we had dressed for war we ate. Priests came to take confession from those who asked and I paid one of Bishop Bek's clergy to bless my men and their weapons. It cost little and I knew it was money well spent. Men fought better with confession made and a clear conscience.

The king had decided to attack one wall. The gatehouse was too well made, as were the other two towers. He stood, encased in mail with a gleaming helm held by one squire, close to the edge of the moat and in front of the trebuchets. A senior lord held his standard aloft. His son and the gaggle of young bloods were close by. They looked like eager pups watching hounds prepare to hunt. The king also had a trumpeter with him and he nodded to him. The strident notes rang out and the three trebuchets all snapped at the same time. The engineers would not wish to upset the king again.

The stones had varying results. One fell at the base. One clipped the top of the wooden hoardings and one smacked into the middle of the wall. The engineers had each watched their own stone. The one that had hit the middle was reloaded and a second stone was sent to hit close to the first strike. There appeared to be no damage from either stone but I knew that was an illusion. The wall would have been weakened. The other two machines took longer to reload as the aim had to be adjusted. The men who worked the machines were as professional as my archers. The one that had struck the base was adjusted so that the second stone hit the height of a man's body up the wall. That satisfied the captain working the machine and soon it sent stone after stone at the same point. The one that had hit the hoardings also made the slightest of adjustments and two stones later the captain of that machine was happy as his stones struck just above the strike of the very first machine. By noon the trebuchets had all broken down at least once and been repaired and the rate of stones had dropped but there were signs of damage. A crack had appeared in the wall and every stone that hit made it more pronounced.

I waved over Gwillim and my archers. Had I asked then the king would have given me command of all the archers who were available, but I did not need them. I needed the knife of a surgeon. My archers would eliminate the odd man who was exposed. "Gwillim, soon stones will be dislodged. Have our men ready to hit any flesh that they see." He nodded. Like me, he knew that the ones who exposed themselves would be the braver ones and if they were slain then it would dishearten the rest. There were brave men on the walls but arrows that plucked men from the walls without giving them the opportunity to fight back sucked the spirit from a man.

The first stone that fell from the wall, showing that it was ready to crumble, came from the parapet. The first strike that had hit the hoarding had appeared to do little, but when first the wood and then a stone crenulation tumbled down the wall to splash into the moat we knew that we were winning. There was a collective cheer from our men. It was Gwillim's arrow that slew the first Scot. The sudden opening exposed one mailed man. I watched as his arms flailed to keep his balance. The bodkin slammed into his chest and he, too, tumbled into the moat.

King Edward was close enough to say, "A fine arrow, archer." He tossed a silver coin towards Gwillim who deftly caught it and bowed.

It was not the end of the attack of the stones but it signalled the ultimate defeat of the Scots in Caerlaverock. The hurling of the stones continued until nightfall and the crack was now a fissure that zigzagged its way down the wall. "My lord Bohun, have the trebuchets close guarded this night. I would not, for all the world, have the Scots make mischief."

"Do not fear, my lord. My men have been spectators this day. We will earn our pay tonight with a close watch."

My men had not hunted for a couple of days and we were reduced to using the bones of the deer, along with gathered greens and our dried venison, to make a thin stew. We were, however, better off than many of the others. Food was scarce and men were already grumbling. The king and the nobles did not go short but more of the infantry began to desert. It was barely a trickle but I recognised the danger. We set a guard around our supplies. If we had to then we could slaughter one of the poorer horses we had taken from the Scots.

The next day was a repeat of the first. It took a few stones for the engineers to get their eyes in. My archers were critical. They needed but one arrow. They stood to and watched for unwary Scotsmen. It was noon when the first section of the wall fell. This time a second fissure appeared and raced up the wall to join the first. The masonry six paces from the top of the wall crashed down in a spectacular fashion to crash and splash in the moat. Two men tumbled to their deaths. One hit the water and the section cracked into the ground at the base of the walls. This time it was Dick whose arrow found the mailed Scot.

King Edward turned, "Bishop Bek, have the rafts prepared. When we have a large enough breach, you can cross the moat and establish a bridgehead. The rest of the army will follow."

Of course, it was not as easy as that. The stones kept hitting but the machines broke down more often. The ropes needed to be replaced and it took time to replace them. The result was that it was close to dusk when the breach was enlarged enough to warrant an attack.

"Do we wait for the morning, my lord?"

The king snapped, "So that they can repair the breach? I think not. Get about your business, my Lord Bishop." He turned to his trumpeter, "Have the army prepare for battle."

The notes rang out. I turned and Jack handed me my helmet and shield. We would not be in the first group across the moat but I would be ready when our turn came.

"Gwillim, it is getting too dark for our arrows to find the mark. When the sergeants have crossed bring the archers. Your swords and daggers can add to ours."

"Yes, my lord." The archers all unstrung their bows and put them in their cases.

Bishop Bek was a brave man, and he led the rafts across. There were embrasures in the walls and it was from them that the Scots sent a few bolts towards the advancing men from the north. The shields of the bishop and his men prevented wounds. As the ladders were placed on the walls so the rafts were punted back across the still, dark waters of the moat. My men and I all fitted on one of them and we punted across. I kept an eye on the walls and saw men ascending the ladders while others picked a precarious path across the rubble from the breach. I stepped ashore with William of Ware, and I did so with a hefted shield held before me. The crossbow bolt that slammed into it told me that the bridgehead was not yet consolidated.

We ran to a ladder which had just two men ascending. That told me the men at the top had a foothold. William tried to ascend first. I shook my head, "I am in command, and I lead."

He was not happy, but he obeyed, "I will be close behind, Sir Gerald."

"Aye, but not close enough to trip me up, eh?" My sword was sheathed and my only defence would be my helmet and my shield. I would need my right hand to keep hold of the ladder.

The danger became clear when, in the darkening gloom, the warrior from Durham who was close to the top suddenly screamed as he was speared and I pressed myself close to the ladder as his body fell perilously close to my head. I hurried up the last few rungs. The Scottish spearman was waiting but so was I. As my body reached the top he thrust with the spear. Had I not been an archer then I might have joined the man from Durham and lie at the foot of the ladder. As it was I leaned my body against the wall and grabbed the spear just behind the head. I pulled. He was not expecting the move and as he was already thrusting he came with the spear. He let go but by then his body was halfway through the crenulation and he screamed his way to the water. He was mailed and he would drown. I stepped over onto the fighting platform. The Scot with the buckler and sword thrust at me. I had the spear the wrong way around and so I punched with my shield at his face. His sword scratched along my mail and I cursed him. I would not be hurt but the mail would need to be repaired. Holding the spear horizontally I pushed him. Already overbalanced by the strike from my shield he fell back into the bailey. By the time William of Ware had joined me, I had turned the spear around to use it offensively.

There was little point in heading towards the breach and, instead, William and I moved towards the tower at the far end of the wall. All along the fighting platform were knots of men attempting to eject the ones who had a toehold on the wall. They were doomed. William and I moved together. He was on the right, close to the edge and I had the battlements to my left. The long spear darted out and speared one Scot

53

in the side. He was wounded and he ran down the platform towards the gate to the tower. His movement sparked a general flight and the half dozen or so defenders ran. It meant that the ones ascending the ladders to join us did so unopposed.

By the time we reached the gate, it was barred. One of the bishop's men had an axe and we brought him forward. It took a few blows but the gate broke and we poured through the narrow entrance. There were no defenders. They had descended already. I let William and the Durham axeman descend first. By the time we reached the bailey, it was dark, but the battle was over. I heard a Scottish voice shout, "We yield, give us quarter."

The king had put Bishop Bek in command of the assault and the Prince Bishop shouted, "Throw down your weapons and your lives shall be spared."

The siege of Caerlaverock had lasted but a few days. The sledgehammer that was King Edward's army had cracked the cobnut that was Caerlaverock.

Chapter 6

We had lost just twenty men in the taking of the castle. We took sixty prisoners, and none was of noble birth which meant no ransom. The men were disarmed, and their boots were taken from them. They were let go. We all knew that they would fight us again but we could not afford to use men to hold them as prisoners. We were haemorrhaging men ourselves. We had five hundred fewer men now than had set out from Chester. Had I been in command I would have left a garrison in Caerlaverock and gone back home. The king could ill afford to pay the men and nobles he had with him. However, once King Edward had divined a course he sailed it, no matter what. He sent away, once they had dismantled them, the trebuchets and returned them to the fleet. The engineers were sent to build a stone castle at Lochmaben. He had listened to me. A small number of men, a hundred, would join the hobilars from Chester. A garrison was left at Caerlaverock. The king took it for his own. Men were also left there to repair it. When we left, a few days later, for Dumfries, we had lost more men to desertions and with the two garrisons earmarked were down to eight thousand men. King Edward was still seeking a battle of note.

"Warbow, take your hounds and sniff out the Scots. Wherever they are gathering I would know."

I sighed, "King Edward, the Scots will hide from us. The men we took here is the largest body of men we have seen thus far."

He nodded, "When we begin to take their animals and occupy their towns then they will fight, they will have to or risk losing all."

I did not agree but I could do nothing more. At least we could raid with impunity. With Bishop Bek and the men of Durham and Yorkshire in the van, we headed for Dumfries. There was a castle which was held by our garrison but the town had been hostile. When the army arrived, the gates were opened and we were given a grudging welcome. We awaited the king for I did not want the gates of Dumfries slammed in his face as they had been when Wallace had pursued the survivors of Stirling.

When the king arrived, he was incandescent with rage as another five hundred men had deserted on the short journey from Caerlaverock. He gave orders that any deserters found would be hanged. All that the decision did was to create brigands who roamed the land taking whatever they wanted. It also did nothing to endear the king to the Scots who saw the deserters as an English blight. We were sent out again to find the enemy. Ralph was becoming more and more depressed at the way the campaign was going. He missed his family and, like the rest of us, could not see why the king was doing what he was doing. I could not explain it either, but I said, in answer, "We are the king's subjects and we do what he commands. You may not like it but, believe me, this king is a better one than was his father. King Edward is decisive while King Henry was not. All that I can suggest is that next time you pay scutage to the king and have another take your place."

"I am not afraid to fight."

I laughed, "And that is the trouble, Ralph, this army will spend many more days marching than it ever will fighting. The Scots know that they will lose if they try to battle us."

A few days later, however, we managed to find some resistance. We were approaching Balmaclellan, a small village a mile or so from Ken Water when we encountered our first opposition. Dick had sharp eyes and he stopped us well before the village and told us what he had seen. I went with him and confirmed that the Scots were making a stand. The village was occupied by about a hundred men. They had a wagon across the road. It was clear to me they were an outpost to a larger force of men. There was a bridge over Ken Water and by occupying the village they would be able to slow an enemy down. The bridge, as I recalled, was a narrow wooden one. It could be destroyed easily and while the river could be forded it would slow down King Edward. I studied the defenders. Most were on foot and while they had helmets and leather jacks I did not see much evidence of mail. Although they outnumbered us, I was confident that we could deal with them. I told my men to prepare for action. I sent James and John back to tell Bishop Bek the news and then the archers dismounted. We had four servants with us and I left them with the archers' horses.

"They have seen us, my lord."

I sighed, "I know, William, but they do not have enough mounted men to challenge us and we need the bridge to be intact. Take the archers and filter through the woods. We will occupy their attention. Once you shower them with arrows we will charge them."

He nodded, "I will wave when we are in position."

He and my archers loped off to the left and right. The ground descended to the valley and the cultivated land lay on the far side, closer to the river. Trees, hedgerows and shrubs were more normal close to the road. The road followed a burn. As they left and to focus the attention of the defenders upon us I had my sergeants form two lines. With my banner and that of Ralph prominently displayed we were tempting the Scots. Taking two knights might result in a good ransom. They had not seen my archers disappear and saw less than a dozen riders. The spears and pole weapons bristled behind the wagon. I saw a bow appear from the wood and it was waved. The trees hid the signal from the Scots but it was clearly aimed at me.

"We keep a steady and measured pace down this slope. Let our arrows do the work for us. We are the bait."

I spurred my horse and we began our descent to the village. Gwillim was a hunter and he knew the best moment to strike. We were less than two hundred paces away when the first of his arrows slammed into the men at the barricade. The ones from my right hit first. That was the signal for the ones hidden on the other side to begin the flight of their own missiles. The Scots were a massed target behind the wagon and arrows found flesh. It is one thing to face a handful of horsemen from behind the protection of a wooden wagon but quite another to have to face two additional and unseen enemies from the flanks. They ran or rather those that could, tried to flee.

"Spread around the village, we will cut them off."

Gwillim and his men were already streaming from the woods and, like us, they trampled across the cultivated fields of Balmaclellan. The legs of our horses were now opened and we gave them their heads. A fleeing man's legs are aided by the fear of death but they cannot outrun a horse and my sergeants rode good horses. Those of Sir Ralph, Jack, and William of Ware were as good as mine and we were the first to reach the fleeing Scots. I struck, not to kill or wound, but to incapacitate. I used the flat of my sword. It rang like a bell when it hit the pot helmet of the first Scotsman I caught. His weapon fell to the ground and his body followed. Ahead I saw the wooden bridge. One man was just fifty paces from it when William of Ware hit him. As my sergeant wheeled to take another I led Jack to the bridge where we reined in on the far side. The bridge over Ken Water was ours. King Edward would have dry feet when he crossed.

We dismounted and allowed our horses to graze on the far side of the water. Gwillim and some of the archers herded the survivors towards us. He jangled a purse, "Not exactly rich pickings, my lord." I nodded. "I have sent for the horses. Do you wish us to keep scouting today?"

I shook my head, "No, for by the time the baggage reaches us it will be dark. This is as good a place to camp as any and the king and his nobles can use the village."

"Right, boys, let us make a temporary home.

Jack was already unsaddling my horse and I said, "When that is done take off my mail." The exertion had made me sweat. John and James arrived with Bishop Bek and the horses. They immediately helped to set up the camp. The youngest men of my company were already becoming old campaigners.

Bishop Bek joined me and Jack poured some ale into our coistrels. The bishop used it to gesture to the sorry group of prisoners, "King Edward will be pleased to have some opposition at last."

"Perhaps, my lord but this hardly constitutes an army. Still, they were defending the bridge and that had to be for a reason."

"What lies to the south and west of us?"

I closed my eyes as I tried to visualise the land. It had been when I had sought Wallace that I had last ridden here. What one remembered were the rivers and bridges. I saw the River Cree, "The road heads south and west until the next bridge, just fifteen miles from here. It crosses the River Cree and ends at Wigtown. There is a castle there."

He smiled, "Good, I will tell the king. The news might please him for the coast is now close."

In the event, the news merely made him just slightly less bad-tempered. The reason for his foul mood was that more men had deserted, despite his commands. His lords were clearly incapable of keeping their own men under control. I wondered then about the wisdom of keeping people like Simon Fraser and John Menteith. Thus far they had done little to aid us and I thought that both men were more than capable of encouraging those beneath them to desert.

The king decided to spend two days in Balmaclellan where his army devoured all that the village had in the way of food. It did not stop the desertions but slowed them. We were sent to the crossing of the Cree. We saw more men but they did not try to stop us. Instead, their numbers grew so that our scouting became slower. Leaving my men to watch them on the far side of the river, I rode to the king.

The pursuivant, Richard, was still with him and he greeted me outside the house he was using, "The king is within and is speaking to his son. If you would just wait, Sir Gerald."

The debate within the thin walls of the mean dwelling merely made the words spoken unclear. Their tone, however, was obvious. It was a row. I knew that fathers and sons had such arguments but Hamo and I had been lucky and the occasions when we argued were few and far between.

"Do you enjoy being a popinjay once more?"

He shook his head, "I know that while I was with you, I was of little use to you but I felt as though I was learning. Any can do what I do now. I am a glorified servant who spends more time waiting upon the whims of my superiors. At least when I was with you and your men I felt like a warrior." He smiled, "Even if I was not one."

Before I had the opportunity to respond the door was flung open and a red-faced Prince Edward emerged. He almost pushed Richard to the ground. I did not like such action and I stood firm. His shoulder came at me in a petulant move intended to show his waiting peers his anger. He bounced back and his eyes raised and locked with mine, "How dare you bar my progress. I am the heir to the crown."

I gave a slight bow, "I am sorry, Prince Edward. I did not recognise you. I thought the king was being robbed. I can now see that you were in great haste." I stepped to one side and made an elaborate gesture with my left hand. I saw Richard smile and King Edward appeared in the doorway.

Prince Edward looked from me to his father and there was hate in both looks. He pranced off towards Piers Gaveston and the other young bloods. The king frowned and then said, "Do you have such problems with your son, Warbow?"

"Hamo, my liege, was brought up as an archer. Like me, he has no airs and graces. We are both blunt men and if there are words spoken between us they are soon forgotten and the air is cleared. I found that the odd time when it was needed the flat of my hand worked."

He shook his head, "But your son is surrounded by yeoman of England and not the prancing ponies of Gascony. Come and brighten my mood. Richard, fetch us food."

Most of the furniture from the house had been moved so that there was just a table and three chairs. He gestured for me to sit at one. He had been alone with his son and seemed happy to remain alone with me. He gestured for me to pour some ale. Wine was in short supply, but every village had an alewife and the king had clearly commandeered whatever ale was to be had. It merely meant less for the men and explained the increasing desertions. The ones who trudged behind the king's banner wanted food and ale. Denying them provender was a mistake. When Richard brought in the platter, I saw that we ate better in my camp than the king.

The king saw my look and shook his head, "Scotland is a poor country and they have hidden their choicest morsels. I would that they stand and fight so that I may defeat them and then get home."

"Then I may have good news, my lord. There are men gathered at the crossing of the Cree. Perhaps they may stand."

"Please tell me that there are more than the rabble you destroyed here."

"They are enough to make us stop. There were at least two hundred." He cocked an eye, "That is more than we found at

Caerlaverock, King Edward. Wigtown lies a short distance away and there is a castle there."

His face lit up, "Then we ride for this crossing and reach it by dawn. I will take just my horsemen and your mounted archers so that we can bring them to battle. Ride back and keep a close watch on the Scots."

"Yes, my lord,"

It was only later that I realised there must have been spies in our camp. Perhaps Fraser and Menteith were colluding with their countrymen. The Scots were still across the river when I reached my men and, indeed, the numbers had grown. I wondered if the King might have his battle.

"We watch them, and the king will be here by dawn."

When the king arrived, it was still dark. The light from the east showed us that the Scots had fled in the night. The king was in no mood to wait. "They were here last night?"

"Yes, King Edward."

"And they had few horses?"

"Yes, King Edward."

"Then we can catch them." He had not dismounted and, waving his arm, he shouted, "Ride with your king and we can destroy this rabble and be home to watch our harvests collected."

There was a collective cheer and the cavalry clattered over the wooden bridge. I cursed the king for we had not yet mounted and now we had to wait until they had all passed. I turned to Hamo, "What is the point of having a hunting dog if you do not use him?"

As we mounted my son said, "The king has more than fifteen hundred horsemen, Father. He can easily see off the men who were at the bridge."

"But who knows what traps our wily enemies have set? Already the army has lost almost two thousand men to desertion. I fear that this action will merely accelerate that action."

We rode in the dust of fifteen hundred horses. There was no opportunity for us to overtake the column of mailed men, largely nobles, who, hitherto had been mere spectators. I had seen Prince Edward and his coterie closer to the king. He would be eager to show his father what he could do. We reached the army just north of Wigtown. The Scots were waiting for us. They had gathered two thousand men, but few were mailed. The king had the chance to have his battle. He would need my archers to soften up the spearmen and I had Gwillim and his archers dismount. James and John held their horses as they tried to make their way through the massed ranks of horsemen.

The Hunt

The Scots were chanting, "Wallace! Wallace! Wallace!" as they banged their spears and sword pommels against their wooden shields. It was a deliberate insult to the king.

Gwillim looked up at me as two Breton horsemen pointedly put their horses' rumps together to bar their progress. I lost my temper, "William, Sir Ralph, let us clear a passage for our archers."

Gwillim grinned and stepped aside as the three of us forced our horses between the Bretons. I used my elbow to strike one Breton in the side of the head. He turned and was about to speak when I growled, "I am an English archer and a baron, if you wish to have satisfaction then see me when this day is over and there will be another Breton mother mourning the loss of a whelp better drowned at birth." He bowed his head. There would be no recriminations. My reputation preceded me.

It was as we neared the rear of Bishop Bek and his men that disaster struck. Prince Edward had endured enough of the insults being shouted by the Scots and he and Piers Gaveston suddenly launched an attack on the Scots. Other young nobles, keen to impress England's heir, followed him. By any standards, it was ill-judged for there was no cohesion to the line. The Scots had their long spears backed by bows and crossbows. They also had men wielding stones tethered to ropes. The arrows and bolts struck first and both horses and men fell. The ones who did not were then greeted by stones which, at the very least, could unhorse a rider. The handful who managed to reach the spears found that their horses, wiser than their riders, refused to charge and more men fell. The king's trumpet was, at last, heeded, and Prince Edward, remarkably still unhurt, led his sorry companions back.

I managed to reach the side of the king and heard the interchange, "Father, why did you not follow me? We could have trounced these Scots and had the victory."

The king was angry, I could see that but this was his son and the next King of England. He merely growled, "Next time, wait for the command." Raising his voice he said, "Have the wounded taken to the healers. Warbow, your archers."

"They are coming, my lord."

The Scottish plan was now clear for, by the time my archers arrived, the Scots, who had rafts at the ready, crossed the Cree and before Gwillim could send a single arrow the enemy had fled. We saw them streaming east. Wigtown was ours but it was not a victory.

Worse news was to follow. We entered the castle and found that most of the food in the town had been taken. We awaited the arrival of the baggage and our infantry. Less than three thousand marched in. The rest had deserted.

The Hunt

When the scale of the disaster became clear the king ordered a council of war. Noticeably absent were his son and Piers Gaveston. I was included in the meeting. The king looked old, "We have not enough men to continue this campaign and I must send for more. The enemy fled east and I fear there will be mischief in those lands we have already taken. We leave tomorrow. I would have this castle slighted and we will return to Dumfries. I will send to those lords who did not commit men and demand that they send replacements." Silence greeted his words. This was, in my view, the end of the campaign. It was now August and by the time men arrived, it would be September. This was not the land for battles when autumn came. The Scots would hide their harvests and the army would starve. We stood to leave.

"Bishop Bek, I would have you and Warbow, remain."

When we were alone, he waved an irritated arm towards the river, "That little demonstration this morning tells me that our enemy is William Wallace. The Scots will use him as a rallying call until he is taken. Even if I manage to defeat the Scots, as we did at Falkirk, they will still not submit so long as the giant lives." He saw the mystified look on the bishop's face. He knew the threat of Wallace but not why I was here. The king continued, "I am sending Warbow to hunt our enemy." Understanding filled the bishop's face. "Have you chosen your men?"

"I had not yet but I can do so quickly."

"Then choose your men and when we head back to Dumfries you can slip away with them. Will your son be one?"

I shook my head, "Hamo will command in my absence for the rest of this contract, unless, of course, they can return home?"

The king smiled and shook his head, "Your men alone have acquitted themselves well thus far, Warbow. They will be paid." I saw that there was a purse on the table. He pushed it towards me, "This is for any expenses that you might need. I know that you are a resourceful warrior and you will manage to acquire more coins on your journey, but know that any further expenses that you incur will be met by me upon your return." He shook his head, "This war has cost me more than I can afford."

"You could have paid for fewer infantrymen and hired more archers."

He frowned, "I do not need the obvious to be stated."

"Sorry, King Edward."

"You will start in Paris?"

"It seems logical."

"And your disguise?"

"The best way to hide is in plain view, Your Majesty. I will take one of my men at arms and I will be his archer. We can say that we are men seeking work. If I let my beard grow and do not wear the livery of a knight, then men will look at my sergeant and not me."

"And where will you seek work?"

My conversation at Chester had yielded some titbits. The Bretons there had spoken of money to be made but it was many leagues hence, in Byzantium. "I have heard that Roger di Fior is recruiting a company to fight for the Byzantines. That conflict is far enough away so that it will not be a threat to the French or the Emperor.

The king looked impressed, "A good story and one that might work. You still intend to take just a few men?"

"The fewer the better, King Edward. Wallace is easily spotted and I would rather remain hidden."

"Good."

"There is one thing, my lord."

"Yes?"

"I will do all in my power to apprehend him and I will follow him wherever he goes but I cannot guarantee success."

He gave me a steely stare, "In a perfect world you would bring him back and he would stand trial but I know that the world is not perfect. If you cannot bring him back, then kill him. I know that you know how to do that."

I was relieved, "Then I will try to obey your former command, my liege, but if not then, if I can find him, he will die."

I saw Bishop Bek make the sign of the cross. Death that came from combat might be forgiven by the church, but murder was another matter. I knew it would not come to murder. Wallace would try to kill me. Even though he was younger than I was I knew that I had the beating of him.

"Your son shall be paid as though he is you, Warbow. He is a good warrior and I have every confidence in him."

I headed out of the castle to the camp my men had made. I would have to tell them of my mission, mainly because I needed Hamo to take command. When I reached the camp I said, "We break camp now. The army will be heading back to Dumfries and I have permission from the king to ride ahead." That pleased them all not least because we would have the first choice of grazing and be able to plunder on our way there. Thanks to the horses we had taken we could make it in one long day. The days, in August, were still long ones. It would give me the chance to speak to my people while we rode. There would be little chance of my words being heard.

The Hunt

With archers at the fore, I rode with Hamo, Sir Ralph, Jack, Gwillim and Willliam of Ware close by. I waited until we had crossed the Cree and then began to speak. When we stopped to change horses, I would tell the others but, for the moment, just my inner circle needed to hear my words.

"When we reach Dumfries then I shall be leaving you." I held up my hand as they all tried to speak at once. "Hear me out and then I promise I will answer all the questions that I am able to. Hamo, you will command in my absence. King Edward will pay you as a baron." He nodded but not a smile cracked his face. "I am ordered to find and arrest William Wallace." Silence greeted those words as I knew they would. "He was last heard of in Paris and that is where my hunt will begin. I plan on taking just two or three men with me. We will travel in disguise. I shall be an archer seeking work with a sergeant as my master. One of my men at arms will come with me and one other. We will say that we seek work in Byzantium where men at arms and archers, not to mention spearmen are being recruited by Roger di Fior." I smiled, "The king likes the plan."

"As he would, Father, for he will not be the one in mortal danger. This is madness. You are known and have many enemies. You will be killed."

"I intend to grow my beard and crop my hair. Wearing old clothes will detract from my appearance. I will ride a simple hackney with an old saddle." I leaned over and patted Hamo's hand, "And I know why you are angry, my son, you would be the one to come with me, but you know that I must leave you here."

His face told me that my words had hit the mark.

Ralph said, "And by the same token I must stay here too for I am a knight and not a man at arms."

"But I could come." We all turned and looked at Jack. He smiled, "I am perfect for this. If Sir Gerald is the old, gnarled warrior then I shall be the keen young man who just wears a leather jack and an old pot helm."

"Jack, this is not sport, it is dangerous."

"Sir Gerald, you took me from a place that was not only dangerous but also humiliating. The life you have given me is one that has been good and this way I can repay you."

"It could cost you your life."

He shook his head, "Sir Gerald, you have no intention of dying and while I cannot see yet, how we might succeed, I have every confidence that you will find a way."

"I could come too, Sir Gerald."

"No, Gwillim. I need a man at arms, and you will be needed to lead my archers."

"I will come, my lord."

I had hoped that William of Ware would for he was the best of my men, "You are sure? You have a wife."

He nodded, "And she is the daughter of Ralph the Fletcher. He holds you in higher esteem than any man. What would he think if you died in this quest, and I was safe at Yarpole?"

"And what would he think if his son-in-law died?"

"Jack is right and you will not die but that is because I will ensure you keep safe."

I was satisfied with their answers, "I will tell the other men when we change the horses. I have to tell them otherwise there will be questions. I trust them all to keep my secrets."

"That they will, Father." We rode in silence for a while. I was planning the journey and they were taking in the enormity of it."

"You will tell Lady Mary, of course."

I nodded, "Aye, Sir Ralph. I have to return to Yarpole in any case. She will understand better than any."

Hamo shook his head, "I am not sure about that, Father." He turned, "How long will this take?"

"It depends on how far he runs. He is busy drumming up support for his country and he will have messages about the unrest. He will want to get home and lead a rebellion sooner rather than later and I must catch him before he has an army to protect him. It could be half a year or it could be two years. I know not."

I had no idea how my men would react to the news but I was touched that all seemed genuinely concerned about me and all of them volunteered. That night, after we had reached Dumfries and I had crawled into the commandeered bed, I reflected that I could not be such a bad leader if so many men wished to follow me on what might turn out to be a suicide mission.

When I parted from my men the next day, the normal banter we enjoyed was missing. Their hearts would not be in the rest of the campaign. Hamo clasped my forearm with his and said, gruffly, "Watch out for yourself, Father. Do not worry about Jack and William, they are both good men and can look after themselves. It is you that none can afford to lose."

"And I will return."

We did not look back, as we took the road to Carlisle. Such an act would have risked a show of emotion and my family did not indulge themselves like that.

Chapter 7

There were tears in Yarpole when I told my wife. She understood the need but the deaths of people like Queen Eleanor from sickness meant that we might be permanently parted without the involvement of violence. She had seen the effects of disease when she had lived amongst the Mongols and when we had lived in the Holy Land. Once the tears had been shed she became all business. She found good clothes but clothes that looked as if they had seen better days. The old buskins she found were scuffed but had good soles. She found, I know not where, a seal skin cape that would not only keep me dry but, in an emergency would make a small tent. She had her women knit me a woollen hat and that, along with my other clothes, not to mention the cropped hair and growing beard, made me almost unrecognisable. The hackney chosen for me had been a good horse but Sal was getting old. She seemed to be the perfect mount for an ageing archer. The rest of the gear I took were my choices. I did not take my best bow but my second-best one. It still had strength and was slightly easier to draw than the new one. More importantly, it looked as if it had seen good service. I had six spare strings inside my new woollen hat. The sword was not the one I had been given when knighted but a slightly shorter one. It was more than serviceable but looked like it was the sword of an archer rather than a knight. I had my rondel dagger as well as a bodkin blade and a dirk taken at Caerlaverock. With a couple of blankets and ale and waterskin, we were ready.

It took two days to prepare for we had to ensure that the story of our departure was believable. The story was that I had returned for a brief furlough but I had to return to the army. It afforded William an extra couple of nights with his wife and child. We left before dawn. This time it was not to surprise an enemy but to fool friends. I wanted no waves and cheers. I did not want questions. My wife would simply tell any who asked that we had returned to the army. By the time Hamo and the men returned we would be lost in France and questions would not matter. All the words that had been needed to be said had been spoken and we slipped silently through my gates and took the road south. It would be a three-day ride to the busy port of Southampton and that gave us enough time to concoct our stories.

William retained his name, we merely added *of Prescot* for that was a place we had passed on our way to Scotland. Jack could still be Jack of Malton. It had been some time since he had used his place of birth and was more normally called Jack of Yarpole. I was more problematic.

The Hunt

I had used a false name after I fled my home following the murder of my father's killer. I could not use that nor Gerald and so we devised a name. Roger of Talacre had been my friend and he had been killed in Gascony. I had never forgotten one of my first friends and I did not think he would mind the stealing of his name. As William pointed out, when I voiced my concerns, I was borrowing it.

Our story was that we had served in the Scottish wars. We were English and it was logical that we would have done so. We had also fought for King Edward in Flanders. That was important as we might well meet men who had fought in the wars. I had been a lord on a horse with fine livery and now I was back to being an archer. They might vaguely recognise William or see in Jack the young lad they had viewed in those wars but without Warbow and his livery, the connection would be hard to make. We would tell the story that we were leaving England as we were disillusioned and sought a better life with more promise in the east. Many Saxons had taken the same journey after the Battle of Hastings and our journey would be understandable. We stayed in mean inns which cost coppers and ate only the cheapest food on the menu. We drank sparingly and kept to ourselves. It was not until we reached Southampton that we tried out our story. It was a necessary one for men were suspicious of anyone who wanted to go to France. None of us had mail although William took his coif. Jack and William wore helmets and while I had one I would only use it in emergencies. It would serve as a cooking pot more than as armour.

After reaching Southampton, we eventually found a small cog whose captain was willing to take us. He was heading for Harfleur and that meant a longer journey overland than the one from Calais but I gave a slight nod to Willliam, who acted as our spokesman when the offer was made. If any were watching for men seeking Wallace it would be close to Calais. William haggled for the cost of carrying the horses and, finally, Captain Hargreaves agreed to our price provided we would defend his ship in case he was attacked by pirates. I wondered if any passenger would sit idly by and not defend himself but the arrangement suited us and we boarded our three horses. Lowering them into the hold was a challenge but Sal, the oldest was lowered first and as she did not baulk too much the others went in easier. Our berth was also in the hold. It would be a test for us all as it stank before we had even begun our voyage. The only saving grace was that the cargo was made up, largely, of sheepskins. Some enterprising Frenchman had decided that he could undercut the price of English wool by buying the raw product. I knew that the Frenchman was being robbed as the sheepskins were not of the best quality but they made for comfortable beds and we took some of the bales to make a nested chamber.

"How long," Jack looked first at me and then William, "for us to get to France?"

It had taken both of my companions the journey to Southampton to rid themselves of the habit of saying 'my lord' and deferring to me. There was no one in the hold but it paid to be careful. Our lives depended upon it.

I answered, "Two to three days, perhaps even four, depending on the winds."

Jack nodded.

There would be no food provided on the voyage for the captain was penny-pinching but we had brought supplies in the bags that hung from our saddles. They were from Yarpole and were there to augment our diet. The voyage across the sea to France would need us to broach them. I had a money belt beneath my clothes. The money from King Edward and silver from my own treasure were secreted there. My two companions also had money belts with their own emergency coins. Bathing was not an option and by the time we returned to Yarpole, if we returned, then we would be smelled from miles away. It would all add to the illusion. My beard had grown well and while the moustache was dark the beard, like the hair I had cropped was white. Each day Jack used a rondel dagger to shave my head. Many archers liked to keep their hair cropped as it stopped wildlife from gathering there. Wearing a hat provided a nice little nest for head lice and the like. Archers needed hats to keep their bowstrings dry. My men told me that I was barely recognisable without my familiar grey-flecked mane and now with the new growth about my face. The poor diet on the road thus far had also made me leaner than I had been. The journey itself was changing me. Men who had been close to me would recognise me and I knew that Wallace, if we managed to get close to him, might not be fooled by my disguise but if we were that close then it would not matter.

The tide determined the time of our leaving and it was a midnight one. We watched England slip by but, once we had passed Wight and Portsmouth the seas became rougher and we headed below decks. Our horses would need comfort and we did not need a soaking from the sea. Jack had a good singing voice and, once in the hold, he sang soothing songs and the horses calmed. I stroked Sal's head and gave her an apple. I had a bag of them from home. They were largely windfalls that would not last long but the horses did not mind the bruising and they all calmed after being given the treat. We had already eaten and when we had been on deck we had made water. We wrapped ourselves in our blankets and settled between the bales of sheepskins where the rough seas rocked us to sleep.

When we were woken it was a rude one. A ship's boy shook William awake, "Master William, bring your men and bring them armed. There is a French pirate and the captain says you are to earn your passage."

"Tell him we will come."

After donning my buskins I took my bow case and drew the bow. Taking one of my strings I strung it. I had a warbag with my arrows and I fastened it to the sword belt with my scabbarded sword hanging from it. I put my precious strings on my head and then donned the woollen hat given to me by my wife. It still smelled of her and although that would fade I smiled at the memory it evoked. The stringing of the bow delayed me and I was the last of the three of us to climb the ladder out of the hold.

The first mate, Dick, was explaining to William what was needed. He pointed to the southwest, "Johnny Frenchman is yonder, Master William. He has the wind and can run us down where he chooses. He will have more men aboard than we do but you three are the captain's surprise." He spied my bow, "If your old man can hold them off with his bow then, perhaps, we can shake the pirate off. Our ship is nimble and the Frenchman will need to be quick if he is to catch us."

I saw that the ship had a sterncastle and a bow castle. The sterncastle was the one I would have to use for the captain had turned us so that we had the wind from the same quarter as the Frenchman. We were being taken off our course but that could not be helped.

William said, "If they close with us they will grapple. Jack and I will wait at the waist."

I nodded and took my bow and twenty arrows to the sterncastle. The captain looked at me dubiously, "Can you still send an arrow where you wish, old man?"

I snorted, "Aye, I can. And can you still steer a ship for you look to be older than I am?"

He laughed, "Aye, perhaps age will do what youth cannot." I took myself to a corner of the sterncastle that was presently unoccupied. One of the crew also had a bow but it was not a longbow and would only be of use when the Frenchman was almost ready to board. I chose my best arrow. They were all good ones. Ralph the Fletcher had given them all to me before we left but there was always one that spoke to an archer. I drew it and, licking my fingers, smoothed the fletch. I gently nocked it and held it in my left hand as I studied the French ship. It was lower in the water than we were and had neither bow nor sterncastle. It was a hunter. We waddled more than she did but the first mate had said that ours was nimble so what tricks did our captain have up his sleeve?

We rose and fell on crests and troughs. Each time the Frenchman's bow dipped then the ones at the fore were doused with sea water. If they had crossbows or bows they would be useless. Distance was hard to gauge at sea but I guessed that the Frenchman was ten lengths behind us. They had oars out and were using them to propel themselves faster. The gap was narrowing. Of course, they would tire but the sight of an English prize would drive them on. France and England were still at war. Pope Boniface had asked the two kings to make peace but as the French king had demanded that Scotland would be part of the peace then hostile action was still permitted. I realised that this would be the first test of my left arm. Since my wounding, I had not even practised at the mark. I would have to rely on the experience of a lifetime. The wind would be slightly against me but as the French pirate would be packed with men then I had a large target at which to aim. Gwillim would have laughed at my nerves. A ship was a huge target compared with a mark. The pirate drew closer. I might not have used a bow for some time but I had been an archer my whole life and my muscles and my memory took over. I just knew when they were in range. I believed that I had chosen the best arrow and as I drew back and my left arm held then confidence rose in me like sap in a tree in spring. I released. There was no need to grab a second for I wanted to see the flight and watch the effect. I had not needed to worry. The wind was slightly against but the pirate was using oars and the wind. They coincided so that the arrow landed in the men at the oars. I knew I had struck one when the oars on the leeward side were thrown into disarray and the bows swung a little. Our crew cheered.

"You are not too old, archer. I have rarely seen an arrow sent as far as that. There is hope."

I saw the seaman draw back his bow and I snapped, "Do not waste an arrow. We shall need them later. I use a longbow! Watch and learn, boy."

I nocked another knowing that the range would be almost the same. I drew and released. I had to husband my arrows for I had just twenty and once they were gone then the best arrows in the world would be lost to me. The second arrow struck. I did not see the effect but a packed ship meant that I would probably have found flesh. Our crew cheered again. If nothing else, I was giving them heart. I nocked a third arrow and waited. The pirate was drawing closer.

"Master archer, why do you wait?"

The Hunt

I did not turn to look at the seaman with the bow but said, "I have eighteen arrows left. I do not want to waste them. There are men aboard the pirate who are more valuable targets than others. Once they are close enough for us to smell their stink then I can send five arrows by the time you count to twenty. Then it will be your opportunity. Choose your targets. A ship's boy is less important than the man who steers or the one with the boarding axe."

The ship was now just five lengths from us and I saw that they did have crossbows and bows. I laughed as the first missiles fell well short of us despite the following wind. Wet strings were an archer's nightmare. I saw a man with a helmet standing at the bowsprit. He was waving a sword and encouraging the rowers. I drew back and watched as my arrow slammed into his chest and he fell amongst the missile men. I knew that would help to demoralise the others. It also made the men with bows and crossbows take cover. They could not hit me but I could hit them. My hit also had the effect of making men with shields protect the helmsman. He would have been my next target for they were close enough for me to target individuals. Instead, I chose the seaman who was clambering up the rigging to tighten a sail. When my arrow hit him he fell, not into the sea, but the waist of the ship. I quickly nocked another arrow and seeing one of the shield bearers lower his shield to see the fallen man I sent an arrow into his shoulder, spinning him around. My age caught up with me for I could not draw, nock and release another arrow quickly enough at the tempting target of the helmsman. The shield was raised and he was safe once more.

The pirate was now gaining. The rowers were giving that extra burst of speed that meant no matter how lively was our ship, they were gaining. The price they would pay was in tiredness but they would outnumber us and, if they boarded, would take us easily. Our captain had done his best and held them off for long enough but they were gaining and when the wind began to veer then I knew that they would catch us. As the pirate began to draw alongside us so I drew, nocked and released as I had at Crécy. My muscles burned but I steeled myself.

"Now, is your turn!" I spoke without turning my head and soon the seaman was sending his arrows into the pirate ship. Our ship's boys were in the rigging and they hurled stones from their slings. Some of the pirates were wearing helmets and the stones pinging from them sounded like hailstones. Every one of my arrows found flesh. Not all were mortal strikes, but they would take a pirate from the fight.

I kept one arrow and as the pirate drew next to us I aimed at the pirate captain. He had a helmet and was protecting himself with a shield but now that the wind was no longer against me and they were close enough for me to spit at I sent the arrow at his head. He thought he was safe, peering over the edge of his shield as my last arrow entered his cheek and drove into the back of his skull. He fell. I slung my bow and, drawing my sword, hurried to the waist and my companions.

William shook his head, "That was as fine a display of archery as I have ever seen but I fear that our quest ends here in the English Channel."

"Will, you should know better than any that it is not over until the bodies are buried. We have hope and they have to ascend our ship."

"Repel boarders."

The crew who were not needed to attend to the sails now ran to grab weapons. Had the seaman and I not thinned their numbers then the battle would have been a foregone conclusion but I had slain the two leaders and we had thinned their numbers so that we were slightly more evenly matched.

The first mate joined us and said, "We owe you a mighty debt, archer. Now let us see if we can surprise these Frenchmen." He bent down and picked up a stone; I had not noticed them before but there was a line of stones close to the gunwale. The other seamen picked them up as grappling hooks were thrown. We did not need telling and the three of us raced to the nearest rope to hack into it. More were thrown and then I heard the first mate shout, "Now!" ten huge rocks were hurled and I could not help but peer over the side. The stones had hit men but, more importantly, a couple had struck the deck and I saw water.

One grappling hook still tethered us and four pirates raced up and leapt aboard. This was a job for warriors and not sailors. I held my sword two handed as Jack and William advanced with swords and daggers. The pirates held boarding pikes which afforded them longer range but our weapons were sharp. Two pirates went for William. He blocked one blow with his dagger whilst hacking the end off the other. I used brute strength to knock the boarding pike to the side and then backhanded it to hack into the man's neck. Jack had improved so much that his sword held the pike whilst his dagger gutted the pirate. The two pirates who were left were faced by three men with swords. Only one had a pike and as he reached for his short sword I rammed my sword into his throat and William finished off the other.

The first mate yelled, "She is holed!"

Without ropes to tie her to us and with the crew trying to stem the flow of water we began to pull away. The four pirates who had boarded were dead. We took their purses and weapons before hurling their bodies over the side. The fish would feed on their corpses. The crew cheered as the captain turned us to rejoin our original course and we were able to enjoy the sight of the pirates trying to save their ship. Our slow turn meant we watched as they dropped an old sail over the side and then began to bail. They would make the coast although it would take them days. They might go a-pirating again but they would need to repair their ship first.

The captain approached us and he had a beaming smile on his face, "I thought we were doomed." He was speaking to William but he nodded to me, "You have a mighty archer in this one, my friend, keep him safe and you shall earn a good living."

The voyage took another two days but the atmosphere was a happy one. The crew shared their food and their wine, saving our supplies for when we would need them. They chatted to us and, it seemed, we were part of the crew. When we docked, not long after dawn, the captain offered to speak to the innkeeper in the port and get us a discounted rate for a room. William told him that we needed to get to Byzantium before the hiring ended. It seemed a plausible answer and as we walked our horses east the crew seemed genuinely sad to see us part. The reason we walked our horses was to allow us and our animals to get back our land legs that three days at sea had taken from us. It also allowed us to talk on the empty road, about our plans and the events of the voyage.

"We saved ourselves but I lost my good arrows."

William said, "The captain gave you a sheaf of arrows, did he not?"

"He did but they are poorly made ones. The arrows have badly made heads and the flights are tatty. The wood is slightly warped. I can use them but not well."

William laughed, "You do not actually seek work, Roger of Talacre, you play a part."

I reddened a little in embarrassment, "But who knows if we may need them again?"

"Your sword will be of more use. You showed on the pitching deck of the cog that you have lost nothing of your skill." William looked ahead, "Now we have many miles to travel."

I had studied maps and knew that we had roughly the same journey across France as we had in England. The difference was that France was at war with England and here every man was a potential enemy.

We walked our horses until we came to the tiny hamlet of Rogerville. There was a water trough and we watered our horses. I was the one who spoke the best French although that was not saying much and I spoke to a local woman to ask for directions and to buy food. I suppose living this close to the coast brought the people into contact with the English and this had been part of England for so long that there was less resentment to us. King John and his son King Henry had lost Normandy to the French and that had come about in my lifetime. Perhaps the Normans thought King Edward was not the same as his father and might recover his lost lands. Whatever the reason she was friendly and did not rob us. We headed east and found an inn at Lillebonne. Once more there was less resentment to us but we were overcharged for the chamber, the food and the stabling but we were safer than I had expected.

It was as we neared Rouen that I began to become more fearful. This had been the capital of Normandy and the French had a strong garrison. There was no way of avoiding the city as any attempts to do so would have made us look suspicious. The guards at the city gates saw our weapons and stiffened, "What is your business here?"

William's poor French actually helped us. He said, "We are passing through on our way to Byzantium to seek work with the Roman Emperor."

I saw them visibly relax. If we had ulterior motives then we would have spoken better French. They knew us as English. My bow case had not helped. One of them, the captain, I assume, switched to English, "And why would the emperor need three such warriors? There is not a hauberk between you and those nags will be lucky to get to Paris, let alone, Marseille."

I growled, "He needs archers and stout Englishmen, that is why and if our horses die then we shall walk."

"Peace, Roger." He smiled at the man, "My friend is old and cantankerous. I apologise for him and his words but he is right. There is no work for us in England, not that pays well anyway, and so we need to earn money as swords for hire. The Byzantines are rich."

One of the others said, in French, "He is right Captain Jean, perhaps we should join them. The pay here is…"

He got no further for the captain of the guard snapped, "Robbers, pirates, brigands: any and all of them will stop these three. They will die on the road." Turning back to William he said, "You may pass and I wish you well on your journey but I fear it will end badly for you."

We were in the city and our story had held. We chose an inn by the river. They were the cheapest and the roughest. Luckily for us, we found one which had an owner sympathetic to the English. He confided in us that Englishmen paid better. He also implied that the French judged his food badly and he did not like that. I understood his comments for the food suited us; it was plain, wholesome and there was plenty of it. The French had pickier palates. Once again, we were not robbed. It did not matter for we had plenty of coins but we were saving money and that could only be a good thing.

That night in our tiny room we discussed, very quietly, how it was going. I was aware that poor Jack was new to all of this and needed reassurance that we would survive. "We have seventy miles to go. The first two days were easy ones and that means we can reach Paris in two. Being down at heel makes us appear less dangerous." They both nodded, "Your French is improving, William."

He smiled, "I know, the more I speak it the more I seem to understand. I know I am butchering their language but that cannot be helped."

"I think they just like it when we do try. By the way, you play the captain well. Continue to berate me whenever you wish. Men will not associate me with Gerald Warbow, Lord Edward's Archer."

Chapter 8

We had used the market to augment our dwindling supplies as we hoped to avoid any more crowded places. Rouen had felt threatening and even though nothing had happened we all felt as though danger or discovery was just around the corner. So long as we were in disguise we were relatively safe but once our identity was known then our lives would be measured in hours. We were increasingly wary as we rode on the road from Rouen. What we noticed was the larger number of men we encountered who spoke English. What was worse was that some spoke with a Welsh accent and some with a Scottish one. Few were soldiers, and in that, I took some comfort, but there were more men from my homeland than I liked. We were also wary because of the larger numbers on the road. That was partly because of our later start due to our use of the markets. Our time of departure was also constrained by the time they opened the gates of the city. This was not Lillebonne where we could leave when we liked. Another consideration was that there were many travellers heading for the capital of France. Some merchants used the river to transport their goods to the city where they would fetch a higher price but there were many who risked the road for a profit. There were others who, as in England, were heading to a major city to seek their fortune, or perhaps a change in them.

Five miles out of Rouen we stopped at a stream that ran close to the road and watered our horses. There was a throng of men on the road and they not only barred our path, they prevented us from speaking. I knew we had a choice; barge through them and find a clear and open road or wait until they had moved on. I knew the former would ingrain us in their minds. If we delayed, then while we might reach our bed for the night late, we could make an earlier start and get ahead of them.

Half a mile from the road I saw what looked like a small, abandoned church. The ground close to the stream suggested that there had been houses here at some time in the past but some violence or, perhaps, disease had destroyed it. Perhaps the church had been used by the locals. I nodded to it and began to lead my horse there. If people saw us they might think we sought to commune with God. I had seen pilgrims on the road to Paris and in Rouen had spied and heard a couple of warriors who were heading for the Holy Land to take the cross. Our action would not be seen as sinister. We walked in a line with heads bowed. A boggy patch of ground meant we had to take a detour and I wondered at the wisdom of my decision. We picked our way across a dry line of ground and found ourselves approaching the church from the west and not the south. The detour also dropped us below the sight of those on the road.

The raised voices from within the ruined church made me stop. Although they were French we could understand them. Our time in Normandy was improving our language every day. The others were alert too and, after dropping their reins, both Jack and William drew their swords. Leaving Sal to graze, I slipped my bow from its case and strung it. I nocked an arrow.

The voices ahead were threatening, "You are a priest and we know that you have money. You have hidden your coins. Where are they?"

The voice that replied was filled with terror, "I am a poor pilgrim and I have nothing. If I had coins would I have slept in this abandoned church where you found me?"

"Just slit his throat and we will sell his buskins and this cross. This nag of his we can sell to the horsemeat man."

We were trying to stay hidden, but we had stumbled upon violence and it was not in our nature to walk away from those in peril. We exchanged looks and the other two flanked me and moved apart so that when we moved closer, I would have a clear line of sight of whatever was happening. The church had been built on a slightly higher piece of ground and so was above us. As we edged around the sides we watched for anything that would make a noise.

I drew the string back a little. It was far from a full draw but it would enable me to send an arrow quickly. As we began to ascend, I saw a young priest, he was tonsured. A man had his arm wrapped around the priest's head and a knife was at his throat. A second man held the reins of the sorriest-looking horse I had ever seen. It was all skin and bones. A third man held a short sword. It was the horse that gave us away. It neighed and the man with the sword whipped his head around.

The man's eyes narrowed and he waved his sword contemptuously at us, "Leave us to our work lest we turn our attention to you."

William had now fully assumed the role of leader and he said, "Let the priest go. Walk away while you can, my friend."

"I am not your friend and if you think I am afraid of an old man with a bow then you are mistaken."

The man holding the priest was grinning for he had a human shield. He called out, "Henri, shall I slit this throat and then we take these three. They look to have purses that are worth taking."

The man holding the horse had dropped the reins and drawn his sword. The leader began to advance. My disguise was working. He did not recognise me as a seasoned archer. He saw me as an old man with a bow. He thought my reactions would be slow.

William saw the signs too and he sighed, "Do not step down this path for it will end badly."

"Gaston, do it."

I was drawing back even as William said, "Roger."

The range was just twenty paces and even with a poorly made arrow I could not miss. Gaston had obliged me by moving his head back so that he would not be splattered with the priest's blood when he cut his throat. The arrow struck him in his right eye. I was annoyed with myself for I had aimed at the centre of his forehead. The result was the same. The head flew back, and the knife fell from lifeless hands. The other two just stared as the man lay on the ground, his arms spread like a crucifix. As I nocked another arrow, I reflected that he had fallen where the altar would have been. The priest slumped to the ground and sat staring at us.

I swung my bow so that I was facing the leader, "Henri, is it?" The man nodded, "Then drop your sword before you join Gaston there. You have seen my skill and know that I am an archer."

The man dropped his sword.

William said, "And you, too." The last man obeyed. William looked at me and I nodded. There was little point in killing these two. They had no animals and could not pursue us. Besides which, I had seen the look of terror on the faces of the two men. Our shabby clothes and my white beard had fooled them. They now saw us for what we were. "Take off your boots." The men looked puzzled but obeyed. William remembered how we had dealt with the Scots. A man without boots was not a threat. "Now pick up your friend and take him hence. Return at noon and your swords and boots will be close by. Unless, of course, you wish to try a bout with one of us. Perhaps you can defeat us."

The bandit shook his head, "Our lives are all that we seek." They hurried to their dead friend and picked him up. William pointed to the north and they headed towards a stand of trees that stood there.

I shouted, "The crucifix."

They still had the priest's cross and the man holding it threw it to us. The priest caught it deftly.

William said, "Jack, the horses."

As Jack left I tracked the men with my bow and nocked arrow. The one called Henri saw my movement and they moved more quickly. I did not lower the bow until they entered the wood. Then I returned the arrow to my belt and unstrung my bow. William had poured some ale from his skin into a coistrel. The priest was shaken, and his wide eyes showed his terror. I spoke calmly, "Whither are you bound, priest?"

He drank the whole coistrel and then, taking the outstretched arm of William, pulled himself upright. "Paris. I was heading for the cathedral there. I have a penance to perform."

William said, "We heard your words but there are safer places to sleep than an abandoned church far from the road."

He gave a sad smile, "I thought that I would be safe in a church, I was wrong." He took the reins of his horse and stroked the animal's head, "Marie here gave me away. She neighed at the wrong time and they burst upon me."

Jack had arrived with the horses. Fate had intervened but it had upset our plans. We were now responsible for the young man and until we found a place to stay we had to watch over him. I spoke, "Ride with us then, at least until the next town." I bowed my head, "If our leader agrees, we can pay for a meal for you and some oats for your horse." Jack had produced one of our windfalls and Marie greedily gobbled it. "It seems she needs a good meal too."

"And you can entertain us with your tale." William looked at me, "Perhaps the road will now be clear."

After hurling the boots and the swords closer to the bog we walked our animals back towards the road. As soon as we rose from the dip I saw that the road was now emptier. In fact, the traffic was now heading to Rouen rather than away from it. We mounted and William said, "I am William, the leader of our little group, this is Roger of Talacre, as you saw, he is an archer, and this is Jack. We are heading first for Paris and then for Marseille where we will take ship for Byzantium and Constantinople. We are swords for hire."

He looked from me to William and then nodded, "You are English. Would it not have been faster and easier for you to travel first to Bordeaux where you could travel through Gascony which still belongs to your king?"

The priest was clever and that, perhaps, was no surprise. He had seen the flaw in our plan.

Jack laughed, "And had we done that, my friend, then your corpse would be lying in the church and your horse would be butchered for meat."

William nodded, "Thank you might have been a better response rather than questioning our motives."

"I am sorry, and you are right. I am grateful but perhaps I deserved to have my throat cut." He leaned forward and stroked Marie's mane, "But Marie here does not deserve such an end. Let us begin again and I will curb my natural curiosity. It was always a failing of mine. I am Robert d'Arbre. My father is a knight with a small manor. I was the second son and not martially minded nor did I enjoy farming. I loved books and reading and in that lay my doom."

I was intrigued and entertained by the story. Robert was a natural storyteller and he already had me wanting to know more. I could tell that William and Jack felt the same by their wrapt looks.

"There was a monastery close to my home and the abbot there allowed me to become a novice. My father did not want a priest for a son and he thought that once I had sampled the life in a Franciscan monastery, I would decide that a secular life was better than a monastic one." He shrugged, "Perhaps he was right. I enjoyed reading and I loved the copying of manuscripts." He smiled, "I am told that I have a good hand. What I did not like were the hours. Rising for lauds never appealed. I did not mind the frugal fare but I tired of the company of serious men who never smiled. When I was not copying manuscripts, I worked in the infirmary where I learned how to tend to men. Sometimes it was simple injuries, such as broken limbs, whilst at others we looked after those whom God had smitten with disease. I helped men to live but I also saw men die. It helped me to grow up and become a man."

Jack jumped in for he thought he saw the end of the story, "So you left the monastery."

William glared at my foster son. Robert just gave a sad smile, "I suppose I should have done and that may have been a good decision, but I did not. I was stubborn and determined to prove my family wrong."

I asked, "Your mother?"

He nodded, "You are clever, archer, aye, my mother is dead. The plague took her and the softness she imparted to our family was gone. Had she been alive then..." he made the sign of the cross. "We choose a path and some paths cannot be retraced. The abbot was not an unkind man and he saw my unhappiness. The priest in the local church was not a kind man and the abbot saw that too. He asked me to minister to the villagers. It meant that I did not have to pray as much in the monastery and I met people who smiled and spoke of mundane matters and the weather. I still spent many hours transcribing holy works and that was a joy but I also left the silence of the monastery. I heard the laughter of children."

Jack could not help himself, "Could you not have become a priest in the village?"

"That might have been a good choice, but Father Bertholt did not like me." He shook his head, "I am not sure that Father Bertholt liked

80

anybody. His sermons were always about burning in hell. He used Latin like a weapon to intimidate all. It did not work with me as I can both read and write Latin and Greek." He saw the question forming on Jack's lips, "When my mother was alive, she taught me. She was a learned woman. I was close to her and my brother was closer to my father." He shrugged, "Such things happen."

"I was an only child but I can see what you mean."

William and Jack looked at me as I revealed a hidden part of my life. I never spoke of my upbringing. They knew not about the killing of a knight in revenge for the hanging of my father.

"Father Bertholt regarded the villagers as being beneath him, however, I enjoyed it. I found pleasure in speaking to them all. I was not a priest and could not hear confession but the younger ones in the village confided in me. One of them, Anna, was most troubled and her tale was the one that concerned me the most. It took some time to win her confidence but after a month when I saw her every day, she confided her darkest secret to me. She had no mother, and that made us both closer, but her father worked as a charcoal burner. It meant she lived alone in the mean home that they shared. He would spend a week or more in the woods and then return for a few days. I had noticed that she was putting on weight and as her diet was as poor as the other villagers that surprised me. She eventually confided in me that she was with child. I was delighted but she was not. I asked her who the father was, and she was reluctant to say. It took two days of badgering and then she told me that it was Father Bertholt."

"The priest!" Jack, like me, was shocked.

"Aye, he is a most venal man and took advantage of the young girl." He was silent for a while.

William said, "While I would hear the end of this tale I can tell that it upsets you. You need not continue if you do not wish to."

He shook his head, "No, I need to confess to someone for it was my sin of pride that caused the tragedy. I thought I was wiser than I was. I confronted Father Bertholt, and it was a mistake. He called me a liar and went to the abbot to tell him that I was spreading lies about him and he wanted me whipped."

"But the girl, surely, she would have backed up your story?" Jack was young and his innocence made him see a world that was ideal and not real.

Robert shook his head, "When the news emerged and I was taken before the abbot, Anna took herself to the pond, weighed herself down with stones and took her own life." The three of us made the sign of the cross. The troubled girl would never get to heaven.

81

Even I was shocked and we rode in silence. The clip-clop of our horses' hooves seemed like a funeral march.

William said, "And you were sent away because of that?"

"No, I was sent away for when burial was refused I lost my temper and I struck the evil man that had caused this. I struck him so many times that he was rendered unconscious and I had to be pulled away. My father wanted me punished severely. He wanted me to be whipped. The abbot intervened and said that I was to do penance by travelling to Notre Dame in Paris. He said I was to ask God what I needed to do. My father agreed but said that I was no longer his son." He shook his head, "He must have felt something for me as he let me take Marie, although she was of little use to him so perhaps not." He looked at William, "My tale is almost at an end. I persuaded the abbot to let me bury Anna in a quiet corner of the monastery. I was the one who spoke the words for Marie and her unborn child. The rest you know. I had little money and I travelled for two weeks. I worked twice for a meal but most of the time I have eaten from the hedgerows and slept where I could. It has allowed me to contemplate my life and my future."

I said, "You no longer wish to be a priest."

"You are a clever man. Those grey hairs in your beard signify wisdom. I will do as the abbot said but my mind is made up. I will seek a life where I can help others. After Paris…? I know not."

We stopped a few miles later at Abbaye Notre-Dame de Fontaine-Guérard. We did not know the name when we found the place but the priory seemed a good place to stop and to pay for refreshment. The nuns were Cistercians and we were afforded a limited welcome. We were not allowed in the priory but there was a water trough and we paid for bread, honey cakes and cheese. When Robert discovered the name of the priory he dropped to his knees.

"Perhaps this is a sign."

The nun who had brought out the food was an older nun and she smiled and put her hand on Robert's head, "I can see, by your garb and your hair that you have been in holy orders but travelling with men of war seems a little incongruous."

It had taken time to hear his full story but he told it to the nun in a few words. Perhaps it was the habit that encouraged him, "I struck a priest who had abused an innocent girl and caused her death. I am to go to Notre Dame and do penance." He nodded at us, "These men saved my life when I was attacked on the road."

Her face became serious and then she nodded, "I cannot condone violence nor can I sanction abuse, even from a man of the cloth." She made the sign of the cross and said, "Go and do your penance but know that you are not a bad man. I can see that." She turned to us, "And I can see that despite their weapons and rugged features these are good men. Journey together and find solace in each other. God has put you together, you, young pilgrim and these unlikely Samaritans."

Just then a nun came out and said, "Abbess Elizabeth."

"I come." William held out some coins and she shook her head and folded his fingers around them. "The food is a gift as are my words. Mayhap all will be well for you."

That meeting in the priory changed us all. It was as though the abbess had spun a spell and bound us together.

The rescue and halt at the priory meant we only reached the hamlet of Les Thilliers-en-Vexin. There was no inn there but that also meant there were no other travellers. It was the presence of Robert that gained us shelter and food. The headman of the village had a farm and seeing that Robert was a priest, he let us use his barn and his wife provided a meal for which we paid. The barn proved to be a godsend, especially for Marie as it had been used to store oats and barley. The four horses wandered the barn eating the grains that remained. There were many of them.

I nodded to his head, "Your tonsure marks you as a priest, as does your garb."

Although he wore boots, obviously from his home, his clothes were just a brown habit and a cloak. He did not even have a hat.

"I will grow out my hair and, as you can see, the lack of a razor means that my beard is growing. Once I have visited the cathedral I will find other clothes."

Jack was the most curious of us all, probably because Robert was not much older than he was, "And you do not know what you will do with your life?"

"I could go to the Holy Land. There I could serve God and others."

I shook my head, "Therein lies madness. I have been to the Holy Land and the crusades are a war we cannot win."

"Yet you three travel to the Roman Empire."

I smiled, "For payment. You would seek to serve God and people in a land where the ones who rule it do so with religion in their hearts and those who seek to take it do so for money."

"And the pilgrims?"

I shook my head, "Are deluded. Most never reach the Holy Land and those that do are preyed upon and, at best, disappointed."

"You are a cynic."

"I speak from experience." I decided that I had said enough and I remained silent.

William glanced at me and said, "Stay with us until Paris. We will pray with you at Notre Dame and then, if God wills it we will go our separate ways. The three of us will need God's help if we are to perform the task we have set ourselves."

I nodded, "Amen to that."

Robert gave us a curious look but smiled and said, "I shall enjoy your company and getting to know your story."

Chapter 9

We were now just over forty miles from Paris and had there only been the three of us then we might have made it in one day. Marie was still an unfit animal and it meant we would have to stop in Pontoise. We would have to use coins to pay for the inn and for food. I did not object to the expense for I liked Robert and such an act of kindness could only help me enter the next world. The problem was that he was bright and he was curious. My men and I had no opportunities to speak to each other. We could have spoken in English, he knew that was what we were, but I was unsure how much he would understand. I just had to hope that the others would not make a slip. What I did and I prayed the others did, too, was to listen for any word of Wallace and it was in Pontoise, as we ate a stew with tripe and slowed cooked meat of some description, that we heard the first whisper.

There were some merchants at the next table and they were heading for the coast. As we were speaking French, for the benefit of Robert, they did not know we were English.

The younger of the merchants was speaking, "Do you think, Richard, that any will pay us for the news that William Wallace has returned from Rome to Paris?"

The older man to whom the question was addressed snorted, "King Edward will know soon enough, for I heard that Pope Boniface has sent a missive to the king to tell him to halt his invasion of Scotland, which he determines to be a sovereign state. Besides, I do not wish to incur the wrath of the Scots. Let sleeping dogs lie. What is it to do with us? Our business is the making of money. We would make more if there was no war between France and England. If King Edward is forced to cease his invasion then there might be a peace."

The conversation ended when they paid their bill and retired. Merchants made money not by wasting it in inns but by eating frugally and retiring early. As much as I wished to speak to the others the presence of Robert prevented it.

Robert showed that he understood English, at least when he said, "Is that why you left England? King Edward's wars will soon be over."

William smiled, "The wars against the Scots were never profitable. We knew not that the war might end."

The answer seemed to satisfy the novice priest but was a warning to me to be even more close-mouthed than we had been. The sooner we were at Notre Dame and could rid ourselves of the affable young man the better.

The Hunt

I had to confess that having Robert with us did make life easier. For some reason, we were more trusted because we had a priest with us. His French was also far better than ours and whilst the rest of us sometimes missed out on the nuances of a phrase, Robert did not. He also had a good ear and reported conversations he thought we might find interesting. That was also a little worrying as I thought he might suspect more than was good for us. He was grateful for all that we did for him. Marie, in particular, had regained some of her strength. Our store of apples did not last long but we were able to buy carrots when we found markets and being fed grain helped her.

As we left Pontoise, having bought more supplies for the prices would be higher in Paris, he said, as we left the town and headed on the road east, "I know that I would not have made it this far without your help. A traveller alone might be rooked at best and death was almost my fate. If there is anything I can do to help you then I beg you to ask."

William, like me, was suspicious but he smiled, "You keep translating for us while we are in Paris and that is repayment enough. Our French is improving but we still sound like foreigners and that puts us at a disadvantage."

"Of course. How long do you stay in Paris?"

That was a tricky question. William shrugged, "A few days for we need to find the best route. Do we head for Marseille and take a ship? Lyon and head down the Rhône? Or will a route across land serve us best? There are men in Paris who will know. We will seek out men like us, swords for hire. I fear that we may well have to use inns that are rougher than you would like. Once we reach the cathedral, we shall part, eh? Go our separate ways?"

He shook his head, "You wish to pray in the cathedral, and it will not take me long to do penance. The abbot told me the words to say. Do not worry about the inn being rough. I am hardier than you think and besides, four can live as cheaply as three."

My heart sank. He was like a puppy and had adopted us. How would we shake him off? I realised that I had changed. When I was younger I would have discarded him quickly. Marrying Mary and becoming a father had changed me. I felt responsible for others. I would wrestle with guilt long after an event. We were now tethered to the young man.

Our experience at the gates of Paris showed me that we still had need of him. As he was French we let him speak whenever speech was necessary to smooth our passage. The guards at the gate were suspicious of us but Robert chattered away like a magpie and they smiled.

"I come to Paris to do penance at the cathedral of our lady."

The elder of the guards laughed, "And for what should a priest so young do penance?"

Robert smiled and shook his head, "Even a priest commits sins and the penance of a priest needs something as magnificent as a cathedral as a means of speaking with God."

"Aye, they say it will be finished in my lifetime but finished or not it is still the finest church this side of Rome!

One of the others shook his head, "It may be better than the one in Rome, we have never been there."

The other stood his ground, "It stands to reason, that it must be better. The Pope resides there."

The sergeant turned his attention to us, "And why does a priest need to ride with three armed men?"

Robert became serious, "These men travel to fight for the Emperor of Rome and besides, they saved my life and rescued me from bandits. I owe them much."

The simple truth of the answer persuaded the men and the leader nodded and they moved aside, "Go with God."

As simple as that and we were in.

We rode directly across the bridges of the Seine to the Île de la Cité and the cathedral of Notre Dame. It was a magnificent edifice but it still had scaffolding around it and men were working on the south transept. What struck me were the buttresses which supported the walls. They looked to me like the wings of some sort of enormous bird and made it look as though the cathedral might fly to heaven. They also added to the size making even an old cynical warrior like me make the sign of the cross. It made me think of God and my mortality. The towers and flèche, spires, that rose high into the sky seemed to almost touch the clouds. When you looked up they melded into the sky and heaven. I felt small before the towers. We dismounted and walked our horses for the last two hundred paces. There was a practical reason for that. Most people were on foot and we stood out. We were too visible. Anyone could be watching and we had to see our enemies before they saw us. With our horses flanking us we walked across the cobbles to the doors of the church.

As with all such buildings the entrance was festooned with beggars and, I do not doubt, thieves. Our weapons made the latter wary of us but beggars, some, apparently horribly disfigured, cried pitifully for alms. Robert was young and I worried that he might be taken in by the ones who faked injuries but he turned to me, "The abbot warned me about those who crawl here each morning and beg during the day and who, miraculously, are cured by the end of the day for they scamper home, only to be afflicted by the same disease each morning. We will seek those who are able-bodied." He saw William's questioning look and explained, "We need to go within and that necessitates leaving our animals outside. I fear that without some guard for them, you would be walking to the emperor." He nodded to Willliam's purse, "This will cost some copper coins."

He headed for a man and his son. Both were whole but clearly needed alms for their clothes were tattered and they looked thin and emaciated. Neither was as loud as the fake beggars, the professionals, and simply stood. As we neared them, for it was clear that we were heading in their direction, the man said, quietly and humbly, "A sous, sirs for my son and I to eat this night."

Robert said, "We would pay you to watch our horses whilst we are within. Can you be trusted with them?"

The man stiffened, "I was a soldier of France and fought against her enemies. Had not my wife died and I not suffered dysentery then I would not be reduced to this impoverished state. If I say your horses will be safe then they will be."

Robert nodded, "I meant no offence but," he glanced at a beggar whose injuries were clearly fake, "you are in the company of those who prey on the innocent."

"I understand but we will watch them for you."

What impressed me was that he did not hold out a palm for coins but stood there, patiently. I gave a slight nod to Willilam who counted out six copper coins. "There will be more when we return."

The beaming smile on the man was greater than the worth of the coins, "Thank you, they will be here." He nodded to the water trough that was nearby, "We will wait there where the animals can drink and it is less crowded."

He and his son led the four animals away and with uncovered heads we entered the darkness that was Notre Dame. Inside it was noisier than I expected. The noise was the murmur of prayers being intoned but such was the number that it sounded like the buzzing of bees. As soon as we stepped from the vestibule then we were bathed in the colourful light from the jewelled glass of the windows that flooded the interior of the church. The walls were a blonde colour, and they reflected the light back into the church. We were in Robert's hands. The abbot had given him clear instructions and the young man followed them. He did not head for the altar where people were cheek by jowl but for one of the side chapels. He sought one where there was just a woman with a cloth over her head. She was kneeling and mumbling a prayer. He turned to us, "Here is where I will pray. I shall see you back outside?"

We nodded and watched him as he walked to the chapel with the statue and sank to his knees. I did not wish to intrude on his penance nor did I wish to leave without speaking to God. I saw another chapel, closer to the entrance where no one knelt. I headed there. The others followed me. I saw why it was devoid of people. There was neither a rail nor a statue. I did not need a statue. I just needed the cathedral. I sank to my knees and held my palms together in prayer. I was speaking to God and while I knew that he would hear my thoughts I wanted to give voice to my words. I said them so quietly that Willliam and Jack who flanked me could not hear them. They joined in the buzz of supplication that rose to the rafters.

"Almighty God, I am not a godless man and yet I have done things in my life that I should not. Men have died at my hands and it was not in battle. For that, I ask forgiveness. I did what I did for my king and my country. I pray that when my time comes, such acts will not bar me from the joy of heaven. I have tried to be a good man and I have helped others when they were in need." I sighed for the words had tumbled out and I felt much better for having said them. "I pray that you watch over my family: my wife, son, daughters, and grandchildren. They have not committed the crimes that I know I am guilty of." Once more the simple saying of the words brought me an ease. "I pray for the man I have served my whole adult life. King Edward is not a perfect man but he is the finest of kings. I pray that you give him guidance as he steers the ship of England through stormy waters." Suddenly there was no more to be said. Jack and Willliam would be asking for God's help in their own ways and I simply said, "Amen." I closed my eyes and kept my head still. I listened to the noise around me and thought of God in heaven, hearing all the words as they rose into the skies. I prayed that he would hear at least some of mine.

I stood and saw that Jack and William had risen already. Not a word was spoken. It was as though there was an unspoken thought that made us all move towards the door. We left and headed for the horses. The man and his son were stroking them. I murmured, "Pay them well. We gave nothing to the church, let us pay those two for the peace that I feel."

William gave me a shy smile, "Aye, for I feel as though I am cleansed in some way. I do not understand it."

I said, "I do, God was within those walls. I felt him and I was humbled."

William gave the man two silver coins and his eyes widened, "Thank you, my lord."

William said, "I am not a lord but a simple soldier like you. Let us say that any of us could have suffered as you have and if I had then I would hope for kindness from some stranger."

He slipped the coins into a purse secreted beneath his tunic, "You are English."

"We are." William's voice was wary.

The man nodded, "I fought against you and I saw this," he tapped my bow case. He nodded to me, "You have the build of an archer. We may have fought against one another."

I smiled, "Aye, we may but we are both here and the ones alongside whom we fought may well be dead, eh?"

He smiled too, "And had we spoken before we fought then who knows, we may have been friends."

I was doubtful but I nodded, "Perhaps."

"I am Michel, and this is my son Jean-Michel. What brings you to Paris?"

"We are heading for the east where we will serve the emperor." The man was speaking to me. I think it was the bond that we may have fought against one another rather than a recognition of my position. "We are looking for other warriors who may be able to give us sage advice."

He gestured to the south of the river, "There are others like you, swords for hire, they frequent the inns close to the College of Sorbonne. There are Germans, Hungarians, Bretons and some from your homeland, the Welsh and the Scots."

I tried to keep a straight face and was glad that he was speaking to me for Jack's eyes widened when the Frenchman said 'Ecosse'.

"Then, when our friend returns, if you would guide us there we shall give you more coins."

He shook his head, "We will do it for nothing. Already you have given us more than we might expect in a week of such begging. Soon we shall have enough to leave this cruel city and head back to Senonche where I was born."

I put my hand on his forearm, "We will pay you again for William is quite right. Any of the three of us could be in the same position as you and besides, we still have the coins in our purses we earned in England."

"Then our prayers have been answered and my son and I can leave on the morrow." All we need are the few belongings we have. If you will wait here we shall fetch them."

He and his son hurried off along the side of the north transept. "A stroke of luck, eh?"

I nodded, "Aye, William, but we cannot endanger either Robert or this man and his son." I nodded towards the cathedral, "We spoke to God and such an act might jeopardise all that we have done thus far."

Jack said, "And yet I will miss Robert. I like him."

"And that is why we must make him leave us. If he stays with us then his life will be in danger." William and I understood that which Jack did not. Innocents would always be the first to die.

When the father and son returned with their meagre belongings my heart sank. The pair had next to nothing. The tatty blanket would barely keep them warm in summer, and in winter… The two wooden bowls, spoons and their coistrels were all that they had in the way of supplies. They did not even have a skin for water. That meant they would have to use horse troughs. I realised that I was already thinking of taking responsibility for them and yet their plight had nothing to do with me. As they neared us, I realised why. The hunt for William Wallace was not important, not in the grand scheme of things. I knew that he was a poor general and as a symbol for people to rally behind, he lacked the support of the nobles. No matter what the outcome of our hunt Wallace would not spoil King Edward's plans to take over Scotland. This Frenchman and his son were of more relevance for we could do something to change their lives. I did not know it in the church but God had spoken to me and planted a seed in my head.

Robert was away longer than we expected. While we waited Jack poured ale into their coistrels and we shared with them the stale bread from Pontoise. It was as though we had given them a feast. The two remained silent while they ate and drank but the looks between them showed their joy. I knew why they were silent. If they spoke then their luck might change. When you had nothing, you believed in such superstitions. They had been lucky and they would not jeopardise that luck.

When Robert walked towards us he had a look upon his face which made him appear oblivious to all around him. He almost floated towards us with a beatific smile and wide eyes. We waited for him to speak. I suppose we were like Michel and his son. Speaking might break the spell that bound the priest.

"I had a vision." None of us spoke. "Well, it was more of a visitation. I heard voices in my head as I prayed to God for forgiveness and guidance. He told me to help you." He pointed at all five of us. "He said that I ought to help those who were close to me before I even thought of helping others." He grinned, "I will help you to find your way to Constantinople and you, friend," he smiled at Michel, "I will seek to find you clothes and shelter. I know that, at the moment, I am poor and can offer little but having done my penance I can now begin my life anew." He grasped William's arm, "Thank you for saving me and to all of you for giving me a purpose."

We smiled but inside I was almost weeping. We had dug our own hole and could not now get out of it. We could not refuse his help for we had admitted that we needed to find a way to get to the empire.

William nodded, "Then let us go. Michel, here, knows where mercenaries are to be found. Let us cross the river and seek rooms and a stable."

Michel gestured with his arm, "If you would follow us."

We led our horses and, as before, made them a barrier at the side of us. Jack asked, "Michel, where do you normally sleep?"

The boy pointed at the flying buttresses, "Beneath those. We use our blankets to make a shelter. It is cosy."

I did not believe him for a moment. It was a hard life. I had lived rough when I had crossed England to take a ship to France but sleeping out in a wood was more comfortable. A man could easily make a hovel from branches and leaves. A good one could keep out both rain and wind. Food could be foraged and there was always fresh water. How the two had not succumbed to an illness was beyond me.

The bridge was crowded but our horses helped to keep us somewhat protected. Once on the other side, it became easier but the buildings and homes there were not the fine ones we had seen on the Île de la Cité nor at the northern side of the river. Rubbish was simply thrown on the street and piles of excrement littered the road. I wondered why someone had begun a college in this part of the city.

"Michel, why is there a college here? It seems to me to be a poor part of the city."

"Robert de Sorbon was chaplain to the king and he established it for the poor. What better place than close to where they live? Priests from the cathedral come to teach here. It is a good arrangement."

"Perhaps you could find employment here, Robert. That way you could help people and yourself." I clutched at the straw.

Robert shook his head, "First, I aid those close to me, as God told me to do, and when that is done I may well offer to help at the college."

My little band was growing and there was nothing that I could do about it. As Robert had said, there were some footsteps that cannot be retraced.

Chapter 10

We reached a wide street and Michel said, proudly, as though he owned it, "The Rue St Jacques." He pointed down the straight road, "There is a Dominican Monastery close to the gate of the city and this is the start of the pilgrim's trail to Santiago de Compostela. It is why there are so many inns. Some cater for pilgrims, they are safe but there are some, a handful, that serve soldiers such as yourselves." He pointed to a painted sign above one which emanated a loud and raucous noise. The sign showed an axe and a sword across a shield. They were crudely painted. "The Crossed Blades is the largest and it has a stable."

I nodded and looked at William. He took the hint and said, "Roger, you are the oldest of us and while I am the leader, I would appreciate your advice."

"I think that this will do but, if I might suggest," he nodded, "as this looks a rough place might we not pay Michel and his son to watch our horses? We could buy them a meal too."

"You have done enough for us but if it would help you then we would gladly watch your horses and do so for free. A stable is a warm and comfortable place in which to sleep."

William beamed, "A fine idea."

Robert clapped his hands together, "Better and better for I would not disperse this company yet. I feel we are stronger together than we are apart."

William said, "If you would enter and negotiate. It may be that a priest gets better rates. Explain that we have two servants who would sleep in the stables." He handed him four silver coins. It was too much but Robert would be more comfortable with an excess of silver.

We handed the reins of our animals to Michel and his son. Jean-Michel, in particular, had taken a shine to the horses. Sal seemed to reciprocate. Dogs and horses are good judges of character. Robert was in longer than we expected and when he came back to us, he was red-faced.

He shook his head, "I am sorry my friends. I am guilty of hubris." He pointed back to the inn and said, "I said I would help you, but the price is too high."

"What it is?" He answered William who said, "You are right. Michel is there another?"

Before Michel could answer I said, "The price he demands is high but we have paid more in England." I pointed to the sun which told us that the day was passing. The bells from the cathedral confirmed it. "It is but one night and we might find the information that we seek."

Robert gave me a curious look as William said, "Very well. Michel, take the animals to the stable and we will go and meet this robber. We will leave our bags on the horses in case we leave quickly."

"Very well. Come, my son. Let us see if we can find some oats for these animals."

When we entered, I was surprised. From the noise I had expected it to be rammed to the rafters but there were just eight men within and they sat at a table close to the far end of the bar. They were clearly the innkeeper's cronies. He looked to be the man who was leaning on the bar and laughing with them. When we entered, he turned to look at us and the chatter ceased. They were trying to intimidate us and that was confirmed when Robert almost cowered behind me.

We walked to the bar and William drew himself to his full height. He said, "Our friend here tells us that without even meeting us you wish to rob us. Why?"

The man's eyes narrowed, and he strode over. His coterie began to rise but he waved an arm and said, "I will deal with these Goddams." He used the insulting term that some French men used towards the English. "Firstly, I charge what I like because this is my inn and if you object then go somewhere else."

I had the measure of this man now. He was clearly an ex-soldier and one who was used to using his fists to get his way. His nose had been broken more than once and there was a wicked-looking scar that ran from beneath one eye and ended in his beard. He might have been a powerful man once but lack of exercise and eating and drinking his way through his profits had made him into a tub of lard.

William must have recognised the bluster too for he said, "You have a stable and that is why we chose this place, empty though it is." He nodded to the men, "Is this handful of human lice enough to keep you in business?"

The man said, "Your French is execrable."

I moved to the bar and put my hands on it, close to his. I was the same height as the man but I still had muscle, "For that, we apologise." The man grinned and his sycophants laughed. "After all, when we fought the French, and despite the enormous belly you now possess, you were once a soldier, the only French words we encountered were, 'I surrender!'" I smiled. "Now, my portly friend, give us a more reasonable price."

I thought, at first, that he would become violent, but the grim look became a grin, "You have balls, my friend, I will give you that. I thought, when your young priest entered that you were the kind of men who enjoyed the company of other men." Out of the corner of my eye, I saw Robert blush. "We hate that kind but now that I see you for what you are let us say a silver piece a night for the four of you, your horses and the two servants."

William said, "Let me suggest a silver piece for tonight and the food for us as well as grain for the animals. Then we will decide if we stay a second night."

It was still too much but we needed a bed and the people we met seemed so villainous that I knew we would find what we needed here. They all had the looks of men who would know such things.

The innkeeper held out his hand, not to William, but to me, "It is a deal. I will shake the hand of the archer for you are right, we did fear the English, not because of their horsemen but their archers. I lost many friends to ash-fletched arrows." He turned to the others, "These are welcome. Treat them well."

It was clear they were his gang and that explained why there were so few other people in the inn during the middle of the day.

He called, "Eloise."

A woman with sunken eyes, thin straggly hair and her two front teeth missing emerged. She could have been any age from thirty to sixty. It was hard to tell. "Yes, Henri?"

"These men will have number two room," he looked at William, "one room will be enough?"

"So long as there are beds within aye, but we do not sleep on the floor."

"One bed and two palliases. When you are settled come down and Eloise will prepare food."

"Do not forget our two servants."

He nodded to the woman, "Aye, there are two in the stables. When you return, we will crack open a pichet of wine and you can tell me what three Englishmen and a pretty priest are doing in Paris. It may be a tale with which I can regale my customers."

We headed through a narrow, low door into a corridor so narrow that my shoulders brushed the side. We passed one door and within I heard the sound of what might have passed for lovemaking and she stopped at the second door. She pushed it open.

"There is a jug of water and a bowl. I will fetch a towel."

William gestured at the first room with his thumb, "Is this a whorehouse?"

In answer, she put her hands on her hips and gave him a lascivious look, "Why, do you like what you see?"

William saw that she was mocking him and shook his head, "No, for I fear that you would eat me alive."

She laughed, "Aye, that I would and then spit out the bones."

"Is there a key?"

We all turned to look at Robert. Only he had expected one. Eloise shook her head, "You will not need one."

We entered the chamber. It would be cosy. Robert started to open his mouth and William shook his head and put his finger on Robert's lips.

I said, loudly, "It is a rat-infested cesspit."

William answered just as loudly, "We will give it one night and then seek another."

We laid our cloaks on the bed but retained our swords and daggers. And without exchanging further words we headed back to the main room. A couple more people had arrived. They were clearly soldiers too. I recognised the buskins they wore, and they each had a short sword hanging from a baldric. They did not look prosperous, and I became more optimistic that we might find information in this inn. Robert might become suspicious at our choice of questions for they would be more about the Scots than a road to Byzantium. William led us to a table with a wall at our back. It was always our practice to do so when dining in a strange inn.

Henri came over with a pichet of wine, "Here is your wine. You pay for more than this and if you want drinking vessels that will be extra."

We each had our own coistrel. Even Robert had one. It was always safer drinking from your own vessel. Eloise came over, followed by a scrawny serving girl. Eloise carried a pot and the girl had wooden bowls and spoons along with four loaves. The smell they imparted told me that they were relatively fresh. There was a bakery just a few doors from the inn. Perhaps they had an arrangement. The smell made me realise how hungry I was. Eloise ladled the stew into our bowls. It looked hearty and I recognised beans, greens and vegetables. There were also pieces of meat, but their identity was harder to determine. In all likelihood, it could be a horse but, equally, it could be a dog. I had learned not to be squeamish about such things. Whatever the animal had been it was now dead and food was food. The bread was deposited and Eloise said, "There is salt on the table. If you need anything else you will need to provide it."

William said, "Our servants?"

She said, over her back, "I am heading there now."

The Hunt

If Michel and his son were given the same provender, they would think that they had died and gone to heaven. If nothing else our visit to this inn would serve to feed the two and give them a chance to survive.

We ate in silence. The stew was tasty but needed a sprinkling of salt. The old soldier in me required that I use the last of the bread to clear the final traces of food from the bowl. That done we tasted the wine. It was, as I expected, rough, but it had not been too heavily watered. I said, quietly, "Nurse the wine."

Robert pulled a face and I smiled. Living in a monastery he was used to better wine. He pushed his coistrel away and said, "Should I ask questions?"

He spoke to William who shook his head, "Let us listen first." He nodded his head towards the half a dozen soldiers who were eating the same fare as we.

The other occupied tables were just a pace or two from ours. The ones further from the bar were more popular for when the inn filled up, and more people were arriving, then they would be less comfortable.

We listened while it was still relatively quiet.

"Did you find any work today?"

"There was a lord who wanted to hire a sword but he was paying little more than he would pay a farm labourer."

"Work is work."

"I still have the coins we took in Flanders and I will survive for another week or so. Something will turn up and, if not, I might head to Castile. They pay well."

"Aye, and there is often work in Gascony which is on the way, I might join you."

The four men who had been speaking were at a table close to two other soldiers. One of the two leaned over and said, "Excuse me, did you say you fought in Flanders?"

The man who had said so nodded.

"Then it must have been the war before this one."

"Why do you say that?"

"Did you not hear how a Flemish army of peasants destroyed a French army at Courtrai in July? The king may well need an army but first he has to ransom his lords."

The four men at the first table shook their heads in disbelief. "We never lose to the Flemish."

"Aye, well perhaps that was what the nobles thought. It is like when the Ecosse destroyed the Earl of Surrey and his men at Stirling Bridge."

The conversation was now between the two tables.

"You are well informed, my friend."

The speaker shrugged, "I was talking to some Scotsmen across the river in the inn close to the Conciergerie. They had been trying to enlist the help of the king and they said we could earn money in Scotland."

My ears pricked up at the word, Scotland.

"They offered to pay?"

The speaker laughed, "The Scots are as poor as church mice. They promised loot from the dead English."

"And first you have to weather the storm of their arrows. No, my friend, your words have confirmed what I already thought. I shall head to the sunny lands of Castile where there will be pay and profit."

A large party entered the inn. They were not soldiers but looked to me like carters. Such men were tough and rough. I had not seen it but I worked out that there must be some sort of warehouse off the Rue St Jacques. The noise level rose so that we could no longer hear the conversation. It did mean, however, that we could put our heads together and speak.

We were still deceiving Robert and that made our words somewhat strained. My foster son asked, "What is the Conciergerie?"

I looked at Jack, "It is a palace on the north side of the Seine. The king uses it."

Robert nodded, "Perhaps you should have gone there."

"I think, Robert, that Michel has brought us to a good place. We can always visit the inn close to the Conciergerie, but I suspect it will be more expensive to stay there than here. This is a rough place but it has brought us news already."

Robert was like a dog with a bone, "But not about Byzantium."

I leaned closer to him, "Robert, we are grateful for your presence, your French has helped us enormously, but we know what we are about. Like those men we spoke to our purses still have a few coins and, who knows, it might be that Castile is a better opportunity. Aquitaine is still English and that might be a shorter and easier journey."

I could see Robert was disappointed, "I had thought to come with you to the east. It might not be a crusade, but we would be treading the path of crusaders."

William said, "Then take that road yourself."

"I need the protection of warriors."

"We are warriors, Robert, but we serve ourselves and not God."

"Roger, we all serve God in one way or another." He picked up his coistrel and drank a little, hoping perhaps that it had improved. It had not. He put it down, "Anyway, God spoke to me and wherever you go I shall follow wherever that is."

We had heard enough. I stood, "I will go and make water and speak to Michel. If you wish more wine do not get any for me. I have had enough. I shall retire."

I went back through the narrow corridor and emerged in the yard. Others were making water in the large pot that they would use to either clean clothes or to sell to men making gunpowder. I waited my turn and emptied my bladder. That done I headed to the stables. I did not see either Michel or his son.

"Hello?" Two heads appeared from the manger above the stalls, "Were you fed?"

Michel grinned, "Yes and we thank you."

I looked around, "There is no ostler here?"

He shook his head, "And yours are the only horses. I fear that if we were not watching them then they might have been taken."

"Then it is good that we hired you." I was thinking on my feet. We would not be leaving the next day. We would have to visit the Conciergerie and seek out the Scotsmen. "We will not be leaving tomorrow. Can you watch our horses for another day?"

"For a hot meal, wine and a roof, of course."

"And we will pay you. You have to gain enough coins to make a new life, Michel."

"Already the arrival of Englishmen has changed our lives. A new life is within touching distance. You have done enough."

I headed back to the room. It was as I stepped from the stables that two men jumped me. One pinioned my arms and the other swung his fist at my stomach. I had been taken by surprise, but I reacted immediately. I stiffened my stomach and when the man's fist hit my muscles he looked up in surprise. My arms were pinned but not my head, nor my feet. I brought up my knee between the man's legs and he could not help but double up. I hurled my head back and felt it smash into the other man's nose. His grip loosened and I elbowed him in the ribs. I heard bones crack, and he cried out in pain. The man I had kneed tried to rise and I swung my boot to connect with his rising head. He fell backwards, clearly unconscious.

Michel and his son ran from the stable as I turned and punched the man with the broken nose hard in the stomach, "No more! No more!"

The landlord emerged, Eloise had probably reported the shout and he looked at the two men. I said, "Do you know them?"

He nodded, "Sadly I do. They are thieves. How they got past me I do not know. I will deal with them."

"Not yet." I turned, "Michel, you and your son need better boots and weapons and a cloak. Take them from these two." I reached down

99

and took their purses. I tossed one, the heavier one, to Jean-Michel. The other I kept. "Tell them that the next time I see them will be their last on earth."

The man with the broken nose who was trying to stem the bleeding said, "I swear, Englishman, that you have seen the last of us."

Henri smiled, "I will spread the word, Englishman, that you are worth the hire. These two have slit throats before now and you took them as easily as a cat takes a mouse."

Michel and his son had taken all that they needed. "Keep a close watch on the animals. There may be thieves other than these." I was looking at Henri as I spoke.

"If you stay another night, we may be able to offer a lower rate." He kicked the one who was lying on the ground and said, "Wake, I shall not carry you." The one with the broken nose helped his companion to rise and I waited until Henri had shoved them out of the rear gate which he had unbarred.

Michel said, "We will take turns to stay awake."

I reached the room, and the others were there. Robert saw my bloody knuckles, "What happened?"

I told them. William said, "From now on we travel in pairs."

I snorted, "They were not a problem."

"But next time there may be others who are better."

Jack said, moving one of the palliases, "I shall be as a chamberlain and sleep behind the door."

I nodded, "I think we will be safe enough but so long as you are happy."

"I will sleep easier knowing that any who try to enter have to push me away."

Our journey was proving to be eventful and, thus far, we had not even had a sniff of William Wallace. I doubted that the next day would see us any closer to the elusive man. If he had been seen then the soldiers would have commented. Wallace was a giant and once seen was hard to forget.

Chapter 11

Eloise was cleaning the inn along with the scrawny girl when we emerged from our room. The room next door to ours had been noisy all night and it confirmed what we all thought, Number One room was used by the whores. We had not seen any yet but that was not surprising. Henri would have clients who used the same women.

Robert asked, "Breakfast?"

Eloise shrugged, "If you want it then Henri will send us to the bakery and charge you double. I can do without the walk if it is all the same to you."

That decided us. William said, "Let us tell Michel what we are about." The two were up and grooming our horses. "There is no need to do that, Michel."

"We enjoy it and besides this feels more like honest labour than begging. You have paid us well. Let us earn the coins you have given us."

William nodded, "We will be across the river and return this afternoon."

Robert could not understand why we were going to a different inn. "You did not ask about getting to Byzantium last night. Why go somewhere different?"

William could not think quickly enough to give an instant response. I said, "We heard, last night, that there were Scotsmen in this inn. They speak English and as they are this close to the French king, they may have more knowledge."

He took the wrong inference from my words, "So you do not need me."

William smiled, "Of course we do and your sharp ears may hear things that ours do not. Roger is right. We have a week or so before we need to worry about money. If we can earn before we get to Byzantium then so much the better."

He seemed mollified by the answer but I still felt as though he was a millstone around our necks. At least, when we left the inn, Michel and his son would head off to start a new home but our puppy would still trot along behind us.

We headed out onto the busy Rue St Jacques. The smell from the bakery was enticing and so we queued with others to buy freshly baked bread. It was tasty and more than filled us as we crossed the bridge back to the cathedral. The builders were already scurrying up the scaffolding as they strove to finish the edifice. We headed to the bridge that led to the more prosperous side of the city. The king had his palace and his nobles made their homes close to it. We spied the inn that had been mentioned. It looked more expensive. The walk had not taken long but we were thirsty. We entered and found it busy already. There were guards from the Conciergerie who, coming off duty, were availing themselves of food and drink. There were others too, pilgrims heading for the cathedral. There were no tables available and so the four of us went to the bar and William ordered ales. Although of much better quality than the wine we had endured the night before it was also twice the price and reflected the inn's position so close to a royal residence.

I felt we had to counsel Robert and I said, as the drinks were brought, "We speak French. When we need to speak English, William will make that decision."

Once again, I was given a look of curiosity. I did not care for this was the reason we had come to Paris. If we could discover if Wallace was here then half of our task, the hardest part, would be completed. I did not expect to see Wallace himself. He would stay hidden but his presence could not be masked. The four Scots who entered were clearly nobles, albeit younger ones. They were loud and they were ebullient. They did not even bother to try to speak French, "A jug of your best wine, some bread and some ham."

The inn was clearly used to such behaviour and the innkeeper said, in English, "Of course, my lord."

They had chosen a table that was close enough for us to both study and hear them. The innkeeper said, as he poured the wine, "And what do you celebrate, my lords?"

"Pope Boniface has told the English king that he cannot subjugate our people and his words have had an effect. He has withdrawn his army from Scotland. William Wallace's mission to Rome has worked."

Our ears all pricked up. The Scotsman's words meant that Hamo and our men would be heading home and that Wallace had been in Rome. Was he still there?

The innkeeper left and the Scots toasted each other before one said, "Now William just needs to persuade the French king to do more than give vocal support; it is time for the French to send soldiers."

Another said, "He will do his best but when I saw him yesterday, he said that he wanted to return to Scotland. Now that Longshanks has left, he can move around the country without the fear of being hunted."

"William is needed here. The French like him and if any can persuade them to support us it is William Wallace."

Their own words took some of the joy from the moment. They ate some of the bread and ham. One said, "I would return home too. We were just unlucky at Falkirk. I think we have the beating of the English."

Another laughed, "Their knights? Aye, that we do. We showed that at Stirling Bridge but their archers? At Falkirk, we were protected by mail and armour but the ordinary men, the schiltrons, they were butchered. Once those yew bows are drawn then the men with spears will think of flight."

"Alan, you are so pessimistic. Besides, light horsemen can deal with the archers as we did at Stirling Bridge."

"Perhaps, but Longshanks did not lead them there, Surrey did."

"Longshanks is getting old. He cannot live forever."

Our silence was becoming noticed and so I said, in French, "I think I will take a walk around the island." I put a coin on the table. "I will see you back at the inn later on."

Robert rose, "I will come with you, Roger."

William shook his head, "No, we may need your skills with words. Roger is able to look after himself." He nodded at me. He knew what I was about. I would scout out the Conciergerie and see what information I could gather.

We had our cloaks with us and they each had a hood. I slipped my cloak about my shoulders and then, after I had left the inn, pulled up the hood. Many men wore hoods for they protected their heads from the sun. For some reason wearing a cloak made a man feel cooler. I did not understand it but I knew that it worked.

I walked on the opposite side of the street from the royal home. There were many businesses and the buildings afforded shade. As the streets were crowded I hoped that I would be invisible. I was seeking a place to watch, not the main entrance, but the sally port further along the wall. It was guarded but if anyone wished to exit or enter unseen it would be through that doorway.

I found a building which had been damaged in a fire. It was boarded up but there was an alley that led to the back and I secreted myself there. When I had been younger, I had often stood a long watch. I was ready for the boredom that came with such seemingly pointless watching. It was not long after noon that my waiting and aching legs were rewarded. The sally port opened and I saw first Jack Short and then his brother, Robert emerge. That they were known to the guard who stood there was clear. The two men scanned up and down the street and only when they were satisfied did they wave to one within. Wallace emerged. Like me, he was cloaked and hooded but he could not disguise his size. Wallace was in Paris and if it was just the two brothers who were his guards then we had a chance to take him.

The Hunt

They left and headed north. If they left the city then I would not be able to follow. It was only the crowded streets of the city that afforded me cover. If he saw me then Wallace would recognise me. I had hunted him before. I had to stay far enough behind the three of them and his two companions were like hunting hounds. They kept turning and almost sniffing the air. I used others to disguise my movement. I walked behind pairs of people and I crouched. When I spied a cart or a horse I moved closer to it. If there was a doorway I stepped into it. I paused at stalls to examine the goods and I never came closer than fifty paces to my prey. That proved to be my undoing for as I glanced down at a stall selling crucifixes they must have turned off. When my gaze returned to the street they had disappeared.

I did not panic. They had to have turned off and there was just one junction. It led to the right and I headed along it. I had to be careful for if I was in their position and wished to see if I was being followed then I would turn off and wait to watch for the follower. Luckily for me, a man carrying long loaves over his right shoulder came from a baker's and turned down the road. I stepped close to him. There were no watchers nor was there a giant and two dwarves. I had lost them. I headed back to the bakery. I joined the queue of people. Most were buying bread for the day. The bakery would keep baking until it was dark. The bakery was hot and the shutters were wide open. It afforded me a view of the street and I was able to keep an eye out for the three men. I bought a small loaf and a pastry. Stepping out I put the bread in the satchel I carried and then leaned against the wall to eat the pastry. It was warm and it was sweet. I studied the houses and one stood out. It was a large house with a couple of guards outside. Some lord lived there. As I licked my fingers to remove the delicious stickiness of the honey coating, I let my mind work out what Wallace might have done. He could have carried on down the road but he had not been in sight when I had turned. He was not an easy man to miss. He had to have entered one of the houses.

One who had been in the queue behind me came out of the bakery. He had bread stuffed with ham and cheese. It was a popular delicacy in the city and he began to eat it. I nodded, politely, I said, "Is that good?"

He grinned as he licked the melted cheese that had oozed onto his beard, "The best in Paris. You English should try them,"

"You know I am English?"

He smiled and swallowed, "You are trying to speak our language, but you butcher it and by your shape, you are an archer."

"You were a soldier?"

"In Flanders." He popped the last piece into his mouth and shook his head, "Only a fool fights. A wise man finds other ways to earn a living."

"And you have found one?"

"I can use a blade well and became a butcher." He pointed down the road, "I work there. The pay is good and I get to take home offal and offcuts. I eat well and no one tries to stick a sword in me," he nodded at me, "or sends an arrow at me."

"Then you are wise. Tell me, as you work so close, who lives in that fine house with the guards?"

"A countryman of yours. He is a knight, Sir Geoffrey of Baldon. He lives here in Paris." He leaned in, conspiratorially, "I believe his father fell out with your king. He supported someone called de Montfort?" I nodded. "He came here some years ago and brought his family fortune with him. The father died four years ago and the young lord has inherited." He smiled, "It was good talking with you, but I have animals to butcher."

I knew then that Wallace had entered the house. To confirm it I walked down the street and passing the entrance to the house found somewhere I could watch. There was a stall selling ale and wine. The owner had put a couple of upturned barrels on the street as impromptu tables. I bought a pichet of wine and sat there. I was forced to remove my hood as it looked strange otherwise, but I kept hidden by sitting close to one of the wine barrels. I could still see the entrance, but I was masked.

I was on my second pichet and had almost consumed it all when they emerged. The owner of the stall had demanded payment first and so as they came out I downed my wine and wiped my mouth. Jack Short and his brother sniffed the air and scanned the street. Only when there satisfied did Wallace emerge and they headed back to the Conciergerie. I knew now where they were going and I was able to keep Wallace's head in sight. Even when they ducked into a shop for a few minutes I was able to stay hidden knowing that they would come out. They entered the sally port. I did not move and watched for a while. When Jack Short came back out a few moments later and scanned the street, then I knew I had been wise to do so. I headed down an alley and came out close to a small bridge over the Seine. I crossed back to the cathedral. I slipped inside and used a side door to emerge. Making sure that no one was following me I headed back to the inn on the Rue St Jacques. We now had our prey and we had to work out how to take him.

The Hunt

The others were in the half-empty room in the inn. Henri gave a wave as I walked in. My face gave me away and Robert said, "You have news of Byzantium?"

I smiled and said, enigmatically, "It was a good day. Did you learn any more after I left?"

Robert shook his head, "All that those men spoke of was fighting in England for this man called Wallace. Perhaps you should return to England, William, it seems to me that you will be able to earn a good living there."

I spied the opportunity to be rid of Robert, "Perhaps our priestly friend is right, William. Thus far we have found no others who seek this new route to riches. We have enough money to get home and this way Robert can pursue his dream of helping others and becoming a teacher at the College."

Robert grinned, "I like this company and I will stay with you for a while longer." A frown appeared, "You do not want rid of me, do you?"

William shook his head, "Of course not but we would not have you waste your life following three mercenaries across France and then England."

"Then you have decided to return to England?"

We looked at each other and I shook my head, "We will debate that later. Now, I am ready for food. Just a small loaf and a pastry have passed my lips since this morning and my stomach thinks that my throat has been cut." I waved my hand, "Henri, is there food ready?"

Eloise was lounging at the bar and Henri looked at her, "Shortly." She left.

"I will go to the chamber and deposit my cloak, I shall not need it again."

"And I will go to speak with Michel. Even though he seems quite happy to sit in the stable and watch the horses I am not sure." William was clever and this way we could talk without being overheard.

We both entered the bedchamber, "I found Wallace. He and two of those we freed at Lochmaben are with him." William nodded as he digested that information. "He was with an English renegade, Geoffrey of Baldon."

"I have never heard of him."

"Me neither but it is a clue. What if the Scotsman enlisted the help of the disaffected? Montfort's supporters."

"That was thirty years since."

I shrugged, "Some people have long memories and the opposition in parliament has to come from somewhere."

"Can we take him?"

I shook my head, "He would need to be on the move and away from Paris. He was careful. He went down a busy street and his two men were watching. We need the darkness of night or a lonely road and I cannot see the wily Wallace risking the night."

"Then we wait here."

I nodded, "Tomorrow you go and take Jack with you. Get there early. They use a sally port and then turn down the Rue Dominque. There is a large house there, that is Geoffrey of Baldon's. I believe that they will go there. I will take Robert and see some of the sights but to give credence to our story about seeking information we will use the same inn. Who knows the Scots may come again with even more information?"

There was slightly more food when it was finally served, an hour after Eloise disappeared. William reported that both father and son were happy with their employment. The coins we gave them were more than five times what they might have had by begging. As they were being fed and were safe in the stables then they were in a better place than by the cathedral.

Robert kept probing. He had questions about our future and would not let go. I was glad when we were able to retire. We had paid Henri and told him that we would be there another night. As the only other occupants of his rooms appeared to be whores and their clients, he was happy with the income. Especially as he did not have to hire an ostler.

William and Jack left early. Robert asked where they had gone and I told him that they were going to find Greeks in the Jewish quarter of the city. "I could go with them, I speak Greek."

I feigned disappointment, "Had I known that then you might have gone with them. As it is, what say you and I visit the market. When we part from Michel and his son I would that they had cloaks. Perhaps we can find them some that are not expensive."

"For soldiers, you are kind men, Roger."

"We are just being Christians."

As it turned out we found a stall selling second-hand clothes. From some of the stains I suspected that they had come from a battlefield, but we found two that whilst dirty, had neither blood nor cut marks and would suffice. They were also cheap. We saw some of the churches in Paris, there were many and I managed to take a route for us to end up close to the Conciergerie. "Let us try some of the better wine they have here, eh, Robert?"

"I know not how I will repay you for your kindness."

The innkeeper was effusively welcoming. I preferred the sourness of Henri, "Welcome, you return for a second visit but where are your friends?"

"I waved an airy hand, "Out, around. A pichet of wine for my young friend and me."

"Of course, something special so that you will return again."

I was regretting already this second visit. William and Jack would probably be heading back to Rue St Jacques, and we would be better placed there.

"I need to go and make water, Roger."

"Of course. Once I begin, I cannot stop. I will wait until we have consumed this wine."

The innkeeper returned with the wine and he frowned, "Where is your young friend?"

"He has gone to make water."

The innkeeper recovered his composure. "I will pour you the two goblets." He said it as though the pewter pots were cut glass. He poured and then hovered nearby.

"I am sure the wine will be acceptable."

"Of course." He backed off to the bar.

I picked up the goblet and sniffed it. It smelled sweet. I did not like sweet wines. I saw Robert returning and decided to taste it. I could always send it back if it was sweet. I sipped the wine and confirmed that it had been honeyed but there was something more.

Robert saw my face and said, "Is something wrong?"

"The man has given us sweet wine and…" Just then it was as though I had swallowed a bag of writhing, biting snakes. I was wracked with pain such as I have never endured. I tried to stand and found that my legs would not hold me. Just before darkness consumed me I realised that I had been poisoned and then all went black.

Interlude

King Edward was not a happy man. The pope had commanded him to leave Scotland and to begin talks with the French about a lasting peace. Pope Boniface, as guardian of John Balliol, the claimant to the throne, had issued a papal bull and the king's hands were tied. He did not dare risk excommunication. In addition, Parliament was becoming increasingly bullish. His demands for money were scrutinised and questioned. Simon Montfort had shown the barons what they could achieve if they kept tight purse strings. The king was also suffering from illness. It was no surprise for he was getting old but it annoyed him. Not for the first time he missed his first queen. Eleanor had been the love of his life. It was as he thought of her that he also thought of the man that Queen Eleanor had regarded as King Edward's rock, Gerald Warbow. The king missed the irascible archer. For one thing, his archer understood the men that the king led and could give King Edward sage advice. He was also the most loyal of men. When Warbow was around the king felt safer. Even his own son made King Edward fear a knife in the back. He regretted sending Warbow to France but he could not recall him as he had no idea where he was. King Edward realised that Wallace had already done his work. He had persuaded the pope to issue a papal bull and King Philip of France was belligerently banging the drum of war. If France actively supported Scotland by sending soldiers to fight then he would need Gerald Warbow and Wallace would be an irrelevance. He needed the man who was still known as Lord Edward's Archer.

In Yarpole Mary was glad that Hamo was home. He and the men from Yarpole had returned without losses. Sir Ralph was whole and it should have been a joyous time but it was not. Her husband, the love of her life, was God knows where and he had but two men with him. She knew from Hamo's words that he would have to be in hiding and for a man of his age that was not as easy as it had been. She did not curse the king but she did question his poor decision making. William Wallace was a brigand and a bandit, a rabble-rouser. She knew that from Gerald's words and her husband never lied to her. Each night she prayed for him to be returned safely.

Hamo knew that his father had been given no choice in the hunting of the Scot. He understood why he had to stay with the army but Hamo also knew that if he was with his father then Baron Warbow would have a better chance of survival. William of Ware was good but not as good as Hamo. Jack was improving but he was still raw clay that needed to be shaped and moulded. The foray into France might make better men of both Jack and William but Gerald Warbow had nothing to gain from it.

Chapter 12

I swam in a black sea that threatened to choke me. I sank to the bottom and struggled to breathe. I coughed and retched but all that came forth was not water but black bile. The snakes attacked and bit me once more. It went black again and I found myself whirling and spinning in space. I thought I was dead already but I had so much pain that I knew that I was clinging onto life. As I rose through the murk and darkness I wondered if I was between heaven and hell. Was my past coming to haunt me? Even though I was in pain I wondered at the arrival of Robert. I could have used the young priest as a confessor. Then my passage to heaven would be assured. I knew that Robert had been sent to us as a sort of chaplain. I should have been honest with him and given him the truth. Had I, then now I would not be between eternal joy and everlasting damnation. I saw light and forced myself to reach it. The light might be heaven. My throat filled with, who knew what? I found myself retching once more. Would I be able to reach the light?

"Bring it up, Sir Gerald, bring forth the blackness."

I realised that I could hear the urgent plea of William of Ware and that meant I was not dying. I began to throw up the contents of my stomach. It was painful beyond words and even when my stomach was empty, I still felt as though I wanted to retch.

I heard the voice of the old crone, Eloise, "It is working. Pour more of the liquid into his mouth. You, young one, hold his arms. Priest, pour and pray as you do so."

My nose was held and a foul-tasting concoction was poured into my mouth. It tasted disgusting but with my nose held I had no choice and I swallowed. It made my eyes open and the bright light made me close them again. It felt as though I was choking. When I retched my motion was so powerful that even Jack could not hold me, and the vomit spewed into the pot that was laid below me.

Eloise cackled, "That is it. The poison is gone. See the green bile. He will live."

I opened my eyes and saw that I was in our chamber. My men along with Robert, Michel and his son were gathered around me. Eloise patted the back of my hand, "You are a strong one, Englishman. You fought for life. We thought the priest here would have to give you the last rites but you thought other. I will bring a bowl of gruel later. You need something light."

I croaked, "Thank you."

She shrugged, "I was paid well." She closed the door and left us.

"Ale or water. I am parched."

Jack gave me the ale skin and I drank. I feared, as it slipped down, that I might retch again but I did not. I lay back and closed my eyes. I was alive. Without opening my eyes, I said, "Now tell me all."

It was William who spoke. "Wallace knows we are on to him." I opened my eyes and William nodded, "We told them the truth. Had Robert not gone to make water then both of you might have been poisoned. While Eloise saved your life Jack and I told them all." He was right, of course, and my black dream had told me so. "We followed him and his two men to that house and hid. They emerged on horses and with laden sumpters. Four men accompanied them. The one called Jack Short waved cheekily as they passed us. They knew where we were hiding."

Jack took up the story. "We were heading back here when we passed the tavern and saw you on the ground and Robert cradling you. We carried you here and when we told Henri that you had been poisoned he sent for Eloise." He shook his head, "He said that the sweetening of wine with honey was a common trick."

Robert said, "She gave you the first of the charcoal in water, yesterday. We watched over you all night. She returned this morning and it was the last two doses that worked."

"So, while we watched, I thought it incumbent upon me to tell the truth. If I did wrong, I am sorry but I would do it again. I like not the subterfuge."

I shook my head. It was a mistake, "You did the right thing and I apologise to you three. I should have been honest."

Michel smiled, "For my part, it would have made no difference. You have changed the lives of my son and me. For that, we are grateful beyond words and we are happy to serve an English lord."

I looked at Robert who shook his head, "And I feel a fool, Sir Gerald. I knew you were not who you said you were but I had all sorts of fantastical thoughts in my head. The truth is more mundane and like Michel I am happy to serve you."

"It is a moot point, Robert, as our quest is over. Wallace knows the hounds are behind him and he will have fled. I feel like a newborn and helpless but tomorrow we pay our bill and head back to England." They nodded, "After we have visited a certain innkeeper."

Robert asked, "You would return there, knowing that they are enemies?"

"Aye, and it is not just for vengeance. I do not like to leave a job half done. I want to know his connection to Wallace and I would visit this Geoffrey of Baldon. He is clearly an enemy to our king." I could see them taking that in. "And you three, you have done enough. I will give you all money to begin new lives for without the three of you..."

"Did you not hear Michel and I when we spoke, Sir Gerald? We spoke in the dark of night. The three of us are bound to you. Jack has told us that you are a lord with a manor. I realise that we are presumptuous but if we help you to get back to England then perhaps there will be places for us."

"Of course, and you need not ask. There is land I can give you but, Michel, it will be in England and not France."

"And France has done little for us. It was three Englishmen who gave us hope and dignity, not Frenchmen. Besides from what Jack has told us, Yarpole," he managed to mangle the word, "sounds like the garden of Eden and your Lady Mary a saint."

I looked at Jack who shrugged, "Well she is, my lord."

I smiled, "Tomorrow, you three shall watch our horses while William, Jack and I discover the truth. Buy food from the market and wait beyond the walls for us."

Robert asked, "Are you sure you can handle the enemy? Who knows how many there are?"

William answered him, "Do not worry, my friend. We have a score to settle. Jack and I are oathsworn and Sir Gerald will want vengeance. We will meet you and then we head home. Perhaps we shall be there by Christmas."

Eloise returned with the gruel and Michel and his son went to the stable. The old woman said, "There is food in the inn for you. I will feed the invalid."

I saw them hesitate, "Go. I will be safe enough."

The door closed and she began to feed me. She did so with great gentleness, "You know, Sir Gerald is it?" I nodded. "They say that you judge a man by the company he keeps and a leader by his followers. You have five men there who would give their lives for you and that is quite remarkable." I swallowed and said nothing. "When I was young and still had my looks." She laughed, "Aye, I was not always a toothless old crone. There was a young lord and I loved him. He was Henri's father, and I would have married him. He was like you, a good leader whom men would follow to the ends of the earth. He died in the

113

Crusades against the Cathars. How my life might have been different had he survived."

The gruel was gone, "You have done well, you have this inn."

"Henri might have his father's name, but he does not have his other qualities." She shrugged as she rose, "My fault, I fear. I brought him up alone and did what I had to. I am not proud of all that I did but I was young. I had Henri when I was but fifteen." She kissed me on the cheek. "Your men told me of your ride through the land of the Mongols and how you rescued the woman who is now your wife. My Henri would have done that had God spared him. I am glad that I have met you for you show me a future I never had and now I can dream of what that life would have been like."

I slept better than I had expected I would but when I woke I still felt as weak as a baby. Eloise had a good breakfast ready for us. Now that I had heard her story, I viewed her in a different way. Even her son appeared different. I wondered how many other people had been misjudged by me. Was William Wallace someone I might have liked had things turned out differently? The breakfast helped and after we had eaten I went to the bar to pay our bill. Eloise wanted us to pay less but I shook my head, "The money I pay is well spent. When next I am in Paris then we shall return here."

"And you will be welcome, my friend."

We left the inn. It was early but the Rue St Jacques was busy. We parted from our three companions at the cathedral. Michel and his son had goodbyes to make and Robert wanted to pray one last time. We waited with the four animals while they did so and then planned our course of action. I had said vengeance but more important was the information we sought about Wallace. That an attempt had been made on my life at exactly the same time as Wallace was fleeing could not be a coincidence. The inn catered for nobles who were not renowned for being early risers. We gambled on the inn being quiet. By the time our friends returned, we had our plan. "We will join you by noon. You know where to wait?"

Robert nodded, "By the big tree on the Pontoise road. Take care. We would not lose an employer so soon after gaining him."

They led the four horses across the bridge and cowled and cloaked we followed. We did not head to the Conciergerie but to the rear of the inn. We had not scouted it out but we knew that there had to be another way in to allow wine and food to be brought. The back door was closed but not barred. Presumably, there would be those who worked in the inn arriving. Hearing no one we slipped into the yard which was filled with the usual detritus of inns: empty barrels, baskets of spoiled food and the like. With drawn swords, we went to the rear door which was open. I guessed that the fire would have been lit ready for cooking and the open door would keep it cooler. As we stepped into the corridor we heard voices. There were two, a woman and the innkeeper. They were discussing the menu. We had planned for all eventualities, this one included. As we stepped into the kitchen Jack went to the other door, the one that led to the main room while William and I headed to the couple. The woman put her hand to her mouth.

I growled, "Not a word."

The man went white and dropped to his knees, "You should be dead... spare me, I beg of you."

The woman ignored my words and spat out at her husband, "I told you that it was a mistake!"

I said to her, "Be silent and you shall live. As for you," I pricked his throat with the tip of my sword. He moved his head back but I had nicked him and blood dripped down his neck, "your life hangs in the balance. Much as mine did when you tried to murder me. I seek information. If it is worth your pitiful life then I may well let you live. If not..."

"I will tell you all, I swear I had no choice. I was told that if I did not poison you then my life would be made a living hell."

"Then who threatened you?"

"An English milord. He lives close by. Sir Geoffrey is his name."

"And why me?"

"You were seen following the Scottish giant but you evaded them when they sought you. They know your name, it is Warbow?" I said nothing but he took my silence as acknowledgement. "I was told that if you returned I was to poison you and any who were with you."

"And you were to do this out of the goodness of your heart?"

"No, I was paid."

I had heard enough. I moved my sword hand and his wife said, "He deserves death but let him live I beg of you. We have three children and I would not have them orphans. I swear we will change."

I nodded, "But the world must know of your crime." My hand was quick, and I sliced down the middle of his nose. "People will know what you have done."

He nodded, the blood dripping to the floor, "Thank you, my lord."

Sheathing my sword I said, "We have men watching your inn. If any leaves within an hour of our departure..." I let the words hang.

"We will not move." It was his wife who spoke. She knew that they had been lucky and we could have taken their lives.

We left the same way we had entered. We had already planned on visiting Geoffrey of Baldon and we headed, not up the main street, but an alley which brought us out close to the house. There were two guards at the front but, like the inn, there had to be a rear entrance and we found it. This time it was barred but not guarded. William and I boosted Jack over the wall and he unbarred the gate. It was a large house but not a fortress. The guards at the front were to discourage visitors. We passed a stable and heard horses. William peered in but there was no ostler. It was still relatively early and when we opened the back door we were greeted by silence. With swords drawn, we headed through the opulently furnished house. A wide set of stairs led up to the first floor. There was a room at the foot of the stairs and when we heard a couple of voices then we knew it was occupied. Leaving me to watch the stairs William and Jack threw open the door and entered. I heard the noise as they rendered the men they found there unconscious, but I doubted that the guards on the other side of the front door or those upstairs would have heard anything. They did not emerge for some time. When they did William mimed tying hands. The men would not bother us.

I led the way upstairs. There were just two rooms and one was unoccupied. We could tell as the door was ajar and when we peered in we saw a bed and no one had slept in it. That left one room. Jack took the handle and, after turning it, threw it open. I leapt in and found a couple in the bed. The man woke but the woman remained blissfully asleep. While Jack raced around to stifle any cry I put my sword to the English nobleman's neck, "Geoffrey of Baldon?"

"Sir Geoffrey of Baldon and what do you mean by breaking into my home?"

I smiled a wolfish smile, "I thought that your attempt on my life warranted the invite, or was I wrong?" He tried to pull back. I pushed the sword closer to him. The wall behind the bed prevented any further movement. "So renegade Englishman, why do you want me dead?"

The movement in the bed woke the woman but Jack's finger pressed to his lips silenced her.

The noble was terrified and his words poured out in a torrent, "Wallace said that Warbow was a threat to me. He said if I did not kill you then you would kill me."

"And you believed him?"

"I know that you are King Edward's man and a killer. What else was I to believe?"

"And where is Wallace now?" He tried to shake his head and found he could not. "He is in England."

"Where in England?" I kept my voice calm but if he was in England then we had the chance to do as the king wished and take him. "Tell me and you might live."

"Toot Baldon, in Oxfordshire. It is my manor."

"There, that was not so hard, was it?"

I withdrew the sword and he became emboldened, "The Scots will rise, Warbow, and Longshanks will be defeated."

"But you will not witness it for when I return and give the news to King Edward then the name of Geoffrey of Baldon, which might have been forgotten, will be remembered and if I ever see you in England then you will die." I leaned in, "Do you believe me?" He nodded and his eyes told me that he did. "Now we are going to tie you up and as payment for the attempt on my life, we shall take your horses. The woman is witness." She nodded.

Jack and William bound the pair while I looked for evidence to take back to King Edward. I found the noble's signet ring with the family crest. That would do. We slipped down the stairs and headed through the kitchen once more. Jack saw the pantry and headed inside. He emerged with a round of cheese and a ham. There were four horses in the stables and three saddles. We saddled the three bigger horses and Jack, having fastened panniers he found on the fourth, packed the ham and cheese and he led that animal. We went to the rear gates and opened them. I knew that when the servants arrived, they would realise that something was amiss and so we needed to make haste while we could. We mounted and rode towards the northern gate.

This time we had no priest as cover but riding good horses we would not look as suspicious as we might. The sergeant at the gate held up his hand to arrest our progress. "Have you permission to leave the city?"

I frowned, "Permission?"

He nodded at the horses, "I recognise those animals. They belong to the English knight who lives close to the Conciergerie. He is a friend to the king."

I had not planned on this and then I remembered the signet ring. Drawing it out I showed it to him and said, "Sir Geoffrey sends us on a most delicate mission. He wished us to leave quietly. I hope that this inspection will not jeopardise a task which will benefit King Philip."

Thinking that we were spies he beamed and swept an arm, "I am sorry, my lord, good luck and none shall know whence you left the city."

We had travelled half a mile and the road was empty when Jack said, "Sir Gerald, how were you able to think of such a story so quickly?"

"Since coming to Paris I have realised that it is a hotbed of conspirators, and I gambled that Sir Geoffrey is an agent of the French. His house is so close to the Conciergerie that it is a perfect place for clandestine meetings that could be hosted by Sir Geoffrey and attended by King Philip's men. Now the guards at the front make sense."

William said, "And by now they will have found the pair and there will be a hue and cry."

"You are right. Let us put spurs to beasts and make haste."

Robert and the other two were waiting in the shade of the tree. Upon reaching it we dismounted, "This is the point of no return. I thank you for what you have done but if you come with us now there will be no turning back. We will ride hard for Harfleur and seek a ship. If you wish to leave us then take a horse and our good wishes."

It was Michel who spoke, "While we have waited, Sir Gerald, we have spoken of our future. It seems to all three of us that your coming was necessary. Had you not then Master Robert would lie gutted in a ditch and my son and I would be slowly dying of starvation. With you we have a life and without you, none. We are now your men."

I mounted my horse, "Then choose your horses and let us ride."

We had come this way when heading to Paris and I knew we had two or three days of hard riding. We only had one spare horse now and while Sal was in a healthier condition than she had been I did not want to have Robert ride her into the ground. We rode steadily and used every moment of sunlight. The ham and the cheese meant we did not need to use inns and the first night saw us seek shelter in a farmer's barn. The three Frenchmen with us made us less suspicious and the farmer even sold us some cider. I did not wish to risk Rouen and that meant a detour to the north of the city. It added an hour to our journey and that night saw us sleeping under the stars.

As we ate the last of the ham and the cheese with bread we had bought from a bakery, I reflected that we had, effectively, disappeared. We had yet to use an inn or a monastery. If we were followed, then our hunters would find our trail hard to follow.

William pointed west, "Wallace could be just ahead of us, my lord. Have you thought of that?"

I nodded, "But like us, he has a choice of routes. He might seek a boat from Dieppe or Boulogne. It would be a longer ride but a shorter crossing." William nodded. "Do not get me wrong, I would love to catch up with him and take him back to the king. He tried to have me killed and I do not forget such things."

"Do you think he did, Sir Gerald?"

"Jack, I think Wallace is a brave man but I also know that he is ruthless. Remember how he fled after Falkirk? He is a survivor and he will do anything to survive. He would not lose sleep over my death and that of Robert."

I watched Robert's face, "I had forgotten that I might have drunk the poison too. I had done nothing to harm the man. Why would he try to kill me?"

"He is a patriot and as such his purpose is the freedom of his homeland. Anyone who gets in the way of that is an enemy." I smiled, "Do not worry, Yarpole is safe from the grasp of Wallace and his countrymen. We just have to get there."

We reached Harfleur after dark but we reached it when there was a high tide and as we rested our weary horses at the water trough by the quay, we watched laden ships arrive. We now had French speakers with us and that meant we could take any ship but I wanted an English one. When I heard English voices I led my weary band down the quay to where the cog was being unloaded. I was recognised, "It is our English archer!"

I spied Captain Hargreaves as his men put down a gangplank to lead horses from the ship. We walked over to him. Our story had been that we were seeking work and I knew he would be curious. I did not want questions to be asked that might put us in danger.

"Captain, this is fortuitous. Can we pay for a passage back to England?"

He frowned, "What happened to the dream of serving the emperor?"

I decided to give a version of the truth, "I was laid low by a sickness. We took it as a sign and we heard that there might be a need for swords and bows in England."

He suddenly saw our French companions, "Your band has grown I see." Neither William nor I said a word and he nodded, "As we have just brought over men and horses the ship would need cleaning in any case. Seven horses and men might just pay our passage back and then we can clean out the ship."

As the men began to follow the horses I saw that it was a knight and his men. There were ten of them. I did not recognise the knight but that meant nothing. It just signified that he had not fought in Scotland nor the Welsh borders. I was plainly dressed and he barely noticed me.

He shook his head at the captain, "Next time that I cross I shall use a better ship. Our animals will need a whole day to recover."

I saw the captain fighting to hold his temper in check, "I am sorry, my lord, but I have no control over the weather."

The knight had made his complaint and the captain was ignored as the horsemen led the horses along the quay.

Captain Hargreaves shook his head, "Nobles! They are never satisfied. If you wish to travel back to England, then board now. I had planned on waiting until the next tide and seeking a cargo but we will just buy some barrels of wine and take this tide."

The crew were just happy that they did not have to muck out the hold and while half went with the captain to procure barrels of wine the other half helped us to board. My skill with a bow ensured a warm welcome. The attitude and ingratitude of the English knight and his men also helped us.

We left Harfleur in the dark. Jean-Michel and Robert were not the best of sailors and from the moment we struck the open sea until we arrived off the English coast, they hurled the contents of their stomachs over the side. I was just relieved that we had escaped France so easily. When we docked, I resisted the temptation to kiss the ground but I felt as though I wanted to.

"What now, Sir Gerald? Yarpole?"

I shook my head, "No, William, we need to tell the king that I have failed." I was never one to hide from unpleasantness. I would be the one to tell the king.

Chapter 13

We headed for London. I had an idea that the king would be there but what I did not know was which castle or palace. There was much speculation amongst those we asked but the monks at the Guildford Black Priory gave us the most reliable news. They said that the king was at Eltham Palace. We were given a warm welcome as I was known at the priory. Queen Eleanor had founded it almost a quarter of a century earlier and my association with the Queen was well known. We now knew where to find the king.

We reached the palace favoured by King Richard in the late afternoon. The royal guards knew me, of course, but the French of my companions made them curious. The captain of the guard allowed me to enter the palace, but my men and our horses were left in the outer bailey. I was taken to the king aware that I was dirty, dishevelled and stank of horse sweat. The royal officials we passed sniffed as I approached. King Edward was with the Earl of Surrey in his solar. Two sentries stood inside the room and another in the corridor.

King Edward was one of the cleverest men that I knew and could pick up on the slightest of clues, "I take it that you failed to take Wallace?"

"I failed, King Edward. I found him but he fled." I would not mention the poisoning. It would merely muddy the waters. "He fled for England. I know where he is to be found."

His eyes lit up at the news, "You do? Then all is not lost. Tell me all."

I was not offered a seat and so I stood and told the tale. I gave him the information that I thought was relevant. When I gave him Sir Geoffrey's signet ring he shook his head, "I had forgotten that family but I can remedy that now." He turned to the Earl of Surrey. "It is too late this night but, on the morrow, we will ride to Toot Baldon. The renegade's last property will be his no longer."

"Yes, King Edward, I will go and inform our men."

Left alone the king said, "You shall come with us, of course. Now tell me the part of the story you omitted."

"Omitted, my lord?"

He chuckled, "You went from watching Wallace at the Conciergerie to binding Sir Geoffrey. I know you and cannot see you letting Wallace slip away so easily."

"They tried to poison me, King Edward, and I was laid low for a day. Had they not done so then Wallace might well be in chains."

The Hunt

The king shook his head, "Perhaps you would have been harder on his heels but since I set you on this perilous path I have realised that it was an impossible one. You have done better than I might have expected, and your news confirms that King Philip's support of the Scots is a greater threat than Wallace. De Brus has entered the cock pit and the man I trusted with Carlisle Castle now seeks the Scottish crown. He is more dangerous to us than Wallace for de Brus has the backing of the nobles. I dare say that Wallace will be used by de Brus to bring the rabble to fight for him, but it is de Brus who is more of a threat." He smiled, "You brought your men here?"

"The captain of the guard was suspicious as three are Frenchmen."

The king nodded and said to one of the guards, "Tell the captain that Sir Gerald's men are our guests. They are to be accommodated in the warrior hall."

"Yes, my liege." He left.

King Edward stood, "And you, my archer, stink. If you are to dine with the queen and me, then you need a bath." He went to the door and shouted, "Steward!"

A liveried servant appeared, "Yes, King Edward?"

"Sir Gerald needs a chamber and a bath. See to it."

"Yes, King Edward. My lord?" I followed him down the corridor, "I will see if we have any garments that might fit but…"

I smiled, "I know, my friend. I am an archer and a freak of nature. Do not worry, whatever you procure will suffice."

Eltham was not as big as Windsor and it was a cosier meal than had the king been at a major castle. Queen Margaret was the daughter of the King of France. I confess that I never really warmed to her but then again, like the king, I had known Queen Eleanor who, to me was the greatest of all queens. This time, perhaps because I had been so recently in France and speaking French, we got on better. She knew I had been to Paris and she asked me about the places she remembered.

When I said we had stayed in an inn on the Rue St. Jacques her hand went to her mouth, "Mon Dieu, you were lucky to come away with your life. That is a perilous place."

King Edward laughed, "Warbow can look after himself."

I nodded, "And to speak truthfully Queen Margaret, whilst it was a rough place, as I discovered there are reasons behind people's behaviour, and I have learned not to judge people because of their appearance."

She studied me and then smiled, "I am warming to you, archer. I thought, because of the king's words, that you were just a brutal warrior but I can see there is more to you than that."

The Hunt

King Edward said, "On the battlefield, there is no fiercer warrior nor an enemy who puts fear in men's hearts, but I have also seen kindness. He is a contradiction."

It was quite a pleasant evening and after the trials and traumas of Paris I was able to relax and, for once in the king's company, enjoy myself. I had not had time to speak to my men but William was more than capable of looking after them. I breakfasted with the king and his familia, his household knights. They had changed over the years but they all knew me and, I like to think, respected me. The king and his men dressed for war. I had warned the king that Wallace could not have known we would discover his link with Toot Baldon for Sir Geoffrey had been surprised. It meant we might be able to catch him unawares. It was just an hour after dawn that we headed for the Oxfordshire village. We had spare horses for it was sixty miles but the king wanted haste. I feared for our men but the king had thoughtfully arranged for four spare horses. The three Frenchmen rode at the rear of the column with the spare horses. Forty men galloped through London and then took the Roman Road west.

I was with the king and the Earl of Surrey. I asked where his son was. It was not a question asked for any other reason than simple curiosity. He had named Edward as his heir and I would have thought he would have kept his son close to train him for kingship. The king's face wrinkled into a frown and he shook his head, "Edward has had it too easy. He surrounds himself with like-minded, empty-headed nobles. They hunt, gamble and practise for the tourney. I tell him that he needs to be ready to take the reins of kingship but he tells me that I am hale and hearty and far from being at the end of my life." He shook his head, "We both know that to be foolish. It is another reason that I wish to end this Scottish problem. I am not sure that he could cope with the likes of Balliol, Wallace and de Brus. Together the three of them are a threat."

One advantage of our speed was that none could get ahead of us to warn Wallace of our arrival. We changed horses every twenty miles. At High Wycombe, he commandeered half a dozen fresh mounts to replace six that were struggling. Remarkably Sal was coping well and showed no signs of fatigue. Of course, Sal, along with Jean-Michel's mount, had the lightest loads. The two riders were slight and the only metal they had were daggers. The rain, which fell in the middle of the afternoon, helped as it cooled down the horses and as the veterans and the king had oiled cloaks, we were dry. The three Frenchmen were the ones who suffered, and I wondered if they regretted their decision to follow me.

The Hunt

Had I been leading then I might have been more circumspect when we approached the manor of Toot Baldon. I would have sent men to the rear of the manor house and ensured that all the exits were watched. In his eagerness to get to grips with Wallace the king and the earl simply galloped into the yard. There were men on watch and crossbows cracked as they sent their bolts at us. It was dusk and the crossbows hastily released. The result was that they did no damage and the men operating them were slain by the king's familia.

"Get me Wallace!"

I threw myself from the back of my horse. When there was no pain as I did so I realised that my healing was complete. I drew my sword and dagger and reached the door just after the last of the watchers had hurled himself through. There were men in the house. Shouts and cries in Scottish accents, augmented by words in French gave me an idea of numbers. Some decided to fight rather than flee or perhaps they were just buying Wallace the time to escape. Whatever the reason, as I passed the door to the room used as a dining hall a spear was rammed in my direction. Had I not the strength of an archer then it might have gone badly for me, but I used my dagger to punch away the head and then slid my sword along the spear shaft into the man's stomach. That none of the men I had seen wore armour told me that we had surprised them. The king, the earl and the king's familia were close behind me and as I stepped over the dead man I saw that more of those we sought were fleeing out of the back of the hall. Some were brave, foolishly so, and they tried to stop us. The king's men were the best of warriors and every man who tried to stop us was slain. The effect was to slow us down and as we reached the rear yard and the stables I saw that we were too late. Wallace, the Short brothers and two men I took to be Frenchmen were mounted and galloping out of the rear gate. The rest would be taken or slain but the prey we sought had escaped. Without horses on the other side of the building and being exhausted, there was no chance of us catching Wallace. He had the advantage of fresher horses and a multitude of directions he could take. He would head to Scotland but we had no way of knowing which route he would take.

I sheathed my sword. The slaughter sickened me, but it was forced on the king's men for the ones who remained fought recklessly as though their lives meant naught. By the time the king thought to halt the slaughter and seek prisoners, it was too late. There were just four wounded men left and three of them would not see the dawn.

My mind went back to Lewes when, with the battle almost won, The Lord Edward had raced off recklessly to pursue the men of London.

It had cost the king the battle and father and son their freedom. This was another such foolish act.

It was my men who discovered the steward and the handful of servants and caretakers who watched over the manor for the exiled knight. The king was ranting and raving to his household knights as though it was their fault that William Wallace had escaped.

Jack appeared at the door, "Sir Gerald, we were putting the horses in the barn when we found the steward and his people sheltering there."

"Bring them in." They might not be prisoners, but they might serve to give the king his answers. I turned, "King Edward."

"Yes, Warbow?"

"My men have found the steward. Perhaps he can give you the information that you seek."

His face brightened, "Bring him in."

The man was old, as old as me and he did not walk well. He bowed, "King Edward, I am John of the Baldons and the steward here."

"Tell me of Wallace and his men. Leave nothing out, no matter how trivial it may appear."

He swallowed, "They arrived two days ago. There were eight of them but within a few hours, another twenty had followed. There were Scots, like Wallace, Frenchmen and Englishmen."

"Englishmen?"

Nodding he hurried on, "Two were his servants but there were others who came with Lord Goven, he is a friend of Sir Geoffrey." He stopped speaking and I could see his face contorting as he sought other nuggets of news that might satisfy the king.

King Edward asked, "And do you know where they will go?"

He shook his head, "I know that they planned on staying here for a week or two. They expected others but when they discussed such matters they sent the servants from the room."

I interjected, "But you heard anyway."

His head whipped around, "Aye, my lord. When your master is an exile then if you want to keep your place you keep your wits about you. I think they planned on leaving here in small groups and heading back to Scotland. I heard Wallace say that they would each take one of three routes: the Norham crossing, the Carlisle one and the Alston pass. He thought that way they had the best chance of avoiding discovery."

The king nodded his thanks to me for the question and then said, "Thank you, Steward. Would you like to keep your position here even though it is a new master?"

He smiled, "I have not seen Sir Geoffrey since I had all my teeth and a full head of hair. I was born close by and the servants are all my

125

family. If we lost this position then we would become paupers. I will serve the manor and," he emphasised, "my king."

"Good, then have food prepared. We cannot leave this night." He pointed to his knights, "Leave the earl and the baron alone with me. We need to speak."

We were left alone. The steward and a woman I took, from her age, to be his wife entered with wine and goblets. She said, "Food will take an hour or so, King Edward. Would you like some bread and ham to ease the pangs of hunger?"

He smiled and was the gracious King Edward once more, "Thank you, mistress, but we can wait, and the food will taste better."

I was the lowliest of the three and I poured the wine. The earl said, "You were just unlucky, King Edward. We almost had Wallace in our grasp."

I could not help my reaction. I rolled my eyes. King Edward saw it and smiled, "Warbow here does not think so, do you?"

I had learned, over the years, that the king preferred the truth. He might snap and be surly but he liked honesty. "No, my lord."

The king sat and took a deep swallow. Sighing he said, "Then illuminate me with my mistakes. Had you been the leader what would you have done?"

I smiled, "Ah, there is the thing, my lord. Had I been the leader then I would have had my ghosts, my archers. All you had was a band of mailed men who are perfect for smashing through enemy lines. My archers would have surrounded the manor. The rear door would have been barred and the thought of a shower of arrows would have ensured that the ones within surrendered."

"You are right and I could have sent my knights around to the rear. True, they would not have had the yew threat of your archers but we would have Wallace. Next time advise me. I keep the old hunting dog with me to do as he has always done, warn me." I nodded. "Sit, the two of you, I am getting a stiff neck and people say I am too stiff-necked in any case." We obeyed. "It is clear that we cannot pursue Wallace for we know not where he goes."

The earl was keen to contribute and he said, "But we could send riders to Norham, Carlisle and Craven. If we use fast riders then as our enemy has to keep hidden and move more slowly, we can bar their escape."

"A good idea and so order it but as Warbow here knows, as do I, they need not cross the border at a major crossing. If they go to the Eden or the Tweed they can ford and there are many passes and paths north of Craven. We might catch the odd one but Wallace is an elusive fish despite his size. What concerns me is the involvement of Englishmen. I can understand an exile but to think that there are men who live here in England who consort with our enemies. The French? It is to be expected." He banged the table, "Come next spring I will take an army north and we will finish what we started. I will use Edward. Perhaps campaigning and leading an army might be the making of him. We will have two armies. I will head up the east coast and the prince can march to the west, through Carlisle. We can sweep through the lowlands and meet at Stirling." He smiled, "Let us end this war where it began to go disastrously wrong." The earl shifted uncomfortably. The king said, "There is little point in beating about the bush, Surrey. While you were unlucky you made mistakes. You will be with me as will Warbow."

"And the pope?"

"I will simply ignore the papal bull. If King Philip supports my enemies and, from Warbow's information, he clearly does as he harboured Wallace, then there can be no peace. Besides, I have heard that the pope and King Philip are set on a collision course." Neither the earl nor myself had heard anything and King Edward smiled when he said, "Philip needs money to pay his army, as do I. He intends to tax his land, including the clergy, churches and holy houses. The pope is not happy." He turned to me, "You are not my only spy, Warbow, although you are the most effective."

I bowed my head at the compliment, "Thank you, King Edward."

He drank from his goblet and before he refilled it he waved it around, "What do you think of this manor, Warbow?"

I shrugged, "I have barely seen it, my lord. It seems cosy enough and the steward is a good man."

"It is yours. You did well in France despite not succeeding as we hoped. This is your reward and I would rather that the income goes to a loyal man than an exiled traitor."

"Thank you, King Edward."

"I have my own motives, Warbow. I know the value of your archers. Wherever you go you attract archers and raise your own. I would have an enclave in Oxfordshire where archers are produced. You are right to chastise me for an overreliance on knights. They have their value but as you showed at Falkirk, it is archers who can break down the will of an enemy. I am just grateful that my enemies rely on long spears and crossbows."

The steward entered, "King Edward, food is ready if we could lay the table?"

He rose, "Of course. I need to make water and to wash."

We rose and followed. I headed for the barn where I knew my men would be. They were all watching for me and I saw expectation on their faces. I smiled, "We eat and then on the morrow, we return to Yarpole. We are not needed again until spring."

The relief on their faces made me smile. Yarpole was a haven and I would be glad to return to my family.

Chapter 14

I had spoken with John of the Baldons before we left. King Edward had let him know that I was the new owner, and I wanted no resentment on his part. "I will be sending one to run the manor for me, John. You will still be the steward, but I need one who can train archers and provide men for the king's wars. Will that arrangement suit?"

He smiled, "Aye, my lord, for Sir Geoffrey used us as a sort of hiding hole for enemies to the crown. I did not say so to the king for I did not wish to lose my place here, but you are known as a fair man. I believe you know that I was under duress when I acted as I did."

"I like to think that I am a good judge of character." I had some of the money left from King Edward's expenses and I gave it to the steward, "I know that there is an income. I would have you detail it on paper," I suddenly stopped, "You can write?"

"Yes, my lord."

"Good. Then when I send my man down he will return it to me. Use this purse to hire men to dig the foundations for a warrior hall. I want it at right angles to the main hall so that with the stables there are two arms. The barn means that at some time in the future we can build a connecting wall and this will be a more secure home. When I have had the opportunity to look at the accounts, I can decide how best to use my new manor."

John looked as though he had been given spurs such was his joy, "Thank you, my lord, and we will all sleep better with you as our lord."

The night of sleep and the reflection of my journey had been fruitful and after we had passed Oxford and were heading for Yarpole I spoke to my men, "William, I know that you have missed your family and I am also aware that Luston has bad memories for you."

"I have missed my family, Sir Gerald, and while Luston reminds me of my dead brother I am a man and I will bear it stoically."

"You need not. I would have you, if you are willing, bring your family and run Toot Baldon for me. John of the Baldons is a good man and he knows how to run a manor. I need you to train men at arms and archers."

"That sounds ideal, my lord, but I am no archer."

"Yet you have been around Gwillim and Dick. You know how they train men. Even more importantly, you know how they are to be used. The other advantage is that when we go to war, in the spring, you will be able to stay with your family."

"My lord, I am not afraid of war."

129

"I know but I owe you for the service you and Jack gave me in France." I turned to my foster son, "I did consider giving Toot Baldon to you, Jack ..."

He shook his head, "I am not yet ready, Sir Gerald, and besides, you, Hamo and Lady Mary are my family and I would not be parted from you."

I was happy, "Then all is well." I turned to Robert, "And I have plans for you, Robert. You shall be my priest in Yarpole and teach my grandchildren but when William returns to Toot Baldon, I would have you return with him. The steward is preparing the accounts and I would have you and William scrutinise them before they are brought back to me. William is a warrior and you are a scholar. That combination may prove fruitful."

Michel and his son had learned some English and they had listened to my words. However, Michel spoke in French when he asked, "And my son and I, Sir Gerald, you have plans for us?"

"You are part of these plans. William has a farm in Yarpole. It shall be your home. You and Jean-Michel can decide if my choice is yours also."

He grinned, "If Captain William is happy then so am I?"

William said, "It is more of a smallholding than a farm, Michel, but I am more than happy for you to have it. Sir Gerald has given me a much richer prize and I will not begrudge you some good fortune."

The mood was a happy one from then on as the others chattered excitedly. I was silent for I realised I was building a legacy. I now had many manors and each one was managed by a warrior alongside whom I had fought. The future of England was out of my hands but the future of those manors was not. The men I had put in charge would run them well. The young archer who had lived in the Clwyd Valley had risen higher than his dead father could have imagined. I hoped that, in heaven, he was proud of me.

Thanks to the towers we had built at Luston and Yarpole our return was signalled and Hamo and my wife were in the yard to greet us as we clattered in through the gates. Mary threw her arms around me. My welcome was always as warm. She hugged me and kissed me hard, oblivious to the bemused stares from the three strangers, "I miss you more every time you are away. I pray you stay now...at least until Christmas."

I pulled away and nodded, "The king does not need us until spring."

"And I see that you have not come home emptyhanded. Who are our guests?"

"This is Robert, a priest from France. He will be our chaplain and teach our grandchildren."

She held out her hand for him to kiss, "You are more than welcome, Robert."

"And I am more than happy to serve such a gallant knight and his beautiful lady."

She laughed, "Old lady, but I thank you for your kind words."

"This is Michel and his son, Jean-Michel. Michel was a soldier abandoned by the French. He and Jean-Michel were beggars at Notre Dame."

My wife had been a slave and I saw her face drop. She held out her arms and embraced the two of them. "Then we will show you here that we do not forget old soldiers and their families."

"William of Ware is to be the one who will manage my new manor. Michel and his son shall have his smallholding."

She laughed, "I can see that the meal we enjoy this night will have a rich diet of news. The three of you are invited, as are you and your wife, William."

"Thank you, my lady, and know that we shall miss you more than any."

I sniffed, "Thank you for that, William."

Mary laughed, "Who would miss a grumpy old man? Come inside and wash the stink of horses from you." She put one arm around me and one around Jack and the three of us entered my hall.

I was now at that age where the comfortable and comforting things in my home made me feel warm and welcomed. My servants filled the bath that we had built just outside the back door. It was close to the kitchens and that meant water could be heated. We had fitted a plug at the side so that the dirty water filled the hogbog and the pigs loved it. In winter it was cool but the hot water always refreshed. Mary entered the bathhouse with me. It just had a wooden wall and a simple door but it was functional. I knew that greater lords had more elaborate bathhouses but this was functional and suited me. Mary, when she had been a slave in the Mongol court, had to make do with water poured over her head in a tent. She was happy with the arrangement.

Mary was in a playful mood and as I soaped myself clean with the soap my women made, she threw cups of cold water at me. We giggled and laughed like children. My childhood had been a hard one, as had Mary's but my children and grandchildren had enjoyed theirs and had it showed in their joyful faces. When the water cooled, I emerged and she towelled me dry. She was gentle. This was a skill she had learned when a slave and had attended on Mongol princesses. She oiled my body with

131

oil infused with rosemary and thyme. There would have been a time when I would have thought such things effeminate but my time in the Holy Land had changed my views. I only used the oils when at home. If I was on campaign then the healthy stench of humankind was an effective disguise. By the time we were done, it was getting on to dusk. Autumn was fast approaching. We went into my hall and the others were there. I saw that my three Frenchmen were now dressed in clothes procured by Hamo and Jack. We had slop chests filled with good clothes and they had enjoyed a simpler bath than I had, in the water trough. With their hair combed with a nit comb and new, clean clothes Michel and Jean-Michel were almost unrecognisable as the two beggars from Notre Dame.

My table was never formal unless the king came, and with Hamo's children enjoying the attention of our guests, it was a lively and somewhat noisy place. I had thought that when I was older, I would resent such noise but I now found that it was reassuring. The wine poured by Hamo helped. I had a good cellar. We sat together and Mary, when she had finished organising the food, would be at the other end. Jack and Alice flanked my wife. Alice got on really well with her mother-in-law and the two would have their heads together like two birds during the meal.

I nodded at Hamo's children. Our three Frenchmen were playing with them but the children would continue to harass them unless stopped. Hamo said, "Children, we have guests. Show them to their seats and then sit and show them how well-behaved you can be."

"Yes, Father."

I smiled, "And if you are still awake when the meal is finished I will tell you the tale of the pirates who attacked us off the coast of France."

Mary had just entered with a platter of bread and, hearing my words said, "Gerald!"

I adopted an innocent look, "All children like to hear tales of pirates and I will not upset them."

Hamo laughed as my wife tut-tutted her way to the kitchen. "Even getting to France is an adventure for you, Father. You need to slow down and enjoy your grandchildren."

"Aye, you are right." I drank some of the wine, "This is a good barrel. Is it fresh or old?"

"We broached it today. It is from the Pays d'Oc."

"Good, then there may still be some left by Christmas."
Occasionally we had a poor barrel. Some wines did not travel well. It would not be wasted. Some would be used for cooking and the rest made into vinegar. "To answer you, Hamo, I will cease my endeavours

132

when the king no longer needs me. This spring campaign is Prince Edward's first command. If he does well then the king can do less and I will be at home more."

"You will not serve the prince?"

"King Edward saved me, when I was a young man, I am oathsworn. From what I have seen of Prince Edward he is not a man I even like. You owe him nothing. When King Edward is taken from us we can just become border knights." He nodded, "I have another manor. I have given it to William." I looked around, "Where is he? The food will be ready soon."

As if he was waiting William, his wife and his two children entered. It was the signal for squeals of delight from Hamo's. I shook my head. Our three French guests looked bemused. I took a loaf from the platter my wife had just fetched and cut off a hunk. I liked the hard crust at the end and taking some butter I smeared it thickly on the still warm bread. I had enjoyed the bread we had eaten in France, but this loaf was made with my flour, milled in my mill, mixed with my yeasty beer and cooked in my bread oven. It was the finest in the world and I closed my eyes and enjoyed the melting butter slipping down my chin. This was my home, and I was not bound by any conventions. It was the place where I was the happiest.

The wine slipped down easily, too easily, and I found myself smiling at the most trivial of things. I was bemused by the reaction of the three Frenchmen to the food that was served. Michel and Jean-Michel had endured hunger and were happy about simply eating but some of the food was new to them and I smiled as they tentatively tasted each titbit before devouring it. I had not planned on telling the story of the poisoning but Jack, too, had enjoyed more wine than was good for him and being seated at the far end of the table had blurted out the start of the story before I could stop him. Michel, Robert and Jean-Michel did not help as they happily contributed to a story which, whilst it had a happy ending, told my wife and daughter-in-law of the danger and the threat to my life.

Hamo said, "Poisoning is a nasty way of killing. I hope you made the innkeeper pay."

I shook my head, "I might have done had I not needed to chase Wallace. I learned a lesson. I was never one who liked an overly sweet wine and now I shall avoid it completely." I shrugged, "I cannot see myself travelling abroad again any time soon. Englishmen are not poisoners."

The stupidity of the statement caused by an excess of wine, made Hamo burst out laughing, "You may have forgotten but there were

Frenchmen at Toot Baldon and the poisoning was ordered by an Englishman. You survived but there is a lesson to be learned. We expect a knife in the night but not poison in our soup."

The look given to me by my wife told me that this was not the end of the matter but, that apart, the evening went well. The children were so tired that they fell asleep and I was spared having to face the wrath of Mary by telling the pirate story. After they had been taken to bed and there were just the men and Mary around the table I spoke to William.

"Is May happy about the move to Toot Baldon?"

"She has mixed feelings for it means leaving her father, but she knows that it will be for the best."

The drink had made me mellow but it also opened doors, "There is another solution. Take Ralph the Fletcher with you. May is his only daughter and his wife is dead. I know that he dotes on his grandchildren and he can train archers as well as any man. In fact," I suddenly saw another benefit, "there may be another advantage for it will make him feel useful once more."

Mary said, "A good idea but he may not wish to go. After all, he has roots here."

Hamo shook his head, "Many of those, like Mordaf, are now living far from here. Others are dead. I know Ralph and he will leap at the opportunity."

William smiled, "The solution appears to be perfect. I will speak to him on the morrow. He may well be abed now."

Hamo said, "You will need a wagon. We have one to carry you hence and that means that Robert need not ride. Gwillim is Ralph's oldest friend. He can drive the wagon and he and Ralph can have a long goodbye. It will take three or four days to make the journey."

Robert said, "We did it in two."

"Riding horses. Toot Baldon is close enough so that we can easily get there in two days if we need to." Hamo was a practical man and he knew that, unlike my Scottish manor, Toot Baldon was within travelling distance and I could keep in contact with my new manor. The Scottish manor of Coldingham would not last much beyond the death of King Edward. I was not a fool. Even if Prince Edward changed and became more like his father, that would take time. I had been King Edward's mentor. Prince Edward's was the peacock that was Piers Gaveston.

It was my falling asleep that ended the evening. One moment I was speaking to Hamo and then next I was shaken awake by my son and my wife, "Time for bed, Father, you have done well to stay awake this long but a combination of the wine, a hard day of riding and the warmth of our home means that the night is ended."

I gave an elaborate bow and almost fell over, "Goodnight, one and all."

Each of them beamed and said goodnight while my wife shook her head, "Come you old fool. I do not want you falling over and breaking something."

Between us, I was undressed and I rolled myself into the bed. My wife undressed and donned her nightgown, speaking to me all the time. "You would not have told me about the poison, would you?"

I gave a silly smile, shook my head and said, "No." She rolled her eyes and I added, by way of mitigation, "I was quickly healed and suffered no ill effects."

She climbed in and kissed me, "Do not leave me first, Gerald. Each time you go to war I fear that I will have seen you for the last time. I knew there might be danger in this hunt for Wallace, but I did not envisage death by poison. You must take care."

I kissed her back, "Fear not, I now lead men. Hamo is the one who is more likely to suffer a wound. The king uses me as an advisor. I do not think that we will suffer another Stirling Bridge. All will be well."

"Do not tempt the Fates, Husband. Do not speak of such things."

I woke chastened. I had needed to rise in the night to make water and I hated that. For one thing, it meant the rooms stinking but also, once awake I found it hard to return to a comfortable sleep. Mary had risen earlier than me and after I dressed I walked down the stairs for my appetite to be roused by the smell of hot bread that had just been brought into the house from the bread ovens. We had a pair of ovens for we allowed the villagers in Yarpole to bake their bread. Once we shared the same oven but it proved to be too small. Hamo, Jack and my grandchildren were up already. Robert along with Michel and his son, were in the warrior hall and William and his family had returned the previous night to their home. Mary had much to do. It made for a more peaceful breakfast.

My ale had already been poured by one of the servants and after drinking deeply to assuage my raging thirst, I broke off the end of a loaf and sliced through it. I smeared butter on it and the bread was so warm that the butter melted into it. I added more.

"Now that Ralph the Fletcher is leaving, we shall need a new fletcher."

I nodded as I chewed the delicious bread topped with homemade butter. "Before he goes, we will ask him to suggest a replacement. He will know such things."

"We do not have long for he is anxious to get to his new home before autumn sets in. William has spoken to me, and he takes this new responsibility very seriously. He wants to supervise the storing of food for winter. He said that the hall there needs work."

I nodded and swallowed, "Sir Geoffrey lives abroad and I think he used tight purse strings. John the Steward might well have wished to keep the hall maintained but the exile just wanted the coin."

"What will happen to the traitor?"

I looked at Jack who had met the man and I shook my head, "If you are asking do I think will the king pursue him then I say no. He is beyond King Edward's reach but Sir Geoffrey will suffer. When his father fled the king confiscated the main manor. Toot Baldon was an oversight. Soon he will only have the house in Paris to maintain his lifestyle. When he becomes reliant upon the goodwill of King Philip he may have to earn his thirty pieces of silver. From the house we saw I think that he is a man of pleasure and leisure. Plotting with malcontents is one thing but actually doing something will bring about his downfall. As for the other English plotters... he has the name of one Lord Goven. I fear that he will flee to France but the king can use the name to seek others."

"And God will punish this renegade." I nodded as Anna brought in the porridge and autumn fruits. Jack made the sign of the cross, "Robert told me that God sees everything and all will be brought to account at the end of days." Jack had grown up in France.

I spooned the steaming, milky oats into my bowl and then drizzled honey into it. "But if he confesses..."

As I dotted the porridge with fruit and hazelnuts he shook his head, "Robert told me that Sir Geoffrey will be punished."

The porridge was too hot to eat and I put down my spoon, "You like Robert, do you not?"

He smiled in a shy way, "I know he is no warrior but he has qualities I admire. Since I came here Lady Mary has educated me but I would learn more. Robert has promised to teach me while he teaches the grandchildren and acts as your chaplain."

Hamo asked, "He will be a chaplain?" I heard the surprise in his voice. I had never been an overtly religious man.

I took a spoonful of porridge. It was ready to eat. "Hamo, you know how it is. We rescued the man and that made us responsible. He saved my life when I was poisoned." I gestured with my spoon to Jack, "Along with William and Jack. I do not need a chaplain but the priest lives in Yarpole and it cannot hurt to have a man of God living under my roof."

He looked relieved, "I feared you were growing morbid. At times you have been more than a little melancholy and maudlin, as though you were contemplating death."

I shook my head, "No, but I am a realist. I have outlived many of my friends. King Edward is of an age with me and he is preparing Prince Edward to take the reins of power."

"As you have with me but King Edward is still actively seeking to make England safer. Emulate him, Father, keep your mind active and look to the future. I would have you as a model for my children as you were for me."

"John is barely a toddler. What can I teach him?"

"Nothing, yet, but he adores you, Father. Tell him stories. You have more to tell than any man alive. Who else travelled so far east that he met the Mongols? You and mother have lived rich lives and that can only help my son, and my daughter, to become like me and my sisters." He smiled, "And my unborn child."

"Alice is with child?" He nodded. "And you hope for another…?"

He grinned, shyly, "A boy I can make into an archer but a daughter, I could bounce on my knee. I do not mind which." His face became serious, "Do not say anything to Alice. She worries that it is bad luck to speak of a child before it is born."

"Of course."

My clan was growing. There had just been my father and me. I knew that I was blessed to have such a healthy and happy family. I still had a purpose and that purpose was far removed from being Lord Edward's archer.

Chapter 15

The parting of my man at arms and his family was a sad one. It was just a two-day journey for me to travel to see him but I knew that the times when we did meet would be rare. William was the best sergeant-at-arms I had ever had, and I would miss him. His father-in-law would be equally missed. I spent some time with Ralph before he left. I needed his advice on a replacement for him. I could make arrows, every archer could, but a fletcher had special skills and an eye that was given to him by God. He and I sat in the front room of my home before a fire, for a chill wind came from the east and the fire was comfortable for two men who suffered aching joints.

"I know that you are happy to go, Ralph, but you leave a hole that needs to be filled. Who can replace you?"

Ralph was a modest man, "I just make arrows, my lord. It is not hard. There are many who can make arrows."

"Ralph, you know what I mean. I can make arrows and they are serviceable but you can make arrows that are true and will fly further than those made by an inferior fletcher. Give me a name that shall be your legacy here while you enjoy the sunset of your years with your grandchildren."

He sipped the ale and then nodded, "Walter of Rhyl, he has a good eye and he has been the one archer who did not just take arrows from me but asked me how to make them. I have been training him."

"He is young." Walter had come to us barefoot and ragged two years since. A Welsh raid on his family while he and his father were hunting had set the pair on a vengeful hunt for their killers. It cost Walter's father his life and when Walter arrived, he had been more dead than alive. He was a good archer but had a tendency to silence.

"He is and he is serious." Ralph shook his head, "I try to make him smile when I teach him how to fletch but he is hurt from within. He is the best. I would leave him my home, with your permission, my lord. It is a cosy one and close to your hall. Lady Mary is kind and if anyone can heal his troubled soul it is she." He suddenly smiled, "The Frenchman you brought, Robert?" I nodded, "He may be able to help. He seems a kind man." He spread his arms, "You asked me, my lord, and my answer is as true as the arrows I make."

"And it is a good answer although I had forgotten the young man." I shook my head, "The time was I would know every man in my mesne as well as I know myself."

He smiled, "I have served you for many years, my lord, since before he became king. You are still Lord Edward's Archer, even though he is king. You have more to do now than when you were younger. Hamo knows him. Ask your son." He smiled, "Walter of Rhyl is my legacy to you."

Hamo knew the young man and nodded his agreement when I broached the subject, "He has a skill, Father. You have not noticed him, well, because you have been away and he just gets on with his job. When we campaigned he was the one who never complained and, never missed. He can make arrows. Ralph was not with us and when arrows needed to be repaired even Gwillim asked Walter to do it. He is the perfect choice and Ralph is quite right, being in Ralph's old home, close to the hall is the perfect place for him. Ralph has seen what you have not. Your French priest is like the missing piece of a puzzle. Despite the fact that he is French he is popular. He has been here but a short time and yet when he walks into a room he is greeted with smiles. He is a priest but not one who chides. He cajoles. Walter likes him and smiles when he is in the presence of the French priest. He will grow. The warrior hall is not the place for him. He is too solitary."

I smiled, "You know my men better than I do."

"You have been away and you have other responsibilities. I know that I am lucky. The king's eye has not lighted on me. When you left for France, I was just another archer. You are still Lord Edward's Archer. I am glad that I go unnoticed."

The day that William and Ralph left, with Gwillim and Robert driving the wagon, was a sad one for all. Ralph, especially, was family. His house was a stone's throw from my hall. The servants all knew him for he was a kind man. My archers formed a guard of honour with bow staves held aloft as he boarded the wagon. Poor Walter had enormous buskins to fill.

When they had gone I felt an emptiness within. Taking Jack, we rode to Wooferton to visit with Sir Ralph. I had not seen him since the campaign, nor my daughter and her children. I would visit Margaret and her children closer to Christmas. Part of the reason to visit was to find out if Ralph's heart was in campaigning. When we had been in Scotland I had sensed, in him, a different attitude. When William, Jack and I had spoken in France of Ralph they had confirmed my view. They knew that his heart was no longer in the fight to enlarge the kingdom. I did not mind but I wanted the air to be cleared. If he no longer wished to war for the king then I would do all that I could to ensure that happened. Hamo was still a warrior and I knew that he was happy to go to war.

The Hunt

After I had greeted my daughter and the grandchildren and played with them for a while I went outside with Ralph. Jack was adored by my grandchildren, and he was more than an acceptable alternative to their grandfather.

Ralph smiled as we stepped out in the chilly air, "So, William of Ware and Ralph have left you?" I nodded, "You will miss them."

I patted my chest, "They will always be here."

"And Wallace, what of him?" He pointed to my head, "Is he still there?"

"He escaped it is true, but in the spring the king goes forth and perhaps the end is in sight for the elusive giant," I told him of Paris and the acquisition of my new men.

He smiled, "You gather men like a forager gathers windfalls, Sir Gerald."

I shrugged, "It is true that I was once alone but when I became Lord Edward's Archer, I seemed to attract others like metal to a lodestone." He smiled and we leaned on the fence by the paddock where his squire and sergeant at arms were working with a couple of young horses. "I will be blunt, Ralph. When we were in Scotland, I had the impression that your heart was not in the campaign."

He flushed, "I fought as hard as any."

"I was not questioning your honour. I was trying to see into your head. You know me, Ralph. I will not judge you. God knows that I have endured much for this royal family, and I have not always been treated well. Speak the truth," I smiled, "and as my father would have said, 'shame the devil'."

He sighed, "Scotland is just a place for men to bleed. If the war was in Wales where there is a threat to my home then I would don mail every day and twice on Sunday but Scotland... the Scots do not want England. They see the land around Carlisle and Newcastle as theirs by right but we both know that they have not the skills to take them. The Romans had the right idea. Put a wall from the Tyne to the Solway and let the Scots have the rest." He suddenly realised what he had said, "I am sorry, Sir Gerald, I have misspoken."

"No, Ralph you have done as I asked and spoken the truth. I came here today because the king intends to march north in spring and make war on the Scots. It will not be a short campaign. I will ask the king if you and your men can stay on the border to protect my family while we campaign. It is my archers that he wants in any case."

"I am not a coward."

"And no one said that you were. I understand. I am unique. I was King Edward's man when he was a youth, and my fate is tied to his. You have not upset me, but rather the reverse. I want honesty from all."

When we left for Yarpole I felt much happier for I had cleared the air and my daughter along with her family would be safe.

That done I could turn my attention to Michel and his son. As with Robert, I felt unaccountably responsible for them. The truth was I had real sympathy for them and their plight. My life could have ended the same way. William and his wife had not taken all the furniture from their home with them. Toot Baldon was relatively well furnished. The smallholding had yielded its summer and autumn crops and I found them both in the fields, scratching their heads. Farming in France and England was different. Even the farms in the north of England were different from those around Yarpole.

"Sir Gerald, this gift is too generous for us. Surely there must be another who might want such a fine home? What about Master Jack?"

I smiled at the generous spirit of the Frenchman, "Jack has Luston when he chooses it but at the moment he is still learning to be a warrior. You understand that, Michel?"

"I do but he is already a much better soldier than some who command others. You have trained him well."

I nodded at the compliment, "And now, Michel, what is it you wish to grow?"

He looked uncomfortable, "I confess that I do not know. I spent fifteen years as a soldier and when I left home I was barely older than Jean-Michel here. What can I grow?"

There were four small fields and each one was separated by a small hedgerow. I pointed to one, "That one grew wheat and so we leave it fallow for a year. That one has winter barley. You have one, there, that was left fallow last year. You could plant oats. They grow well and can be used as both food and fodder. Remember you have two horses now to care for. The last field? Beans. When they are harvested you cut down the stems and the roots will fertilise the ground so that you do not need to leave it fallow. If you let your horses graze in the fallow field it will keep down the weeds and their dung and urine will fertilise it."

"There is much to learn." He scratched his chin, "Goats, I could rear goats and use their milk for cheese."

"It is your farm and you choose what to raise." I waved an arm. There were four more such small holdings close by, "The other small holdings are farmed by my archers and men at arms. Ask them. They had to learn too. If you need a plough I have one and you can use your horses to pull it."

141

"We are grateful but this is all new to us."

I pointed at the nearby wood, "Unlike many lords, I am not precious about my hunting. If you wish to hunt the rabbits and the squirrels you do not need my permission. If you want to take fallen timber or to copse appropriate trees then I also give you my permission. The hunting of deer and wild pigs, however, is something we all do and we all share in the rewards. We will let you know when we hunt." I smiled, "And now I will head back to the hall for I can smell food cooking."

"The beans and the oats, my lord?"

I nodded, "See my steward. He will let you have a bag of each. You will need to save seeds and beans for the next crops but we will start you off."

I had smelled the ham being fried for the wind brought the smell and I hurried back. Father and son would soon learn the pitfalls of farming. We would not see them starve."

It was February when a dishevelled rider rode into my yard. It had rained all morning and I took the opportunity when the rain stopped at noon to get some fresh air. It did not do to stay indoors for days upon end. The rider's normally bright clothes were muddied and sullied by the rain and the roads. It had not been a cold winter, as such, but it had been both wet and windy. The rivers had flooded and while we had not suffered, those who lived along the Severn had. I recognised him and his livery as Richard of Craven, the pursuivant who had been attached to my familia when we had been in the borders. I was in the yard sparring with Jack when he rode in.

Jack smiled, "Why, Master Richard, your fine plumage looks as though it has been dragged through a hedge."

He dismounted and shook both his head and his hat, "Aye, Master Jack, this is not the time of year to ride through lanes that look like rivers and the wind is a lazy one that goes through you and not around."

I nodded, "Jack, take Richard's horse to the stable." I went to the horse and hefted the bag from the back. I slung it over my shoulder.

"Sir Gerald, I can do that."

"You are here on the king's business, and you look weary beyond words." I shouted, "Steward, we have a guest."

Although the words were intended for my steward, I knew that they would carry to Mary and as we entered and she saw the dishevelled official she shook her head, "You will catch your death of cold in those wet things."

Richard looked down at the puddles forming on the floor, "I am sorry, Lady Mary, I…"

"Tush, tush, have Master Richard's bag taken to the guest room. I will have a bath filled."

"No, my lady, it is not necessary. My clothes will dry. My news is urgent." He smiled, "And besides this is my last task as a pursuivant. I am appointed to serve the king as a warrior."

I beamed, "Well done, Richard. We will await you in the dining hall."

Mary said, "I will see that we have good food this night. This is not the day to be riding abroad."

Hamo must have been watching from where he worked with Walter in the barn, sorting arrows for the coming campaign. He entered the hall and said, "I saw a rider. We have a guest?"

Since my falling out with the Mortimer family we had fewer guests. I nodded as Jack arrived, "Richard of Craven. He has been sent by the king."

The three of us took seats in my hall close to the roaring fire. I plunged a poker into it. Hamo said to the servant, "Fetch butter and honey."

"Yes, Master Hamo."

"How goes the arrow count?"

"Ralph had left us a good store although some of the flights need attention. It all depends on how long we will be away. We brought many arrows back last time because of the early end of the campaign. We need no more if it is to be a campaign of the same length but a full season of war will need many more sheaves."

I looked over to Jack. Since William's departure, he had filled the boots of my lieutenant. Despite his youth, he was well thought of and the older sergeants did not mind taking commands from one who was only recently a man. It helped that he was my adopted son but Jack had a mild manner about him and he was popular, "And the mail?"

"Bob Strongarm has repaired all that needed repair." He smiled, "I have a new hauberk for Bob said I had grown so much over the winter that I needed it."

"Good. James and John, are they archers yet?"

Alice's two brothers had been striplings when they had come to us but Hamo had worked with his wife's brothers and they had responded well. "Gwillim thinks so. They cannot yet hit the longest mark but then again few can. They are fast and they are accurate. Length will come with strength."

"Good."

"And Sir Ralph?" Hamo was not afraid to bring up difficulties.

"Unless the king asks for him directly then I will leave him here. He has no wish to war in Scotland and we need this border to be protected. We cannot rely on the Mortimers." I shook my head, "I was sad when Sir Roger and Lady Maud died. I now see that their passing was a tragedy. We needed their strength and not the weakness of their son."

Any further grumbling was ended by both the return of the servant and the entrance of our guest. I saw that his clothes had suffered from the damp on the journey and, as he approached the fire, steam rose.

Hamo poured the ale and Jack cut a hunk of butter to drop into it. When Hamo plunged the poker into the ale it sizzled and spat. My son said, "Get that down you. It will warm your cockles."

We let the pursuivant sit close to the fire and the steam rose even more quickly, "Thank you."

I let him take a good drink. Hot ale infused with butter and honey was more of a meal than anything but it also warmed a man from within. I waited until he placed the pewter mug on the hearth before I spoke, "It must be urgent for the king to send you out when the roads and the weather are so inclement."

"It is, Sir Gerald. I was given this last task to perform, and I was not given it in written form."

I nodded, "The king trusts you."

"He does." I saw him close his eyes briefly, as though to gather his thoughts and then he began, "Prince Edward is now Edward of Caernarfon, the Prince of Wales. He has been given the earldom of Chester. He is to command half of the army when we march north this summer."

I nodded for I now had a date. We would not have to leave before the crops had been planted.

"The prince will command his Welsh subjects and the Irish levies who have been ordered to serve the king."

Hamo said, "Irish?"

I explained, "The Irish are good warriors but can be a little reckless. They need a firm hand."

"And is the prince the hand that they need?"

We all looked at Richard who shrugged, "The king has confidence in his son."

His words did not convince any of us but there was little point in pursuing the matter. However, as the prince would be leading the men of Cheshire and Wales I wondered if he would command me, "And my demesne, we follow the prince's banner?"

144

Richard shook his head, "No, King Edward would have his loyal archers and his elite company follow his banner. His army musters at Berwick in July, St Swithin's Day."

"The men of Yarpole and Luston?"

"Yes, my lord."

I wanted everything to be clear and I pointedly asked, "Wooferton and Toot Baldon?"

He smiled, "No, my lord. King Edward has commanded a thousand landowners to supply men. He said that the ones who served the last time had done their service."

Hamo shook his head, "Clearly we are the exception."

"King Edward thinks well of your father's men."

"And how will this be funded? Does parliament pay?"

His face broke into an enormous smile, "The king was aided by the pope and the King of France."

I could not help but laugh, "And how has he managed that trick?"

The pursuivant finished his ale which Jack refilled and then explained, much as Robert did when speaking to my grandchildren, "Pope Boniface has had a falling out with the King of Sicily, Frederick. He has demanded a tax of ten per cent from every Christian country to fund his war against Frederick. King Edward gets to keep half and as this is demanded by the pope then the church does not object to the tax, indeed it actively supports it and so parliament is unable to oppose it."

"But how does the King of France aid us?"

"King Philip is happy to tax his people but he keeps all the coin for his own purposes. The pope has issued a papal bull so, as you can see, King Edward has the money and he intends to conquer the whole of Scotland. And there is other good news, the Earl of Lincoln, Henry de Lacy, has returned from Rome where John Balliol sought aid. The pope was persuaded to detain Balliol so that he cannot come to his homeland and cause mischief."

I nodded, the king had worked wonders, "That just leaves Wallace and de Brus then."

"Balliol is the one with the legitimate claim, my lord."

"And you, Richard, what of you?"

"I am to be promoted to a knight of the king's household. I shall not carry the banner but I will protect whomsoever the king chooses for that honour."

"Be careful when you drink from that chalice, Richard. The fighting is always the fiercest close to the king's standard."

145

"I know but there may be rewards. You have four manors now, Sir Gerald, one would do me and if we defeat the Scots then there will be rewards for those who serve the king."

"And that is a mighty if, Richard," I did not want to take any of the shine from the glory the young man thought he might achieve, "but if the king has men such as you around him then I am hopeful that we will succeed."

Chapter 16

The months passed so quickly that before we knew it Midsummer was upon us and I still felt ill-prepared. Despite the constant clanging from the weaponsmith and Walter the Fletcher working from dusk until dawn, I was still not sure that we would be fully equipped in time. My wife had new liveries made for my men at arms. My archers preferred the dull colours that would keep them hidden. We spoke constantly, when we ate, about the coming campaign. After Richard left us things became clearer. We would have the furthest to travel for the muster was at Berwick. That meant a march of almost three hundred miles. Even with horses that would take us twice as long as any other cohort. The one thousand landowners commissioned to provide men came from the north midlands, Yorkshire and Durham. They could be at the muster in a much shorter time than we would. Once again, we would need more horses than other contingents. It would not only be the sergeants who needed remounts. The archers and their spare bows, sheaves of arrows and gardyvyans would have to be carried on sumpters which could, at a pinch, be used as replacements.

Robert would be coming with us. Since following us from France he had grown in every sense of the word. He had always been a confident young man but he relished his work as my chaplain. It had little to do with me but he was a great source of comfort to my men and their families. He took a great interest in each and every one of them. He took the ideas from the College of Sorbonne and did not just educate my grandchildren but all of those on my land. He was happy to help the parish priest who welcomed such a learned young man amongst us. When we ate, in my hall, we did not just have Grace trotted out by me but a meaningful one carefully crafted by my chaplain. My wife took to him as she had with no other since Jack. He became her confessor more than mine and the two of them, when he was not educating the young, studied and spoke together. They even wrote poetry too. In short, by the time we had the Midsummer's Eve celebrations, it was hard to think of a time when Robert was not part of our family. He had let his hair and beard grow. As he once said to me, 'I am no longer a monk. I should not adopt the appearance of one.' He dressed as one of us and would carry a short sword when we went to war. He was no warrior but the attack on the road had meant he wanted to defend himself. I thought it a sensible decision. Michel wanted to come to war with me too, but I think it was out of a sense of gratitude for his rescue. I persuaded him that he would be better placed protecting my family. That assuaged his guilt.

I would not be taking my bow with me. The last time I had used it in anger had been when we had rescued Robert and when I had fought the pirates. I had done well but I now realised that I did not need to prove my prowess to anyone, least of all me. Hamo was as good an archer as me and I could not only direct archers but also sergeants. That role might prove crucial in this campaign.

I also had a new horse. He was a courser and was called Felix. The name came from Mary and Robert and was carefully chosen. It meant lucky and Mary decided that I would need all the luck I could get. The fact that he was black, as well, helped. She had procured him in secret. She had Edgar, my horse master, breed from our best stallion and mare. That had been three years since and they had kept the horse a secret until April when the schooled horse was brought forth. I knew he was a great horse as soon as I saw him. He was bigger than any other and could carry my weight, even when mailed. He had been well-schooled. Mary had ensured that Edgar eradicated any reckless tendencies. He was as calm a horse as I had ever ridden. I had ridden him every day since he had been given to me on Lady's Day. I was confident that when we went to war he would get me out of trouble as fast as I got myself into it.

I knew that operating in the borders would give me the chance to visit my manor at Coldingham. Mordaf had been my archer but he was now my steward. I would be interested to see how domestication with Betty, his wife, had changed him. I had not demanded the income from Coldingham in the same way that I allowed William of Ware to use the profits to make his home better but Coldingham might now be in profit. It would be interesting to see. Gwillim was actually looking forward to the campaign if only to see his old friend once more. As Coldingham lay just north of Berwick, I planned on getting there a day or two before the muster. It would enable us to rest and allow my friends to be reunited. Accordingly, we left Yarpole on the 3rd of July. The days were long and I intended to use as much daylight as I could to travel as far as we were able without hurting our horses.

The goodbyes, my wife excepted, were tearful. Ralph and my daughter came over to say goodbye. I saw the guilt on Ralph's face but he had no need to feel guilty. Mary was sad to see me go as well as her son, foster son and confessor but her time with Robert had made her more philosophical. The young man had the ability to impart simple wisdom into everything he said and did. We left as soon after the sun rose as possible. Our first ride took us north of Dorrington, towards

Shrewsbury. We were still in the borders and well known. We were welcomed. I knew that we could not count on such a welcome later in the journey. We then stopped in Nantwich. As it was a centre for the production of salt making, while we were there we bought sacks of salt. It was of high quality and we needed as much salt as we could carry. We planned on hunting in the borders and we would need to preserve the meat. The next leg, to Manchester, took us over the Mersey at Wallintun. Had we used wagons we might have been slowed. The Pennines, north and east of Manchester, brought back memories to me as we crossed that empty land. I had encountered bandits there when, as a young man, I had fled to the Humber to take a ship to France. Neither Jack nor Robert had heard the story. I gave them a slightly sanitised version. The only one who knew the truth was me and I confessed all that I had done to no one. I was relieved when we dropped down to the Vale of York and headed for that bastion of the north. York was a symbol to the Scots. During the time of Matilda, the Scots had tried to take advantage of the discord in the land and brought an army south to take York and use it to regain Northumberland. They got as far as Northallerton before an ageing archbishop and the men of the north trounced them and sent them home. Its solid walls, dating back to the times of the Romans, were reassuring.

Even when we left York we still had a long way to go. For Jack, it meant passing close to the place of his birth, Malton. I wondered if Sir John, one of the men alongside whom I had travelled to the land of the Mongols, would be at the muster. I dismissed the idea immediately. His son might but Sir John was as old as I was and I could not see him enduring the rigours of a campaign. We stayed just south of the river Tees in the deserted manor of Thornaby. It was a derelict reminder of what could happen this close to the Scottish border. When King Sweyn had come to York in 1069 and slaughtered the Norman garrison, the Normans had taken their own revenge and they destroyed the manor and the Danes who lived there. The walls of their burgh remained as did the shell of their hall but the land south of Stockton was filled with ghosts. We would have pushed on to Stockton but it was after dark by the time we reached the river and I chose to stay in the old Danish settlement.

Our uncomfortable night was rewarded by allowing us to reach Durham in less than half a day and there we were afforded a fine welcome by Bishop Bek. Our early journey meant that he had not yet mustered all his men and we slept in the castle and camped before the cathedral. As he had in York, Robert took advantage of the fine edifice to spend an hour on his knees in prayer.

The Hunt

Hamo and I flanked the Bishop of Durham as we ate. "So, Bishop Bek, we go to fight in a land more familiar to you, do you think we can win?"

"I never doubt that, in a formal battle, we will defeat the Scots, not least because of your archers. If they do as they did when we tried the last time and take to the woods, then I fear we will lose our men as we did the last time." He lowered his voice, "Our English men on foot fight battles well but they do not enjoy marching and campaigning. The shorter the campaign the more confident I am."

He was right, of course, and while we might take their towns, the vastness of forests like Selkirk afforded them shelter and protection. Neither of us commented on the prince and his contribution. There was too much we did not know. Whilst the Welsh he commanded were a formidable force, half of his army was an unknown quantity. The Irish could be the deciding factor one way or the other. None of us had seen the prince command as yet and the king was gambling.

Berwick was now English. The king had taken it and Norham was no longer isolated and threatened. I did the castellan at Berwick the courtesy of telling him that we would be staying at my manor of Coldingham. He was relieved as it meant he did not have to find us somewhere to graze our animals. For my men and me, it was the chance to stay somewhere that did not stink of human and animal excrement. Once the whole army was mustered the land around Berwick would become a cesspit.

When we reached Coldingham my former archer looked like a changed man. As one of Sir Gerald's archers, he had been a killer of men and a hunter of the king's enemies. Now he looked to be a farmer. He still had the build of a bowman but his dress was that of a yeoman. He was in the yard, working with his men as they sorted through the beans that they had harvested. Some would be kept as seeds while others would be dried for winter food. The pods would be piled on the compost heap to enrich the soil. The life of a farmer had a rhythm to it. When Betty came out with a child in her arms I could not help but smile. Betty had lost two sons when the Scots had raided and killed her husband, Rafe of Beadnell. She knew not where they were but she and Mordaf had a child now and that was good.

I dismounted and went, first to Mordaf. I clasped his arm, "It is good to see you, Mordaf. I fear that you shall be overcrowded for a few days."

He grinned, "My lord, this is your manor and besides how can I be discomfited when I see so many old friends?"

The Hunt

As Hamo and Gwillim greeted Mordaf I went over to Betty, "How old is the bairn, Betty?"

"Gerald is just twelve months old." She held him for me to get a better look. I was better with children now that I had grandchildren and they no longer frightened me. "We named him after you, my lord. I hope you are not offended."

"Offended? I am honoured." I took out a gold piece from my purse and pressed it into the child's hand, "Here, Gerald, have a gift from your namesake."

"You need not, my lord."

"I know but I choose to and besides is not the giving of a coin to a baby supposed to bring good luck to both?"

Robert appeared and nodded, "Whilst it is a superstition and predates the time of Christ, as our lord said to suffer little children to come unto me, I do not think that he would frown on such a kind act."

I saw Betty's eyes widen. Whilst Robert's English had improved dramatically his accent still marked him as a Frenchman. "This is Robert, my French chaplain and this is Betty, the wife of my archer, Mordaf."

Robert took Betty's spare hand and kissed the back of it, "I am enchanted to meet you."

She blushed and giggled. Mordaf was a fine man but he did not have the words or manners of my Frenchman. "Come within. I will have your room readied, Sir Gerald." She was suddenly aware of the rest of my men as they dismounted. "I fear we cannot seat all in the hall. It is not a big one."

I shook my head, "My sons and Robert are the only ones who will stay in the hall. The rest can fend for themselves. Mordaf understands that."

We entered the manor which seemed tiny in comparison to Yarpole but it also looked more like a castle. This was Scotland where lords did not need to ask to make their homes defensible. The Scotsmen who had built it had a pele tower that could be used as a refuge and a ditch ran around the outside of the hall. We crossed by a bridge that could be removed in times of danger. If nothing else it reminded me of how parlous life was here, north of the Tweed.

Mordaf and Betty had made the hall their own. The furniture was simple and functional as were they. I was comfortable there. Betty enjoyed the attention of Robert who played the perfect gentleman. Jack, for his part, enjoyed entertaining the baby and that allowed Hamo and I to speak to Mordaf.

"And how is Stephen of Dunglass?" He was the steward of my son-in-law's manor. It lay not far away.

"He and I meet once a week. I am teaching him how to hunt with a bow." He shook his head, "You know better than any, Sir Gerald, that you cannot make a silk purse from a sow's ear but at least he can now draw a hunting bow and hit something… so long as it is within fifty paces. We enjoy hunting and talking. He is happy and Sir Ralph, like yourself, does not bother him with letters. We just get on with our manors. The difference is that the Scots expect him to be a patriot and fight for Scotland. They know I am Welsh. The first insult I endured was the last and Angus the blacksmith realised that as strong as he is, a right hand from an archer ends a fight in one blow. I am tolerated."

"Are you in danger?" Hamo understood the problem better than anyone. He had a wife and young children too.

"We are too small to warrant envy and I have trained my men so that we can fight. I keep the ditch clear of rubbish and we keep a good watch." He nodded towards the pele tower. "We keep one man up there during the hours of daylight. We saw you from a mile away. We also have Berwick close by. If a Scottish army came intent upon mischief and I felt we could not safely stay, we have enough horses to be there within an hour. Dunglass has more of a problem."

"And my manor? As you say I do not send letters, but I am interested in how it is run."

"Of course, my lord. There has not been a profit yet for I spent the income from the last couple of years investing in sheep." He smiled, "I am a Welshman and comfortable with our woolly friends. I bought sheep and they graze close to the sea. The salt-rimed grass gives them a good flavour. You shall see tomorrow for I had an old sheep slaughtered. Slow-cooked, salt-fed mutton is a rare treat. The wool gives us a small income and the flock prospers. Oats and barley do well here. It might not have suited the former lord to eat oat and rye bread but we like it. I thought to use the profits from this year to try cattle. If salty grass suits sheep, then why not cattle?"

There was a question in his words and a querulous look on his face. He was seeking reassurance. I smiled, "All is well Mordaf. Tomorrow I shall ride back to Berwick to speak to the king. It will give you the opportunity to speak to old friends."

"And I look forward to that. I did not see Ralph the Fletcher. He is not ill or…"

I shook my head, "His daughter married William of Ware and I gave him the manor of Toot Baldon to manage. Ralph went with him. I have a new fletcher now, Walter of Rhyl. He is young but speak to Gwillim about his skill."

"I will, my lord."

That night I slept in the lord's chamber. I knew that Mordaf and Betty normally used it, but they insisted that the three of us, Hamo, Jack and I slept there.

The next day I rode with Jack back to Berwick. St Swithin's Day was but a day or so away and many more tents had sprung up. The king had not yet arrived but when a sail was sighted at noon, flying the royal standard, then we knew that the king had come. I waited in the outer bailey as the king and his entourage swept in. I saw Richard of Craven, resplendent in royal livery close to the king's standard bearer, Sir Richard Fitzhugh. I was pleased although I knew that Richard would have to learn to fight if he was to survive. The king acknowledged me with a wave but that was all. If he wished to speak to me then he would send for me. I would hang around the castle until the late afternoon and then return to Coldingham.

I had been noticed for the newest member of his household, Richard of Craven, came to seek me out. "Sir Gerald, the king would speak with you."

"Of course." As he led me up some stairs I asked, "And how does the new position suit you?"

He gave me a rueful smile, "You know how it is, Sir Gerald, I am the new man and as such the butt of jokes and the one given the most menial of tasks to perform."

"I am a menial task?" I tried to give a straight face.

He turned appalled, "No, my lord, for the king asked me to seek you out. It is a most honourable task I perform."

I laughed, "Learn to laugh a little more at yourself, Richard. You will learn that such things are inconsequential. Once you have been in battle and they see both your mettle and your worth, then life will become easier."

"Is it the same with your men?"

"I suppose it is. I know that when I was a young archer I was both mocked and humiliated. I grew and my fists did my talking. I cannot remember the last time I endured humiliation."

Richard knocked on the door.

"Enter." The king was alone. "Richard, guard the door."

I sat and King Edward smiled, "Between you, you and the earl of Lincoln have managed to eliminate one of my enemies and I would have you keep an eye open for one of the others."

"Wallace."

154

"Just so. Since we drove him from Toot Baldon there has been nary a sighting of the man but something tells me that his old haunts in Selkirk Forest may be where he is to be found. When we near that haven for brigands take your men and look for signs of him. If nothing else we can stop him from getting comfortable and discourage others from joining him."

"And the other threat, Robert de Brus, my lord?"

"My son along with his Celtic army are attacking Ayr and Turnberry. I hoped that this shall be my son's coming of age. I have given him free rein. We shall see." He smiled, "That is all. You may return to Coldingham."

I did not mind the curt dismissal. I was happier with my men than nobles in any case.

Mordaf shook his head when I told him of our task. "Selkirk Forest is vast, my lord, and we know that Wallace is adept at hiding. You will need luck as well as skill to even get close and he is slippery."

Mordaf was right, of course. "And he seems to have a sixth sense of danger. I know that when I followed him in Paris I was as careful as I could have been and yet he knew he was being followed. How?"

Hamo was more optimistic, "Then we must treat him as we would a wild pig and use every broken leaf and snapped twig to build up a picture of the movement of Wallace and his men through the trees. As we discovered in Galloway, he always has a number of escape routes. We must become as familiar with those trails as we are with the ones in the copse close to Yarpole."

Jack said, "I can see work for archers, Hamo, but what of the men at arms? I know that there are fewer of us but we cannot creep through the forests like wraiths."

"I need you, Jack, and my sergeants to be the opposite of us. You shall be the beaters. Use noise and your horses to let Wallace and his men know where you are. If they are moving then they will leave a trail and we can use our archers' noses to sniff him out."

Robert was new to all this, "What about the battle that the king seeks? When will that take place?"

We all turned to the Frenchman. He was clever and knowledgeable about so many things but here he knew even less than Betty. I explained as though to a child, "If we are lucky then we will pin the Scots to a place where they cannot flee and then they will have to fight, but as Wallace discovered at Falkirk, they do not have the weapons to face heavy cavalry. They will fade before us and be like will o'the wisps."

Hamo nodded, "And our men will also begin to disappear when there is no loot from the battlefield. The king needs victories and quickly too."

For the first week of the campaign, we were with the vanguard as we headed up the east coast. Such was the size of the army that none of the castles was able to hold out against us. They fell without the need for siege engines and war machines. It was clear that the Scots were simply avoiding battle. As we neared Selkirk Forest, we left the army and headed into the dark recesses of the Scots' best fortress. I had Robert, despite his objections, wear a metal studded brigandine and don a helmet.

"Robert, I need Jack to lead my men at arms. You cannot sneak through the forest as I can but you can add to the illusion that you are another warrior. The helmet and brigandine will afford some protection. I do not want Jack looking over his shoulder to see that you are safe. The alternative is for you to return to Coldingham and await us there."

The last argument persuaded him and Jack led my men to harry the villages and farms that lay on the outskirts of the forest. The king and the army lumbered north and west to meet with his son. We had heard that the prince and his Celtic army had already taken Ayr Castle and Turnberry was being besieged. The young man was proving to be a better general than I had thought.

I was with the archers but I had no bow with me. Nor was I at the fore but I walked with the horse holders as Hamo and my best archers fanned out before us, seeking our elusive prey. It was the third day of the hunt and we had not seen a sign of Wallace when we had our first clue that he was around. We were ambushed. That is to say, we would have been ambushed but for Gwillim and Dick's noses and hunter's acumen. The archers all had their bows in their right hands and an arrow was nocked already. It was second nature to them. I led the eight archers who held the reins of the other horses. I had Hamo's mount, Regis, in my left hand. We were thirty paces behind the fan of scouts.

I saw Gwillim and Dick raise their bows and release before the first bolt and arrow was sent at us. That early warning saved the other archers who took cover and then sought targets.

I turned, "Leave the horses here and join our friends. Walter, you mount your horse and come with me. My new fletcher obeyed. He had a short sword. "You and I are going to ride around the ambush. I would have a prisoner or two." We mounted. "Draw your sword. Your task is to stay behind me and watch my back."

"Yes, my lord."

I could see that he was nervous, and I smiled, "This experience will stand you in good stead."

I whipped Felix's head around and rode through the forest, seemingly away from the sound of arrows and bolts whizzing through the air, shredding foliage and slamming into trees. When the sounds faded I turned to ride a parallel course to the one we had been taking before the ambush. I had my drawn sword in my right hand and when I saw the Scot ahead of me raise his cumbersome crossbow, I rode at him and struck him in the back of the head with the flat of my sword. His cry alerted those before him and seeing horses assumed that they were surrounded.

"We are undone, every man for himself."

The men I could see, turned and ran. I did not move for I did not want to spoil the flight of an arrow from one of my archers. Men fell with arrows in their unprotected backs. I dismounted, "Ride back the way we came and bring the other horses."

"Yes, my lord." He sheathed his sword and disappeared into the forest.

I dismounted and after sheathing my sword hurled the crossbow into the forest. I heard it crack and break against a tree. I disarmed the man and put his weapons in my belt. I took my own rondel dagger out and, with my knee on his chest, held it to his nose. The noise of the chase had dissipated when his eyes opened and he saw me before him.

"Now, my friend, I could have killed you, but I wanted to ask you some questions. You will live if you answer me honestly." His eyes narrowed. "Do you understand me?"

"Aye. You are Longshanks' butcher."

"You know me then?"

"I have heard of you. Your name was spoken around the campfire."

"Ah, by Jack Short, no doubt."

It was a stab in the dark but it caught him out. His eyes widened, "Aye, but how did you know?"

Had I used Wallace's name he might have been silent but I now knew that if Short was in the forest then so was Wallace. "Let us say that I know my enemies. Is William Wallace there too?"

I saw the lie in his eyes before it left his mouth, "No, he is far from here. His lands are in Galloway."

Just then Hamo and my archers returned. I stood and put away my dagger. "Hob, Ned, bind this man, we have a prisoner."

"You said I would live if I spoke the truth."

I smiled, it was not a warm smile but the smile of the wolf before it sinks its teeth into its prey, "But you did not tell the truth, did you?

157

Wallace was in the forest and you lied. I will let the king decide what to do with you."

As he was led away Hamo said, "Wallace was here?"

I shook my head, "Not in the ambush but he organised it. We now look for clues as to his whereabouts."

The ambush caused two minor wounds to my archers and yielded us eight Scottish corpses. More importantly, it told us that Wallace was in the forest and the next day we renewed our search. The trail of the fleeing men led us to a campsite. It was there we found more evidence of Wallace's presence. They had made hovels and when we found one big enough to fit a giant we knew where he had slept. Gwillim found the mark of a boot that had to have been made by Wallace. He followed it. The footprints led off down a side trail.

Hob shouted from the other side of the camp, "I have found where they fled. They are heading southeast down the main trail."

Hamo shouted, "Ignore them, we have Wallace's smell in our nostrils. We follow the giant."

My men were good, and they established that there were four men with Wallace. "Two will be the Short brothers."

"It is good that you let them go after Lochmaben, Father. They mark Wallace's presence no matter how well he hides."

The hunt moved much faster after that. We found clues as to his movements when we found branches broken above the height of a normal man. Even without Wallace's boot prints, Gwillim could have tracked him. They were moving fast and they had a six-hour lead over us. We were forced to camp when darkness came, and we just prayed that it did not rain. They tried to lose us close to Yarrow Water but my archers were the best of scouts and we picked up the trail close to Sundhope. Peebles lay to the north and I wondered if he would make for it. I hoped he would as that was one of the places we had chosen for Jack to raid.

No rain came and when we resumed our hunt the next day, we discovered that Wallace was turning to head more westerly than northerly. We found his camp and although it was a dry one, the place where one of them had emptied his bowels told us that we were closing in on them. They were just two hours ahead of us.

I began to hope that we might finally take the elusive symbol of Scottish independence but when we found the farm where animals had been tethered and Wallace was joined by another two men my heart sank; instead of heading north and west, the trail of the horses now headed south and west. The trail was clearer but we were no longer gaining on them. They were heading, for we were now on a trackway, for Wallace's old hunting ground, Annandale.

The rains came when we were close to the tiny hamlet of Cappercleuch. It was an August storm that filled the sky with black thunderclouds and the rain was so heavy that it hurt. We took shelter in the lee of a barn and endured the savage storm. When it finally ceased, night was upon us but further pursuit was pointless. Mud had slid from the side of the hills and engulfed the track we were following. Not only did it hide any trail that might have been there, it would need half a day to clear.

We lit a fire to dry our clothes and to cook the sheep we had butchered, "The hunt is over."

"We can try to follow him again, tomorrow, Father. We know where he is headed, Annandale."

Wallace is clever and he knows that we are following him. He will use the storm to change direction. We have upset his plans, that is clear, and the threat from him whilst not gone, is not what it might have been. We will rejoin the army."

Chapter 17

It took almost a week for us to rejoin King Edward. We found Jack at Peebles. He and the men at arms had raided and we were now well stocked with supplies. We found the king at Wishaw not far from the Castle of Bothwell. I was shocked at King Edward's appearance when we met. He looked ancient and weary. I wondered if I looked the same. He and Aymer de Valance were sat with his household knights as I dismounted and approached.

"Give me good news, Warbow. Tell me that you have Wallace."

I shook my head, "We caught his smell, King Edward, but a storm helped him to escape. He is further south in Annandale."

I saw him sigh, "Then perhaps my son, when he has done with his pilgrimage to St Ninian's at Whithorn, may find him."

I frowned, "Pilgrimage, my lord?"

The king nodded, "He won great victories at Turnberry and Ayr. The west coast is ours and de Brus' power is broken. He goes to pray at the shrine and to give thanks to God."

"What is it that you now wish of me and my men, my lord?"

The weary king waved an arm at the camp. "As you can see, Warbow, we have suffered from spineless men deserting us. The garrison at Berwick mutinied because they had not been paid and we are waiting here for the siege engines that will enable us to take Bothwell."

Aymer de Valence, the earl of Pembroke shook his head, "'Twas ours and it controlled the Clyde. If we are to move north to Stirling, then we must reduce it. We shall need your archers to fight alongside my Welshmen."

"Yes, my lord, we will find our camp for we are weary."

It was depressing news. Scotland was like an ulcer that seemed to weaken our army when we campaigned. Sir Ralph had the best idea. We made our camp. Robert sensed our mood and he did his best to cheer us up. That he succeeded showed me a number of things. One, that his inclusion in my familia was vital and second, that my men still had mettle and spirit. The rest of the king's army might be in danger of crumbling but not the men of Yarpole.

Bothwell Castle was a well-made castle overlooking the Clyde. The donjon was a mighty one and we had to wait for our trebuchets to arrive before we could begin the assault. I hated sieges and this one was no different from the others we had endured. Caerlaverock held out for just two days but it took a fortnight for us to reduce Bothwell. When it finally fell, we were sent the unwelcome news that a Scottish army had appeared at Lochmaben Castle and the English garrison there was being besieged. As Prince Edward's Irish contingent had left for Ireland, having served their allotted time, I was sent to help Prince Edward with a thousand men from Bishop Bek's palatinate army.

"Warbow, I will push on to Stirling. I would have the memory of Surrey's defeat ended. You retake Lochmaben and then bring my son and his Welshmen to Stirling."

"Yes, my lord."

It was the end of September and a campaign in Galloway would be plagued by the biting insects and an enemy that I suspected would flee at our approach. I was given command of the Durham men. I was lucky that the bishop had given me good men. I fear that had I others I might have had desertions on the march south. We had to move at the pace of the men on foot and the journey was longer than I would have liked but the Durham men were hardy folk and we reached the castle before the Scots knew we were there. We camped at Thornhill a few miles north of the castle. My archers captured the village before word could be sent to the besiegers that we were close.

Gathering my leaders around me I explained my plan, "We rise at the third hour when it is still dark. I have no intentions of chasing shadows and I want the castle surrounded before dawn. My archers will be to the north and the Durham archers, who are also mounted, to the south. Our foot soldiers and mounted men will complete the circle. The archers are there to keep the Scots penned. I want none to escape. The Scots have, hitherto, avoided a battle. This will be as close as we come to one and I intend to make them pay." I was, in truth, merely obeying King Edward's orders. He was in a bad mood because of the delays as well as the desertions and the Scots would pay the price.

I went over the role of each of the elements of the army with the leaders. I wanted no misunderstandings or confusion.

After they had departed, I sat with Hamo, Jack and Robert. "Your first real command, Father."

I sniffed and ate some of the salted mutton, "It will hardly be mentioned no matter what the outcome. If we win, we merely regain the castle we took in the first place."

"It is now a stone castle, Father."

"I know, and that is why it must not fall to the besiegers. As Berwick showed, some of those who are in garrisons are not reliable men."

Jack asked, "And when it is over?"

"I hear the question beneath your question, Jack. No, we do not return home. We make the castle stronger and then head back north to rejoin the king at Stirling."

His face told me that I had hit the mark.

We rode through the darkness. My archers took the village of Lochmaben before the villagers were awake. The two bodies of horsemen rode around the loch, keeping the besiegers' fires far enough away so that we were invisible. The Durham archers would be in position already. The signal would be the sounding of my hunting horn three times. Sir Richard of Rede House was in command of the other horsemen and I allowed him extra time to get into position. I drew my sword and raised it. Peter, my standard bearer and trumpeter sounded the three blasts when I dropped my sword.

Spurring Felix, we launched our attack. Although the two bands of archers were loosing in the dark the fires of the besiegers illuminated the camp enough for them to see the fall of arrows. It was the arrows that alerted the Scots and not our horses, for the ground was not hard and it softened the sound of hooves. The cries of alarm from the Scots and cheers from the new walls of the castle told me that the defenders were alert and their arrows and bolts would ensure that the Scots were assaulted from two sides.

One Scottish knight tried to rally his men. They grabbed shields and tried to form a shield wall. It was too little and too late. With Jack on one side of me and Robert of Luston on the other, we ploughed into them. They had not had time to grab their long spears and their swords were too short to hurt. I brought my sword to strike at the shoulder of the knight whose own sword had merely scraped and scratched along my hauberk. He had good mail but it was my right hand that struck him, my archer's hand and I heard the bone break. His right arm hung uselessly from his side. I reined in Felix and his excellent schooling came to the fore. He stopped in an instant.

"Sir knight, yield." My sword was pointing at his face, and he nodded.

The men with him were his retainers and they dropped their weapons too. As the sun rose above the trees to the east the rest of the Scots threw down their weapons. We had retaken Lochmaben Castle and I had a knight that I could ransom.

The prisoners were rounded up and I had their boots taken from them. Not all wore boots but by taking them I ensured that they would not run. They had to be fed but I only needed to do that for a couple of days. I sent them to the king two days later escorted by the Durham men. "Tell the king that I will wait until we have repaired the damage done by the Scots and then return myself. I will send word to the prince."

Sir Richard nodded, "An easy victory and enough purses to keep my men happy. I would follow your banner again, Sir Gerald."

"I fear it will not be this campaigning season. The delays thus far mean that unless the king can take Stirling quickly, we will all have an uncomfortably cold winter in Scotland."

He agreed, "And we would lose more men. We should have begun earlier."

I chuckled, "Do not make the mistake of telling the king that."

Prince Edward was close enough to have heard of our victory and he and his army arrived while we were finishing the repairs to the walls.

I bowed and said, "Your army is smaller than I expected, Prince Edward."

He nodded, "The Irish lords decided that having taken two castles they had done all that was deemed necessary. They went home as did half of my Welshmen. Having made my pilgrimage, I shall rejoin my father." He smacked at the side of his head, "These damned insects are worse than the Scots."

"They are, indeed, my lord." My men had fought here before and we used a salve that seemed to deter them.

He stayed a night and was gone by noon the next day. We had planned on leaving two days later but that departure was delayed when Robert de Brus arrived at the castle. He wished to surrender. I think he thought that Prince Edward was there and was slightly disappointed that it was just Lord Edward's archer.

I accepted it, of course. I told him that I would escort him to the king. He nodded sullenly, "And now King Edward has my poor country. He shook his head, "Why he should want it when he has England and Aquitaine is beyond me."

One problem caused by his arrival was that he had to be afforded quarters that were fitting for a man of his rank. I think any other lord would have baulked at giving up his bed but I was made of sterner stuff. In the event, it was only for two nights as, the day after the ransom arrived, so a messenger, Richard of Craven, arrived to tell me that the king had abandoned his plans to besiege Stirling and intended to overwinter what remained of his army at Linlithgow. It meant we had a journey northeast before we could return home. Before we left I ensured that the garrison at Lochmaben as well as Dumfries were well supplied, and then we left for Linlithgow.

Without the men of Durham and with horses captured from the besiegers we made Jedburgh in three days, although the rain and the wind made it a most unpleasant journey. We stayed in the priory attached to the Abbey. This was Comyn country and the Comyn family backed John Balliol. That meant that Robert de Brus was viewed by the townsfolk with suspicion. We were lucky that the abbot was a fair-minded and honest man. He welcomed us. The English had raided his abbey too many times in the past for him to offer any opposition.

Robert left us, as he always did when we were near a holy place, to pray. As he once told me he knew he could speak to God any time but the magnificence of man-made edifices seemed to make it easier to do so. We ate in the refectory. The monks ate well at Jedburgh for it was a royal borough but with no king, they were free, for the moment, from royal whims.

I had got to know de Brus a little better on the road and whilst I never liked him I found him an interesting character. He was in a lively mood and so I asked him a question that had been on my mind for many years, "My lord, I am just an ill-educated archer and an Englishman to boot."

He smiled, "Some would say the two go hand in hand..."

"Just so. I know that King Alexander's line died out when Margaret of Norway died. How do you have a claim to the throne?" I realised that the question might seem offensive, "If you do not wish to answer then ignore my curiosity."

"I do not mind. You can blame King Henry the 1st for he married his illegitimate daughter Elizabeth to Fergus, the Lord of Galloway. The marriage elevated the lords of Galloway. The family had a claim to the Scottish throne as did the other lords of the Scottish kingdoms but the line of kings was descended from King Duncan. Fergus had two sons, Uhtred and Gilbert. I am descended from Gilbert and Balliol and Comyn from Uhtred. My great-grandfather was the Earl of Carrick and so I have two claims to the crown, Galloway and Carrick. In the absence of any other contender..." he spread his arms.

"Surely the strength of King Edward would make life in Scotland easier. It is less than twenty years since you regained the islands from the Vikings. They would never dare to take on King Edward."

It was then that I saw the veil slip over the eyes of de Brus. He spoke words but I could not see the truth in his eyes. "We are a young country but we do not wish to be ruled from London. We like to be independent."

"Yet you have surrendered and you will be at the mercy of King Edward."

"Your Prince of Wales took my castles and without men how can I fight? I fought for King Edward once before when I was the constable of Carlisle."

I did not say that he had done a poor job of it as he had allowed William Wallace a free hand.

"I will offer my sword to him again. Who knows he might recognise my claim to the Scottish crown and if I cannot be king of an independent Scotland then it may be that he lets me rule as a client kingdom."

"And that would satisfy you?"

He sighed and, for the first time, I believed his words were sincere, "I have been brought up to believe that I have a claim to the Scottish crown. I believe that I would be a good king. You and I are different, Gerald Warbow. You rose from nothing to become an important man. I was born with expectations on my shoulders. That is the real difference between us."

I nodded, "And William Wallace?"

"Ah, the enigma of the one man who might save Scotland from King Edward and yet the one with neither a claim nor a desire for the crown. I can tell you that none of the men with a claim to the crown would use him for he might want a different Scotland than the one we seek. Besides, he is elusive. He is protected by the people who adore him. They see him as one of them. I tried to find him to make him an ally but I could not find any sign of him and he lives in the land I am supposed to control. No, Wallace will be found when he chooses to be and not before."

Robert entered and he looked agitated. He put his head close to my ear, "My lord, if I might have a word," he looked at de Brus, "in private?"

"Of course. If you will excuse me, Sir Robert, my chaplain needs to speak to me."

He took me out to the cloisters which were deserted. "My lord, there is danger."

My hand went to my sword, "Here? In this holy place?"

He shook his head, "Let me explain, Sir Gerald. I was in the abbey as is my usual practice and, as I normally do, I found a quiet alcove where I could commune with God. I heard two men come in and, thinking they were alone they began to speak. The church was empty and their words, although spoken in hushed tones carried to me. One was a Frenchman and they spoke in French. Someone called Lord Comyn?" He looked at me and I nodded. "He had sent the man to meet with the Frenchman. From his accent he was Norman. The pope, it seems, has released John Balliol and he is raising an army in France. They did not expect to see us here but the man sent by Comyn thought it a good opportunity to have a rival killed and blamed on the English. You."

"I was named?"

"You were named. The man sent by Comyn said that there were many places along the Tweed where you could be ambushed and they would make it look as though you had killed the Earl of Carrick."

"Where are they now?"

"I had to wait until they had left before I sneaked out. They were gone but I heard the sound of horses. I came as soon as I could."

"Find Gwillim and tell him the same as you told me." My archer would know how best to obviate the danger.

"We change our plans then, Sir Gerald?"

I smiled, "Of course not, we walk into their trap but the difference is we are the spider that is hunting and the wasp will get a rude shock."

The abbot, Hamo and Robert de Brus all stared up at me as I entered. I knew not if there were spies in the abbey and so I smiled, "Robert worries about nothing. He thought his horse was going lame."

Sir Robert said, "And he asked a baron to help?"

I shrugged, "He is a stranger to our land and to all matters equine. He did not wish to slow us up. He is a good man and I do not mind giving the time." I smiled, "Besides, I needed to make water too."

The abbot smiled and nodded, "Aye, Sir Gerald, when we were younger, we had bladders that could go all day without being emptied but now…"

Hamo recognised the lie in my words, but he kept a straight face. We had been given a cell that we shared and once in the cell he said, "And now, Father, the true story."

I nodded and as I undressed told him. "Gwillim is also aware of the danger. He will have chosen the scouts to find the ambushers. We will ride with our captive in the middle of our sergeants and you and the archers can be ready to attack the ambushers. If they intend to make it look as though we are the attackers, then they will use bows. I have yet to meet a Scotsman who can use a bow."

"There is still a danger."

"When we are on the road then I will tell the earl of the danger so that he is prepared but here there are too many ears."

The monks prayed often and I was awake and dressed by lauds. I fetched Jack and Gwillim and we went to the stables where we could talk. I told Jack of my plan. Gwillim nodded, "I have sent Dick with Ned and Hob already. They have spent the night in the forest to the north of us. They will let us know where the ambush will take place. I thought to have half of the archers follow a parallel route to the sergeants, my lord. If they have counted our men then they might be suspicious but I think that they will see what they expect to see."

"Just so long as our captive is unharmed."

Jack asked, "But he is an enemy, why worry if the Scots kill each other?"

I sighed "King Edward likes to manipulate his enemies. The Earl of Carrick is someone he can use. There are Scots who will follow him and de Brus intends to offer his sword to King Edward."

Jack shook his head, "I would not trust him."

"Nor do I but we are not the King of England."

We left as soon as the sun rose and headed along the road to the west of the Tweed on a frosty morning where our cloaks were tightly wrapped around us. De Brus was a sharp man and he said, "Sir Gerald, you appear to have fewer archers this morning."

I nodded, "And that is the fault of John Comyn and John Balliol." His eyes widened and I explained what Robert had heard.

He nodded, "I thought your story improbable. And you intend to spring the trap with a trap of your own."

"I do. Warn your men that when we are attacked they are to remain protected by my men."

"That will not sit well with them for they are not cowards."

"It is for their own protection. My archers will be deployed ahead of us and while they know my men…"

"Quite. It seems that I am in your hands then, archer."

We were close to Norham which lay on the other side of the river when Gwillim insinuated himself between Hamo and me. He totally ignored de Brus as he spoke, "We have found them, my lord." He chuckled, "They are clever. There is a ford close to Norham and they are on the English side of the river. There are forty of them and half have bows," he shook his head, "not longbows my lord but hunting bows and, I warrant, hunting arrows." I nodded. "Captain Hamo, I have chosen my men."

"Go with God, Gwillim."

My archer made the sign of the cross, "Always, Captain."

Suddenly there were just twelve archers flanking my men at arms. Hamo said, "Walter, take six men and ride at the rear. The rest of you, with me." He nodded to his brothers-in-law, "You two with me." My archers had all strung their bows before we had left the priory but they were hidden on the left side of the horses. The Scots would assume our bows were in their cases.

Jack said, "Keep your hands ready to draw swords. On my command, we charge and not before."

"Aye, Captain."

He was young but he commanded like a veteran.

"Robert, just stay out of trouble. I cannot keep my eyes on you."

My chaplain smiled, "I will pray that God does not wish my unworthy life to end just yet, Sir Gerald."

I slid my sword in and out of the scabbard. Morning frost could make it stick. My open-faced helmet meant I had a good view, but I knew that a lucky arrow could spell disaster for me. The Scots had chosen their ambush site well. They had lined the sides of the ford and sending their arrows at our unprotected right sides meant our shields would be ineffective. However, Gwillim and his men were behind them and, as we rode into the open, by the ford, were heard the distinctive sound of arrows thudding into the ambushers. Gwillim had far fewer men than the Scots but he commanded archers.

Jack shouted, "Follow me."

As Hamo, Walter and my other archers dismounted and began to loose across the river, Jack led my sergeants into the river. The water slowed them but it meant they could swing their shields around for protection. I stayed with de Brus. It was well that I did for the ambushers had another trick to play. A dozen horsemen were on the Scottish side of the river and they suddenly charged us. De Brus was right. His men were not cowards and although outnumbered they turned and faced the mailed men. My chaplain wheeled his horse and rode back down the road. He knew that he would only get in the way.

I hauled up my shield and spurred Felix who relished the opportunity to fight. They came for de Brus whose livery marked him clearly. I rode at his right side and as the lance was thrust at him, I was able to hack through the wooden shaft. The knight, for I saw his spurs, tried to ram his broken weapon at me. My mighty right arm was able to sweep it to the side and then, standing in my stirrups I brought down my sword. I was aiming at his shoulder but his horse flinched when Felix's teeth snapped and, instead, my sword smashed into his helmet. He fell from his horse.

Hamo, Walter and my archers had turned and it was their arrows that drove off the survivors of the attack. Four of the enemy lay on the ground. The rest had fled. Robert de Brus was whole but one of his oathsworn had been speared in the side.

"Robert, tend to the wounded knight."

"Aye, Sir Gerald."

I dismounted. One of the attackers was still alive. He was not a knight. De Brus also dismounted. The man was clearly dying. The sword that had penetrated his mail hauberk had driven into his guts. It was the worst of wounds, one that would give him a slow death.

He looked up and said, in French, "Give me a clean death."

Robert had heard the voice and, giving de Brus' man a cloth to stem the bleeding, knelt and said, "I am a priest. Would you like to confess, first?"

Reassured by the French voice the man nodded. Robert knelt and put his ear to the man's mouth. He listened and then gave absolution. He made the sign of the cross and stood. He nodded. It was de Brus who slit the man's throat. He turned to Robert, "That was a thoughtful act, my friend. Sir Gerald is lucky to have you."

As he went back to his charge he shook his head, "No, I am the lucky one."

We had minor injuries and the Scots, along with their Scottish allies, had lost more than a dozen men. Others had been wounded and had fled. Gwillim took the bodies to Norham so that the constable could scour the land of the survivors and the dead could be buried. We headed for Linlithgow. We did not make it in one day. We had to stay in Edinburgh at the captured castle. It meant we reached King Edward at noon the next day.

He was delighted with the prisoner I brought but less than amused that the pope had apparently colluded with those the king saw as his enemies and released John Balliol. He dismissed the others and I was left alone with him, "You have done, as you always do, Warbow and delivered that which you promised. I will stay here in Scotland. I want my enemies to know that I am not done yet with Scotland. De Brus is an unexpected gift."

"You will use him, King Edward?"

"The ambush attempt told me much. There is an old saying, the enemy of my enemy is my friend. From what you have told me de Brus is not averse to serving me to get that which he wishes, the sole right to the Scottish crown." I nodded. "Perhaps Wallace being at large is not a bad thing, Warbow, for he is the unknown factor. The three contenders need him but clearly do not trust him. When the time is right you shall hunt him again. Until then return to your manor."

My familia headed back the three hundred miles to Yarpole. Autumn would be almost over by the time we arrived, but we would be home for Christmas. We were whole and thanks to the ransom I had taken and our success we had purses and armour. All was well.

Chapter 18

King Edward was a clever man. Through papal intermediaries, he arranged a nine-month truce. He said he would return the lands he had captured to French agents. It was a bold gamble which paid off. The King of France was not willing to send an army into Scotland. Once again, his own armies had been humbled by the Flemish. It would take time to build them up. The king held a tournament in Falkirk to celebrate. It was a clever venue as it was the site of the battle where Wallace had been trounced. We heard all of this second hand as we enjoyed our life in the Welsh marches.

Alice was not the only one pregnant, both my daughters were expecting too. The line of the Warbow would go on. Alice was expecting my next grandchild within a few months. Robert had grown into his role as chaplain and teacher. His life was good. He told me on Twelfth Night that he would say it was perfect but he did not wish to tempt fate. Michel had also changed. He had come into contact with Anna, one of my servant girls. She was a plain and homely girl, and the contact came when he brought the goat's milk to the hall. He had begun to make cheese but as he had a surplus my cook used it too. He fell for Anna who was thought to be beyond marriageable age; she had seen well over twenty-two summers. For her part the kind Frenchman was everything she could have dreamed. They were married in March, a month after Alice was delivered of Robert, named after my chaplain. Mary was pleased for she had a soft spot for Anna who was the kindest and most caring of my servants. She had been the one who had helped to get reluctant grandchildren to eat and was also the one who could be trusted to keep a firm hand on them when their parents' eyes were elsewhere.

As the winter slowly ended, life was good. King Edward's plans appeared to have succeeded. The pope sent messages to his bishops that Scotland should not rebel against King Edward. King Philip and he were still at loggerheads and his support for England was a deliberate insult to the French.

It was Mary who suggested the visit to Ludlow for Margaret was also due to give birth, "You see Hamo and his children every day. You visit Wooferton once a week and see Joan's children but you never see your firstborn. Soon Gerald will have seen more than seven summers. We should visit." She smiled, "Who knows, we may be there in time to see our next grandchild born."

I shook my head, "We have not been invited."

She burst out laughing, "Gerald Warbow that is the most feeble of excuses. Your daughter is due to give birth. Why should we wait for an invitation? What is the real reason?"

I sighed for my wife could read me as easily as she did the books she and Robert pored over. "I fear that my grandson will not be a warrior and that would upset me."

She turned my head so that our eyes locked, "You would have him choose a life such as yours and Hamo where death or injury is just the next campaign away?" I said nothing, "I would rather he took after his father, Richard has a good life. He does not have to go to war and he and his family are comfortable. I would think that a good thing."

She made a good argument but I was and am an obstinate old fool and I continued to dig the hole deeper and deeper, "I am the king's man."

"And that is your choice and, thanks to you, Hamo's."

"But it is the duty of every Englishman to fight for his king and his country."

"What arrant nonsense is that? You have said many times that the fyrd are more trouble than they are worth. Would you rather lead an army of peasants or a small band of professional soldiers? That is what you have created here. Your men are like you and that is good for England. Richard makes money which he pays in taxes to the church and to the king and that is also good for England. Now, when do we leave?"

When Mary made up her mind then I did as she said. Life was easier that way. We took just Jack and Robert with us. Although I had heeded my wife's words, I did take a baldric, short sword and dagger I had taken from the battlefield. I would give it to Gerald. I kept it hidden in my bag. It was not that far from Richard and Margaret's home close to Ludlow Castle but I rarely visited. I thought back to the time when Richard had campaigned with me. It had been I who had advised him to become a merchant. I suppose I thought that it would be a safe life for my daughter but I still wanted my firstborn to emulate me. I knew it was foolish.

Despite having a home in the centre of Ludlow it was almost palatial. He had stables and rooms on two floors. The house was furnished like that of a great lord. I knew that Richard was successful. He bought sheep from Wales and had the animals skinned so that he could sell the wool and then he sold the meat to butchers. He also bought fleeces and he employed women to spin wool. He had an inn in the town, one of my old men at arms, Jack, son of William, ran it for him. I knew how to fight, and Richard knew how to make money.

Mary had, of course, warned my daughter of our imminent arrival so that we were welcomed like potentates. It was warm and my guilt increased. I might have complained that Richard and Margaret did not invite me to their home but I only invited them at Christmas and Easter. I introduced Robert and he proved to be as popular with my grandchildren, Gerald and Eleanor, as he was with Hamo's children. It was partly his accent and partly his infectious sense of humour. While Jack saw to the horses we were taken to the room the family used on a daily basis. It had a fireplace and that was rare and was cosy. While Gerald and Eleanor asked question after question of the priest I studied my grandchildren. Gerald had my build while Eleanor had inherited my wife's stunning looks. They were both children still but you could see the man and woman within their frames. They spoke and moved like young nobles. Hamo's children, more used to roughhousing with archers' and sergeants' children, seemed wilder in comparison. Mary fussed over Margaret who looked beautiful. Pregnancy did that for my daughters.

Richard said, "We do not see enough of you, Sir Gerald."

I nodded, "I am often on the king's business. That is how Robert came to work for me. I shall remedy that whilst I am not needed by the king."

He poured me a goblet of wine. The goblets would have cost a week's wages for a working man. I knew that the wine he served would also be of the best quality. "And does the king go to war again?"

I nodded and sipped the wine. It was delicious and I fought the urge to down it in one. "There is a nine-month truce with the Scots and the French, but as the king is still in Scotland then when the truce is over I shall be called to war again."

He sighed and shook his head, "War costs the country money, Sir Gerald. I have heard, through merchants in King's Lynn, that the king is having built a pontoon bridge to allow him to penetrate deep into Scotland. When finished it will take thirty ships to transport it and has cost a thousand pounds. That is profligate."

Richard never went close to a war and yet he knew more about the king's plans than I did. "It is necessary and with Scotland subjugated then we can take on their allies, the French."

"More war. War makes it hard for men to trade."

I sighed. This was an argument my wife did not want me to have. I saw her glance over and give the subtlest shake of her head. I changed the subject. "The children are growing well. You shall soon have a third child and Gerald will soon be a man. He will be ready to take on the world."

There was an implied question which Richard answered. "He has a natural skill with numbers and he wishes to become a merchant. It is a good thing is it not?"

I sighed, "Aye, I suppose so."

When they tired of Robert's amusements, I took Gerald with me to the stables where Jack had left the sword, baldric, scabbard and dagger. "I have brought you a present."

His eyes widened, "Grandfather, it is a most wonderful gift. What have I done to deserve this?"

I smiled but it was a guilty smile, "For just being my firstborn grandson. I do not see enough of you and if you have this then you will remember the gruff old warrior, eh?"

He threw his arms around me and hugged me, "I know that I will never be a warrior like you, but I swear that I will make you proud of me."

I felt even guiltier, "I am proud of you, Gerald and you need do nothing to impress me. Just be yourself and that is enough."

We re-entered the house and they were all watching for our return. We had fastened the belt around his waist and he strode proudly in. I saw the slight frown on his father's face but Margaret quickly said, "What a fine present. Gerald, you look like a young noble, does he not, Husband?"

"He does but you will have to look after it, Gerald. It is too fine a present to neglect."

Robert knew how to read people and situations and he jumped in, "You know, Gerald, your grandfather gave me a sword too. Of course, I have not used it but it is a handy thing to have, for protection I mean, and practice with it helps to exercise the body. I can tell that your mind is as sharp as a razor."

Everyone smiled and I was grateful, once more, to the Frenchman whose life I had saved.

That evening the three of us gave cleaned-up versions of our hunt for Wallace in Paris and the rescues of Michel and his son. Robert managed to describe Notre Dame so well that it felt as though we were there. The battle with the pirates, which Jack told, made Gerald's face light up. Gerald and Eleanor, for she had been named after the queen, were keen to know about King Edward. That I was often closely closeted must have been a source of pride for them. I told them some of the stories of the Holy Land and his rescue after Lewes. From Richard's face, I realised that he also benefitted from my association with King Edward.

Business was good and my son-in-law made money with or without a war. "We have a fine circle of friends here in Ludlow. The mayor is a good friend and we are all merchants who help each other out when we can." He looked over at Margaret and then said, "If you would be agreeable, we would invite some to dine with us tomorrow."

I knew the reason, it was to impress them with the archer who rode at the side of the king. I nodded, "Of course, although I fear my conversation will be duller than you might expect. My stories are limited."

Mary laughed so loudly that every head swivelled to look at her, "Gerald, you are the most interesting man I have ever met and that includes Mongol princes. Your life has been anything but dull. Do not be so self-deprecating. It does not suit you."

I found myself blushing and I mumbled, "I do not want to embarrass anyone. I am just a rough archer."

"Queen Eleanor did not think so nor do I." She turned to Margaret, "I will help you to plan and prepare it. The only people at our table are the family."

We slept in the guest room. It was better than the best room in most houses and I was comfortable. That surprised me. I rose early and was at breakfast before the rest of the house, Robert and Jack excepted, were awake. The servants scurried about to bring us food. As we ate Robert said, "You are a lucky man, Sir Gerald. You have three families and all get on well. In my home, my father had us constantly vying to outdo the other. There is harmony here."

Jack nodded, "Sir Gerald does not see it but I found peace when I left Malton for Yarpole."

I swallowed the still warm and thickly buttered bread, "Perhaps because my life was so harsh when I was young that I determined, once I married, to make mine easier. I was lucky in that I had money. I have ever been frugal and kept the coins I earned with my bow. What I have not done is to be profligate and waste it. I do not crave fine tapestries, golden rings or delicacies brought from far-off places that cost the earth."

"And what do we do today, Sir Gerald?"

"Robert, you and Jack may do as you please. I came here to see grandchildren that I barely know. I will spend time with them. Ludlow has no cathedral, Robert, but there are churches and you have not seen Ludlow market, Jack. I shall not need either of you until we return to Yarpole."

They nodded and Jack said, "From what we have seen thus far you would never know that just a couple of hundred miles from us there is a war and men fear to leave their homes."

"Aye, the wars we fought against the Welsh finally brought peace. That is what Richard cannot understand. When King Edward has done to Scotland what he did here in the Welsh borders, then the merchants in the north will enjoy the same peace as they do here."

The two had left when the others rose and I was able to watch Gerald and Eleanor eat and talk. They seemed to get on well and I knew from my children that was not always so. I smiled as the two spoke of what they would wear for the feast that night. When Hamo was the same age it was all we could do to get him to wash before such gatherings. They seemed more serious than my other grandchildren and yet they were little older than Hamo and Joan's children. I looked around at the room we were in. It was not the best room in the house and yet it had fine wall hangings and good furniture. The floor had a rug upon it rather than the rushes in my second best room. Richard and Margaret were bringing their children up to be as nobles and yet they would have no titles to inherit. Hamo would have my title and that would pass to his son but Gerald would never be a knight. It was not unknown for a king to bestow a knighthood to a merchant, they were called carpet knights, but it was rare and I had never heard of King Edward giving such an honour. His father had but King Edward was a warrior and he rewarded bravery and not business acumen.

Mary wanted to get to know the children as much as I did and we spent a happy day playing and talking with them. Mary knew more games and we played them. The two children laughed and enjoyed the day so much that I wondered at the dullness of their normal lives.

Jack and Robert returned at noon and they spent the afternoon also playing with the children.

Gerald said, as they were ordered to their rooms to prepare for the meal, "I wish you could stay here forever." He swept an arm around us, "All of you. Today has been the best day of my life."

"And mine."

The two were whisked away and Jack shook his head, "We just played with them as we do with James, Mary and John."

Robert looked around the room, "This is a house to be admired rather than enjoyed. You should invite them to Yarpole, Sir Gerald. They would enjoy the hall."

He was right.

As Mary helped me to dress I sighed. I had enjoyed the day but a feast such as the one we were to endure filled me with dread. I could not talk about the price of wool. I spoke to other men of matters martial. Mary chuckled, "You enjoyed the day now the evening is the price you pay. Richard wishes you to impress his friends. It is the least we can do for them. Margaret has had no coin from you, nor has she had a manor. What she has comes from her husband. This is your opportunity to pay him back." I nodded for she was right. "And do not drink too much. The wine will be strong."

"Anything else?"

"Aye, watch your words. These are not archers and soldiers. These people will have sensibilities."

As we descended I knew that this would be a long night.

We ate in a hall which, had it been in a castle would have been called a Great Hall. It had three tables and there were seats for more than twenty people. I groaned within but kept the smile on my face that my wife had demanded. The other guests were there already and when Mary and I entered we were applauded. I was not expecting it and it brought me up short.

Mary was quicker thinking, "What an unexpected and delightful welcome."

A portly man stepped forward, "I am Edmund Longstreet, mayor of Ludlow and why should we not afford this welcome for the man that has kept our border safe, fought for the king to rid the land of de Montfort and is helping King Edward to bring Scotland to heel?" He bowed, "We are honoured to have you in our town."

I had recovered my composure and I said, "And I am happy to have been of service."

He turned and introduced two immaculately dressed girls, "These are my daughters, Elizabeth and Susanna. Their mother was taken from us when Susanna was born but I have raised them to be ladies." He shook his head at his younger daughter, "I have been more successful with my first born but what can you do, eh, Sir Gerald?"

They curtsied. I was not very good at reading women but I saw a difference in these two immediately. Elizabeth was the elder and looked to be about seventeen. She was beautiful but she knew it and I saw her eyes flicker to Robert and Jack as she gave them a coy smile. Susanna, in contrast, was a little younger but had the look of a frightened deer. She would not make eye contact and whilst pretty, looked plain in comparison with her sister. There was a story here.

Margaret said, "Come and sit. You all know your places."

That was another difference. In my hall Mary and I would sit at either end of the table and our guests simply filled in. Here there was a pecking order and the mayor was seated opposite Richard and me. It meant that Elizabeth and Susanna were sitting across from Robert and Jack. I smiled as the vivacious Elizabeth flirted with Robert. He had no signs that he was a priest. Although he was only titled my chaplain and not a priest, Robert had told me that he would remain celibate and his work was God's work. Her flirtation would be in vain. Jack, in contrast, recognised the shyness in Susanna and he approached her as though she was a nervous foal. The mayor was keen to speak to me but on the rare occasions when he ceased droning, I heard Jack's gentle coaxing of the shy Susanna. He understood her, I think, better than any. Susanna, it was clear, lived in the shadow of her sister. Jack had endured the bullying of Sir John's son and he recognised the source of her unhappiness. I was glad that I had brought him.

"So, Sir Gerald, what is the future for the kingdom?"

"What?" A gentle nudge from Mary reminded me that I had not been paying attention to the self-important mayor.

He sighed and smiled, "I was saying, Sir Gerald, that you have met Prince Edward. When he is king how do you see the kingdom growing?"

"If King Edward can subjugate the Scots then the new king will have an easy time."

"But what of France? Will he wish to regain lost lands there?"

I knew this was a similar conversation to the one I had with Richard, "Perhaps, but young men change. I was King Edward's archer when he was a young prince and he was a different man then. It took Queen Eleanor to make him the king he has become."

Mary took the opportunity to take the conversation in a different direction, "And your daughters, Master Longstreet, they must have suitors banging on your doors for they are as pretty a pair as I have ever seen."

The mayor shook his head, "Elizabeth is a beauty and while I believe she is destined to marry a lord, her suitors are the sons of merchants such as me. I would have my daughter marry into a noble family."

I said, "I was born the son of an archer, I was lucky to have been knighted."

"Is your title hereditary?"

"My son, Hamo, will become baron of Yarpole but he, like me, cares not for titles."

Mary said, "And Susanna? You wish a good marriage for her?"

His daughters were busy in conversation with Jack and Robert. The mayor leaned across the table and said, quietly, "I would be grateful for any who would take her off my hands. She makes no effort to impress any, even the sons of merchants. You have not seen it this night but she has the tongue of an adder. Elizabeth is a much sweeter flower."

I knew my wife and she did not like the comments. The smile she gave the mayor was a thin one without warmth, but he took it as sympathy.

The conversation then shifted as other merchants asked me about Scotland and the prospects of success. I was on more familiar ground and I did not get to speak to the mayor again.

That evening, as Mary and I prepared for bed, we spoke of the mayor. Mary was a sensitive woman, "Elizabeth preens herself as though she is the Queen of Sheba. I do not wonder that Susanna has learned to have a sharp tongue."

I had obviously missed something, "What do you mean?"

"I heard the elder make snide comments about her sister whom she called dull. She was trying to impress Robert with what she thought passed for wit. Susanna endured the comments, but her barbed replies showed me that she has courage. I think she is blamed for the mother's death." She shook her head, "What a shame."

We left the next day and the sadness from Gerald and Eleanor made me yearn to see more of them. Mary nodded to me and I said, "We would have you visit Yarpole any time that you wish. There is always a welcome for all of you. Perhaps when the baby is born and you are ready to travel again…"

Jack said, "And I am more than happy to provide an escort for you." I looked at Jack. What was going on?

Richard said, "A kind offer and one which my wife and children will take up. For my part, I fear that I will have to remain here in Ludlow for business, unlike war, needs constant attention."

Mary seized the moment, "Then let us say that when the baby is a month old, Jack will return with some men and escort you to Yarpole."

Thus it was arranged.

As we headed home, I said, "That was a kind offer, Jack, but whence did it come?"

Robert laughed, "I am a priest but I saw it, Sir Gerald. He and Susanna are enamoured of each other. I have read of such things but never witnessed it until last night."

Jack blushed and I knew the truth, "Robert, you are a priest and know nothing. She is an unhappy girl and I just tried to make her smile."

Mary had seen it too, "And she was smiling by the end of the evening. Husband, you can smell an ambush a mile away but not see what is right under your nose." She leaned from her horse and put her hand on mine. "I remember a rider coming to sweep a slave girl off her feet. Do you not?"

She was right and I smiled and nodded, "If you wish to pursue this girl, Jack, then do so."

He said, rather unconvincingly, "I like her but that is all."

Jane was born two weeks after we left and a month after that Jack went with a wagon and men to bring my daughter and three grandchildren to Yarpole. Jack took the opportunity to call upon Susanna and when he returned with my daughter and her family he did so again. It was clear to everyone, the mayor included, what Jack's intentions were and when his feelings were reciprocated, then it was only a matter of time. The rides to Ludlow were now every three days and it was my wife who said, "Jack, propose. Let us have a wedding and then the two of you can spend time together rather than you getting saddle sore."

My foster son looked at me and I nodded, "I was never apart from your foster mother from the first moment I met her. Seize the moment."

Within three months of meeting her, and much to the chagrin of her elder sister, Susanna and Jack were wed. Her father saw that a marriage to the son of Baron Warbow was preferable to that of a merchant and, Elizabeth apart, everyone was happy. He and Susanna moved into the hall at Luston and the nine months of peace yielded a marriage.

Chapter 19

When Joan had another son, Richard, I was beside myself with joy. I had grandsons and granddaughters. Life was good. It was spoiled of course for war returned, as I had known it would. The king sent out his orders and the men and archers of Luston and Yarpole were summoned. The muster was at Carlisle and Berwick. I decided we would take the western route. Susanna came to Yarpole to live with my wife when it was discovered that Susanna was with child. It was barely a bump but the midwives were confident that she was with child.

It was a changed Jack who rode with Hamo and with me. He had so many questions to ask Hamo that Robert and I were forgotten. The lost boy from Malton had found himself in Ludlow. It seemed to me that Susanna completed Jack. Together they were more than Jack and Susanna apart. The men he led noticed it too. Most were older than Jack and treated him more like a special son than a man at arms. It was a surprisingly happy troupe that headed north.

There were less than five hundred men waiting for us at Carlisle but we were to pick up more men in Galloway. Robert de Brus had kept his word and he brought men to follow the banner of King Edward. Not all were Scotsmen for de Brus held manors in the northeast of England. They had been asked to march across the road built by the Romans to guard Hadrian's Wall. He had a good mix of men and I, for one, was glad that they were on our side. His knights all looked competent and, as I learned on the campaign, unlike some English lords they could obey orders. We met the king close to Glasgow. I had confirmation there of the pontoon bridge he had ordered to be built. However, it had not arrived and we crossed the river by a more conventional bridge. Thankfully we were unopposed. I had expected the king to take Stirling Castle but without siege engines, they were still on their way north, we simply bypassed the castle and its garrison and headed to the northeast of Scotland, Comyn's heartland.

The ambush on the Tweed, by the last of the Guardians still living in Scotland, rankled with Robert de Brus and he was as anxious as the king to bring Comyn to battle. Balliol was still, apparently, organising an army and that just left William Wallace unaccounted for. We met no opposition as we marched through town after town which threw open their gates and, if they did not welcome the king, they did not oppose us. We were beginning to wonder at the apparent subservience when a messenger, weary and with a horse that was almost dead, rode in from

Carlisle. We now knew where Wallace was. An army had appeared from nowhere and was taking castle after castle in Galloway.

I was summoned to the council of war along with Aymer de Valence and Robert de Brus. "If Comyn thinks that he can distract me from my course by this stab in the back he is wrong. Earl," he looked at Aymer de Valance, "take the Earl of Carrick and Baron Warbow, along with their men and deal with this rising." He saw the Earl of Pembroke about to ask a question, "Send to Ireland for men. The wild men did well last time. We shall use them again." The earl nodded. "And Warbow, if you are able, take Wallace. Although I doubt that he will stand and fight us. It may be down to your dogs of war to sniff him out and fetch him for punishment."

"Yes, my lord."

We left the camp to retrace our steps back to Carlisle. Men hate that for they see every weary mile as a waste, but we had, in the main, good men who might grumble but would not desert and would obey orders. I had some sympathy for de Brus for on the one hand Comyn was his avowed enemy and yet it was Carrick lands that were being raided. Robert de Brus could not actually get at Comyn. His rival for the crown was a clever man. I saw a clever Comyn plan in all of this. The king did not try to hide his intentions and once we had crossed the Forth then the Scots had a free hand to make mischief where the army was not. The men led by the Earl of Pembroke were not a large number, but they were the best. I know my view was jaundiced as my men were included but I knew that the Welshmen led by the earl were also good warriors and the archers he brought would augment my men.

We stayed for one night in the earl's new castle at Bothwell. Already the damage done in the attack was being repaired. One reason for the halt was so that the earl could send for the Irishmen promised by the king. They would give us the numbers we needed. As we ate in the Great Hall I cautioned the two men, both were earls and they were senior to me, "If Wallace is with this Scottish army, then he will do all in his power to conserve their numbers and avoid a battle. We will need to use as much cunning as he does."

Aymer de Valence nodded, "I think that is why the king kept the bulk of the horsemen with him. We have your men, Earl Robert, to give us local knowledge and the baron's archers to work with mine to defeat them. All that the horse will need to do is to keep our archers safe."

De Brus shook his head, "They will not like that." He nodded at the horsemen who were all seated at the same table. I recognised one. It was Sir John Menteith, the man appointed by the king to be Constable of Lennox. I studied him and, seeing my gaze, he nodded at me. The king had been suspicious of the knight's loyalties and as the siege of Caerlaverock had shown, he had not joined the attack with any enthusiasm. It would be interesting to see how he fared this time when he was serving under a Scotsman.

We had infantry with us and we moved at their pace. This time it was not my archers who were the scouts but the men of Annandale. They had a vested interest in finding the enemy as it was their homes that were being attacked. They might have been patriotic Scotsmen, but their families were more important than which lord ruled Scotland. Despite the relatively slow speed of our mailed column, we caught the first elements of the raiding army just north of Ayr. De Brus and I had discussed spies in King Edward's camp. We both knew that there would be some and that the enemy would know we had been sent. The spies were confirmed when the vanguard of the Scottish army was caught in line of march, heading to Bothwell Castle. They were less than four hundred paces from us as we reached the crest of the road and saw them marching up the road to Bothwell. Their plan was clear, take the castle before the repairs were completed. Our quick march had caught them out.

Some battles are fought formally. The armies deploy and agree on a time to begin the fight. This was less of a battle and more of a skirmish for we simply encountered one another. The Earl of Pembroke was a clever leader who made quick decisions. He also knew me and my men. As he had never fought alongside de Brus before he used his knowledge to choose the elements who would fight.

"De Brus, gather the sergeants and knights. Put them in a single body and await my command."

"Yes, my lord."

I nodded to Jack. He would ensure that my sergeants were not wilfully wasted.

"Warbow, have your captain of archers take my archers and form a skirmish line."

"Yes, my lord. Hamo, have the archers dismount. Take the earl's archers and form two lines before us. Engage the enemy when you think it right." The earl frowned. He did not like the latitude I had just given my archer, but I knew Hamo and Gwillim and I knew archers. My son would make the right decision.

"For the rest, form a triple line behind the archers."

It was then that our lack of numbers could be seen and it encouraged the Scots. They saw the thin line of Welsh and Scottish spearmen forming what looked like a thin frail line. De Brus had taken our horsemen and fallen back. To the Scots, it would have appeared that we were retreating. I did not see Wallace with the vanguard, but I did spy a handful of mailed and liveried knights. It was one of those who waved his spear and ordered the vanguard to attack. They were a mixture of light horsemen, knights and men on foot. The vanguard outnumbered the archers and the spearmen. They were counting on speed to outrun the fall of arrows.

Hamo had a hundred and twenty archers under his command and the knights and border horse were twice that number. The majority were, however, like Gwillim, Welsh. I heard, from my position forty paces back, the creak of yew as they drew and so I was prepared for the snap of string as the arrows were released. Thoughts of battles past flew through my mind as I recalled standing as they had done and fighting for King Edward or his father. The archers were skilled, and their arrows dropped at the head of the mounted line of men. I nodded in admiration as the second flight was in the air even before the first had scythed down and struck unprotected horses and light horsemen. The knights wore mail and they were protected to some extent but even mail does not help a knight who is thrown from a mortally struck horse. After eight arrows from each of the one hundred and twenty archers the line of horses was broken and the shattered survivors halted. The men on foot who were charging behind had not seen the slaughter. Men charging look to see that they do not step in the wrong place to be trampled by comrades behind. I did not hear the command but knew that my son had given one when the arrows began to slam into men with just a helmet for protection. The shields that might have helped them hung from their sides and by the time they started to pull them up it was too late.

The earl shouted, "Now, de Brus, destroy them. Spearmen, open ranks."

The Welsh were well trained and they turned to allow the horsemen to walk their horses through our men and to form lines. The horn was sounded for the recall of the archers and as the archers and horsemen exchanged positions then the outcome of the skirmish was decided.

Robert had sat silently next to me. As we watched Jack and our sergeants follow the Earl of Carrick to charge into the disrupted and disorientated Scottish vanguard, he said, "How can any army stand against such a combination of archers and cavalrymen?"

I watched as spears rose and fell to strike at the backs of men who were fleeing as fast as they could, discarding their weapons as they ran. "The simple answer, Robert, is that they cannot. It is why the Battle of Stirling Bridge came as such a shock to everyone. Handled as well as our men have been by the earl then the outcome of any fight is decided as soon as the first arrow falls."

He looked at me thoughtfully, "You could have led them as well as the earl."

I nodded for it was true. "The earl knew that and it was why he had me put Hamo in command. I trained my son and my archers."

By dark de Brus returned. He had stopped just shy of his castle of Ayr where the Scottish survivors had fled. He was in an ebullient mood. The sulky look he had given the earl when he had been ordered to the rear was now replaced by a look of triumph. "We must have slaughtered three hundred of their men. Soon Ayr will be in our hands once more."

I said, "Any sign of Wallace?"

He shook his head, "I did not see a giant. The mainward was sizeable and the rear guard had barely left Ayr."

The earl nodded, "Then tomorrow, Earl Robert, take your men to the south of Ayr and prevent their escape."

"Escape? Surely, they will simply hold out in the castle for it is mine and a strong one."

The earl said, mildly, "So strong that the Scots took it easily, despite being held by your men." He sighed, "They will flee south and hope to catch us between Ayr and Turnberry but if you can stop them then this rising will end here at Ayr."

I said, "Why not march south and surround the castle now?"

He shook his head, "Our men are weary as are the Scots. Let them spend the night in the false belief that their castle can hold out. The earl and our heavy horsemen will seal the trap."

I disagreed with the earl. I would have used archers who were faster and better at concealment, but he commanded. As we camped just eight miles from Ayr Castle, I sought out my sergeants. I was relieved when I discovered that none had been hurt. Jack said, "De Brus is a brave leader, Sir Gerald. He leads from the front."

I nodded, "And Sir John Menteith?"

He said, "The Sherriff of Lennox?"

"He is the one."

"He rode at the side of the earl. They rode as though they were one."

I smiled and nodded. My suspicions were confirmed, Sir John was a spy.

Hamo said, "That is the smile of the cat that has just managed to steal the cream, Father. For those of us who are not as clever as you, explain."

Robert was looking on with as much curiosity as my son and Jack. "When Sir John Menteith was with us at Caerlaverock he did not strike me as a warrior but now I see that it was an act. He was and is, de Brus' man. He served King Edward but only to get into a position of power. Now that the Earl of Carrick is King Edward's ally, Sir John can fight as he wants to fight."

Robert asked, "Is this a bad thing, Sir Gerald?"

"That all depends upon the intentions of Robert de Brus. He fights for the king but what does the Earl of Carrick ultimately want? I think that until this land in the southwest of Scotland is back under our control then all will be well but I think that Robert de Brus has his own plans and he strikes me as a patient and thoughtful man." Hamo looked doubtful, "You remember, Hamo, when you were young and we played chess."

He laughed, "Aye, and I could never beat you."

"Nor me." Jack was new to the game.

"That is because I was taught to play, Hamo, by your namesake, Hamo l'Estrange. He taught me to plan moves ahead so that my pawn sacrifices drew you on until, even though you had more pieces, I won for my eye was on the prize, the king. I would not play chess with de Brus for I fear I might lose."

Robert de Brus might be a thinker, but he was also a showman and when the mailed men rode off with flags and banners fluttering it was with such a great noise that they could have heard him in Turnberry. As it turned out the Scots who had fled to Ayr had not even spent the night there. De Brus found his castle abandoned and we took it without a fight. We were all disappointed. I did not mention to either earl that had we surrounded the castle then we would have ended the rebellion immediately.

We invested Ayr and the Earl of Carrick sent out his scouts who confirmed that the Scots had fallen back to Turnberry. I knew that we would not catch them in the open a second time. We had hurt them but the wound had not been mortal. The earl planned on leaving the next day but the arrival of the first of the men from Ireland made him change his plans. "We will wait until our army is enlarged. A greater show of force might help us to cow the enemy into submission."

I did not want to squat in Ayr. "My lord, let me take my men and ride to scout out Turnberry. I know that the Earl of Carrick and his men know the land well, but perhaps fresh eyes might see a way to take Turnberry without a siege."

The castle and town were already overcrowded, and the earl agreed. We left in the afternoon for the fifteen-mile ride south.

Robert asked, "Do not take offence, my lord, but why did you volunteer?"

"Oh, Robert, there are many reasons. Firstly, I do not want to lose the Scots a second time and the only eyes I truly trust are riding with me this day. Secondly, I need to know if Wallace is with this army. I still have the king's commission to bring the traitor to book." I smiled, "And thirdly, the sooner this is over, the sooner we can go home and Jack might be able to see his first child born."

We rode in silence for a while and then Robert, who had clearly listened to my words said, "Strictly speaking William Wallace is not a traitor."

I almost stopped Felix, "What?"

"Perhaps I am an ignorant Frenchman who does not understand the politics of this land but as I understand it William Wallace fought for his country. He never swore allegiance to England. How can he be a traitor?"

Hamo said, "He is right, Father. He never signed the Ragman Roll."

I was annoyed because they were both right and I did not like to be in the wrong. "What difference does it make, enemy, traitor? It is all the same."

Robert said, mildly and quietly, "It affects the punishment when he is caught. Do you execute your enemies after war, Sir Gerald?"

"Of course not." I dismissed from my mind the murder of Simon de Montfort by Roger Mortimer. I now believed that it had been on the orders of King Henry. "They are punished by loss of lands, income and freedom."

There was silence save for the clip-clop of our hooves until Robert asked, "And when you take Wallace for the king, what will the king do to him."

I did not answer but I knew it was to be a more draconian end than that which faced John Balliol or John Comyn. The man who had been part of the slaughter at Stirling Bridge would meet a traitor's end. My mind was filled for the next days with the conflict created by Robert and Hamo's words. We found a wood which straddled the road east from Turnberry. It was on a slightly raised piece of ground and gave us cover and a good line of sight to the castle and encampment that surrounded it. We made a defensive camp and saplings were hewn and embedded in the woods to give us and our horses protection. We used the largest open area to graze our horses and our hovels were dotted between the trees. It would be a cold camp but it was summer and we had taken supplies from Ayr. We would not starve.

The Hunt

The four of us shared two hovels. With the watches set we lay in them. Hamo had just returned from making water and as he lay in his blanket he said, "Jack, I was not in Ludlow when Cupid's arrow struck you so well. Father is, as always, tight-lipped about such things and Robert here is a priest. I would have you tell me how it came about?"

I could not help but smile at my son's blunt words. He had inherited more than my skill in archery. He had also struck home with his words for Robert said, "I may be a priest but I am still a man."

Hamo said, mildly, "A man? Aye, but a man without any interest in a woman, is that not right Robert?"

The Frenchman sighed, "I suppose you are right. I understand men and women but what makes them fall in love is beyond me. As a priest I love men and women but, their minds only. I do not understand their bodily needs." It was rare but Robert looked and sounded foolish and the three of us laughed. Robert saw the reason and smiled, "Jack, explain to me, as well as your foster brother how you went from entering a house never having seen the young woman, to deciding, after a few hours, that you wished to spend your life with her. I know Lady Mary encouraged you but…"

He began, "As soon as I saw her I thought she looked sad and something within me wanted to make her smile. I did not like her sister. She reminded me of Sir John's son. Like him she was a bully." He shook his head, "Susanna has since told me about the things Elizabeth did to her and my first thoughts were confirmed. I did not intend to woo her, just to make her laugh and I did. When she laughed it made my heart sing. She is a clever young lady and when she realised that I was not mocking her she opened up and while the rest of the table talked of… I know not what, we were like two birds who were cosy in a nest of words and smiles. We were cocooned from others. When I looked into her eyes I saw myself and, more, I saw that she saw the same in me. We did not say anything about our feelings but I knew," he patted first his chest and then his head, "first in my heart and then in my head, that this hurt young hart, was meant to be mine. As soon as the chance came for me to return then I did so and when I did I found the time to speak to her alone and I just blurted out my feelings."

Hamo shook his head, "Jack, you have done many brave things in your life but that strikes me as the most dangerous for she could have broken your heart."

I said, "I do not think so, Hamo. When you met Alice you knew, did you not, that she was meant to be your bride?"

"Of course, but that was different."

"How?"

"I knew that she knew and…" he nodded, "I see."

Jack shrugged, "After that it was easy. We both knew that her sister was keen to be rid of her and her father was happy that his second daughter had a match that tied her to Sir Gerald Warbow. Not for the first time, Sir Gerald, I was grateful that you rescued me from Malton."

Our curiosity was satisfied. I had wondered at the haste myself but now it was all clear.

The scouts on the edge of the wood reported riders heading along the road east to Dumfries and Lochmaben. It was clear that none of them was Wallace, but we kept a good watch on the road. Other riders left the castle and the camp to head north and south.

I stood with Hamo, Jack, Robert and Gwillim at the edge of the woods watching with the sentries. I found it useful to have Robert with us for he asked questions that were different from ours. He did not understand war but he was a clever man and he liked to ask questions. Sometimes his questions gave us answers that we had not sought.

Gwillim pointed as the riders returned from the south, "They are clearly border horsemen, my lord, and I think that they will be scouting."

Hamo nodded, "Then we can assume the others are too. I can understand the ones to the north, they seek our army and the ones to the south look for an escape route, but the ones to the east?"

I had an answer, "Either they wish to cause mischief at Lochmaben and Dumfries or they seek an escape route that way."

"Why do they not threaten England?" We all turned to Robert who shrugged, "I am a priest but if I were the enemy leader then would it be not more prudent to attack my enemy, England, rather than my countrymen?"

I suddenly saw that Robert was right. They would not face us at Turnberry. They would head east to Carlisle and the borders. If Wallace was one of their leaders, then this would make perfect sense as he knew the trails and tracks through that land. We had killed or captured many of the knights in the vanguard north of Ayr. The force he had left was better placed to conduct a war behind enemy lines, a war of ambush and raids.

"Jack, send a rider back to the Earl of Pembroke. Tell the earl that Sir Gerald believes that the Scots will head to England. Ask him to send more men to help me prevent it."

"Yes, Sir Gerald."

The riders returned from the east in the late afternoon. When the sentries told us Hamo said, "Then they are heading for England. Dumfries and Lochmaben have garrisons but they cannot stop a

Scottish army. If he crosses the Solway then the whole of the north is laid bare. There is not a man there left to oppose him. The king has emptied the north of soldiers."

Jack's rider had not returned by dark, and I feared foul play. When, the next morning, the gates of Turnberry opened and disgorged the Scottish army, I cursed the earl.

"Do we stop them, Father, or follow them?"

The Earl of Pembroke might not have been decisive enough, but I was, "Both. Hamo, take the archers and line the road. Jack, mount the sergeants. I will lead them."

Hamo smiled, "That is your plan? Even if we emptied every arrow bag we could not begin to dent the resolve of this army."

"We cannot stop them but we can hurt them and we can fetch more arrows. They think they have escaped us. Our arrows snapping at their heels will tell them otherwise."

Robert said, "And what do I do?"

"Keep safe and watch the horses."

He nodded, "And I can pray. That is work on this day for a priest."

The horses were tethered in the trees so that they would not be seen. The archers spread out in a perilously thin line, two hundred paces from the road that wound east. I mounted Felix and took a spear. I could always throw a spear and, for me, a lance was too cumbersome. We had just twenty of us and I knew it was a pathetically small number to do what I wanted us to do. We headed east, paralleling the road. Hamo would choose his moment to attack. I guessed it would not be when the head of the column of men passed, the scouts, but he would save his arrows for the leaders who would lead the mainward. When the scouts headed back to protect their leaders we would charge in their wake. The paltry numbers I led might be an advantage and they might not see us until it was too late.

We were lucky in the landscape. The land did not produce crops and hedges and tree lines had been left to give shelter to animals in winter. We took advantage of that shelter and waited close to some elderberry trees and bushes that had grown in the desolation of a long abandoned dwelling. The walls had fallen many years ago and ivy had made the former walls green and alive. The head of the vanguard was just fifty paces from us when we heard the cries of alarm and then the horn that sounded the warning. As I had predicted, the scouts turned and ran back to the main body. They would be angry with themselves for having failed to spot the ambush. It would make them reckless. We reached the road and I said, "Four lines of five." I was in the centre with Jack to my right. I prayed that my action would not make Susanna a widow.

189

The Hunt

We galloped after the scouts. I saw that the Scots had raised shields and their light horsemen were already charging towards the woods and the ambush. I saw the ones that had been struck by Hamo and the archers. They had done well but in the grand scheme of things had hardly hurt the Scots. I realised that my men had switched their aim to the horsemen and whilst they were falling it would allow the men on foot to close with the woods. If only the earl had sent men we might have achieved something. I had long ago learned not to worry about matters I could not control. I could control what we did and that was to hurt the Scots without losing too many of my men.

As we neared the rear of the light horsemen, oblivious to the danger, I spied Wallace. He stood out and I recognised the Short brothers with him. They were mailed but recognisable even from two hundred paces away for they wore no helmets and had simple coifs for defence. It encouraged me to spur Felix and his leap forward brought me within range of a Scottish light horseman. I leaned forward and rammed my spear into the back of his leather jack. His arms spread and he fell from his horse, releasing my spear. I heard cries from ahead as we were spotted and some of those who had been heading to the woods turned to face the new threat. They knew not the numbers for the Scottish horsemen confused and camouflaged our host. Soon, however, they would see us for what we were, a pinprick. That moment was not yet upon us and so we stabbed, slashed, and speared men who could not defend against us. The handful of knights who bullied their way forward was another matter. I saw Wallace point his long sword at me and shout something. The effect was instantaneous. Ten knights suddenly launched themselves at us. First, they had to clear away the men before them and then catch up with the handful who were coming for us.

"Lock!"

We had practised this manoeuvre and it entailed us slowing and putting our horses' bodies together. As the Scottish knights were coming piecemeal, each determined to end the life of Lord Edward's archer, then we would have more spears and lances facing them. The knight who led had a shield quartered with the lion of Scotland. His family had aspirations to be rulers or had some vague connection in the past with the Scottish royal family. He had a lance and he obliged me by coming directly for Felix's head. A lesser horse might have baulked but Felix was bred from good stock and held his ground. The lance was longer than my spear and I took the hit which was well delivered from between Felix's ears. I angled my shield and although it hurt my arm it did not harm me, sliding to the side. My spear, in contrast, hit him squarely in the face. I have good hand-to-eye coordination and the tip of the spear went through the eye hole. There would be no ransom. The knight fell from his horse. As Felix snapped and bit, his riderless mount now turned and baulked the advance of the next riders. I shifted my grip and hurled the spear at the nearest rider. It caught his upper right arm and shoulder. The tip was sharp and my arm was strong. The spear penetrated to the haft and he used his left hand to guide his horse from the fray. We had an impasse now but men on foot were approaching from the sides. We still held the upper hand and it was the Scottish knights who were falling to the spears and lances of my sergeants. It was at that moment that I heard the horn from the rear of the Scottish column. From Wallace's reaction, I saw him turn and look around, I knew that it had to be our friends. I knew not who they were but when the men who had been chasing my archers began to stream back to the road, I knew that we had attacked their rear.

I drew my sword and spurred Felix on, taking advantage of the distraction. I struck one knight across his back and right shoulder. As he reeled, I lunged with my sword and pushed him from his horse. Had there been fewer horses he might have survived but the milling Scottish horses trampled him.

It was then I heard Wallace's voice as the giant bellowed from the back of his horse, "Fall back! We are undone. Save yourselves."

I shouted, "Men of Yarpole, let us catch this warrior and take him to the king."

My men roared and we urged our horses through the Scottish knights who had been halved already and, seeing their comrades flee, were in a dilemma. After two more were struck from the backs of their mounts the survivors yielded for Hamo and fourteen archers stood less than twenty paces from them with half-drawn bows. They knew what that meant.

With our path clear we galloped, not towards the main army fleeing south and east, but to follow Wallace and his eight followers. They headed across country leaping over the fences in their way. It proved disastrous for two who fell from their mounts but the others managed the feat. I emulated them but my landing was not an elegant one. Jack's was and it was he who took the lead. He had discarded his spear and leaned over his horse to maximise speed. I sheathed my sword and tried to copy Jack but he was a better rider and being slightly smaller and more muscular began to draw away from me.

This was a horse race but only Wallace knew the finishing line. His unerring course told me that he had planned this escape. Suddenly the riders heading to the south the previous day made sense. The leap over the fence had addled my brain and I could not think of the places that lay to the south of Turnberry. The cries of the seabirds overhead told me that the coast was close and when three of the riders suddenly wheeled their horses to turn and face us I knew that they were the pawns Wallace was sacrificing. Jack saw it too and he bravely drew his sword. I urged Felix on for men who were desperate enough to try to stop us would not take prisoners and my foster son was outnumbered. I saw Jack's shield come up as he blocked the blow from one of the men; another thrust his sword at Jack's head while Jack engaged the third with his sword. The men following me would be too far away to help. If I did not reach him then he was a dead man. Jack's horse reared protectively, and his hooves flailed. The thrusting Scottish sword made his horse's head move and, as he did so he became unbalanced and tumbled over. Jack was a good rider and he knew how to fall. He used his shield to break the fall and rolled, his helmet straps breaking so that his helmet rolled away. Although Jack's horse was sacrificed Jack's life was saved by the fall. Two of the Scots had to swerve and that left just one close enough to hurt the recumbent Jack. Even as he shakily struggled to his feet the last Scot was raising his sword. Having seen the fall I had moved Felix's head and my magnificent mount responded well. As the sword came down I swung my sword horizontally. It smashed into the sword when it was just a handspan from Jack's head. Mine was made of the finest steel and as the sparks flew and the metal rang so the Scottish sword bent. The Scot reined in as did I for Felix was now between the other Scots and Jack.

The Scottish warrior hurled his now useless sword at me and, unfastening his hand axe, spat at me, "Your prey is gone, Warbow, and I will end the life of Wallace's Bane!"

I pricked Felix and as he leapt forward swung my sword in an arc. The blade hacked into the man's side and sawed through the mail and into his flesh. Such was the power of the blow that I saw guts hanging from the blade as it came out and the man tumbled to the ground, writhing in that most painful of deaths, a stomach wound.

I wheeled as the last two Scots came at me. Harry and Ralph closed on them so quickly that the two men did not even get a chance to see their killers. I turned and said, "Jack, are you hurt?"

He had discarded his shield and sheathed his sword. He was holding his left arm with his right and he shook his head, "My arm is broken, my lord." I looked beyond him to the fleeing figures in the distance. "Get after him, Father, my life is not in danger."

Robert's voice came from behind me, "Aye, Sir Gerald, you cannot heal but I can."

The Hunt

My priest had disobeyed me and I was grateful, "We will return." I saw that other riders were following from the skirmish on the road. The two would be safe. Leading my men, we hurried after the elusive Wallace and his dwindling band of men. He was clearly heading for the huddle of houses that constituted a settlement. We began to gain ground and I wondered at that for Wallace clearly had a good horse and he could have left his men to outdistance and reach whatever sanctuary that he sought. He was keeping with his men and I admired that. We had a chance, albeit a slim one, to catch him for we would see which house he entered. We might have a battle to take him but I would expect my men to be able to defeat whoever he had with him. I had seen the Short Brothers and they had more cunning than skills.

When I saw the mastheads then I knew that the settlement was a port of some kind. It could not be a large one for I would have known its name. The road descended through mean houses to a beach and I cursed when we were just two hundred paces from it. Wallace and his men threw themselves from the backs of their horses and ran through the surf to be hauled aboard the small, strange-looking ship that was anchored against the tide with a sail ready to be unfurled. I impotently watched as the men were pulled aboard, the anchor raised, and the sail let fly. Had I my bow with me then Wallace's life would have been ended for I was close enough to almost spit at him.

He raised his arm and shouted, "One day, Warbow, you and I shall meet again and only one of us will walk away." The helmsman put over the steering board and Wallace was masked by the sail as it headed out to sea.

"Grab those horses. They are weregeld for Jack's arm."

"Aye, my lord."

I was seething with anger and I dismounted and strode over to the gaggle of men standing there. One was larger than the rest and better dressed. I walked over to him and, grabbing the front of his fishing smock, bodily picked him up, "Now fisherman, whether you live or die depends upon the answers you give me."

"I know nothing, I swear."

I lowered him so that his feet were on the ground, "Who was it waiting for William Wallace?"

He pointed at the departing boat, "They came a week ago in their snekke."

"Snekke?"

"A small ship used by the Vikings from the isles." He pointed to the north and west. Until King Alexander had recovered the islands, they had been Viking and the people who lived there had Viking blood.

"Go on."

"Riders came from the north and spoke with them. The crew were fierce and none of us approached them." He pointed to a blackened patch of sand, "That is where they camped. A rider came an hour since and they prepared their ship for sea. The rest you know, my lord. We could do nothing to stop him."

I let go of the man for he was clearly speaking the truth, "I think, my friend, that, your last statement apart, you have spoken the truth. You could have done something to stop him but you like William Wallace."

The man cast his eyes down, "He is one of us, my lord."

I nodded, "And where do you think they have gone?"

He looked me in the eyes so that I could tell the truth of his words, "I do not think these men, Vikings, my lord, came from close to here. They had strange accents but there are many small islands to the north of us where there is no rule save that of Viking pirates. If the Guardian has gone there then he will be safe."

"He gave up being a guardian, fisherman."

The man smiled, "To us, he is still William Wallace, the Guardian of Scotland and our only hope against the English."

I patted his shoulder, "You are a brave man but I would not speak those words in the hearing of the king or his son. Your life would end swiftly."

He nodded, "We know his son and the men he leads." He shook his head, "They were worse than pirates."

I suddenly remembered that the prince had taken this land. As I had been with King Edward I had not seen how he did so. The prince had merely stoked the fires of rebellion.

We mounted our horses and with the captured animals tethered, we headed back. Wallace had escaped, again. The man had more lives than a black cat.

Chapter 20

Robert had splinted Jack's arm using a long dagger taken from one of the dead Scots. My foster son was in pain yet his first words were about Wallace, "Did you catch him?"

Shaking my head I said, "No, Jack. He has disappeared into the mists that are the islands. I will have to ride to the king and explain my failure."

"It was not your fault."

"I am the leader and the man commissioned to take Wallace. I am to blame. Now, let us help you aboard a new horse. I know not the name of this beast, but he is a good horse and a fine replacement for the one you lost."

We helped Jack onto the back of the horse that had carried William Wallace and as Jack stroked his mane the animal whinnied, "I shall call him William."

With Harry and Ralph flanking him we headed back to Turnberry. The smoke rising in the sky told me that the dead, mainly Scottish, were already being burned. I saw the carrion birds flocking overhead and I knew that when darkness descended then the other creatures would come to devour any unburnt flesh. I saw, in the distance, the standards of Carrick and Pembroke flying above Turnberry. The castle was ours. The only thing in the area was the castle. The village had less than fifteen houses. I knew that Robert de Brus held the castle in high regard for he had been born there and it had been his mother's castle. Our retaking of it was symbolic of the Earl of Carrick.

Robert said, as we climbed to the gate, "He cannot campaign, my lord."

"I can!"

Ignoring Jack I said, "I know. Take him home, Robert. I will send men back with you."

"I shall not go."

I turned to Jack, "I am still your liege lord and I command you to return. We cannot have a passenger with us. You shall return home."

We dismounted and Robert asked the de Brus soldier who held Jack's horse for him, "Is there an infirmary?"

Surprised by the French accent the soldier replied, "Aye, m'sieur." He pointed to a low building in the inner bailey.

"Come, Jack, we will have a second opinion on my handiwork and seek what I need to make a sleeping potion."

I said to the soldier, "Where are the earls?"

"In the Great Hall celebrating our victory, my lord."

I had not yet seen Hamo but I knew that he would find me. I had to speak to the two leaders and do so quickly.

I heard laughter and cheers when I approached the hall. Heads turned and silence descended when I entered. My surcoat was bespattered and besmeared with blood. The men I saw before me, de Brus included, looked as though they wore freshly laundered ones. Had they done any actual fighting?

Aymer de Valance said, hopefully, "You have Wallace?"

I shook my head, "He was spirited away by Vikings. He could be anywhere."

De Brus nodded, "They are mercenaries and will fight for gold and plunder. Wallace will promise both."

"I need to tell the king." I was not seeking permission I was stating a fact.

The Earl of Pembroke nodded, "We now have the Irish and we do not need your men any longer. The work here is to sweep up the remains of the rebellion, stock the castles for winter and then return home ourselves."

Robert de Brus said, "And I am home already." He smiled at me, "You and your men earned great honour today, Warbow. You held the rebels up long enough for me and my men to sweep up their rear and for the earl to take Turnberry without a fight."

I nodded; the clean tunics were because they had not had to fight. The enemy had surrendered or fled.

"Tonight, you will enjoy the hospitality of the Carricks and you shall be the guest of honour. The earl and I insist upon it."

The last thing I needed was another feast but it was a necessary imposition.

I found Hamo with Jack in the infirmary. Jack slept. Robert's drugs had worked. "Well, Father, what now?"

"I will send the sergeants home with Robert and Jack. Did we have any men hurt?"

He nodded, "Edgar, Bob son of Robert and Dai all have slight wounds. They will heal but they will not be able to draw a bow for a while."

"Then they go back to Yarpole, and you and I will lead our depleted company to the north east of Scotland to meet the king. I have news to give him that will sour his appetite."

"Harry told me all. You could have done no more."

I snorted, "Stating the obvious does not help, my son."

He smiled, "Father, you have Wallace on the run. Harry said that you were called Wallace's Bane."

"And another title, along with Warbow, is the last thing I need."

Harry led my sergeants as they headed back, first to Carlisle and then south to Yarpole. Jack's injuries would make for a slower journey, but he would be home in time to see his child born.

It was fortunate that it was August and with long days we ate up the almost two hundred and fifty miles to find the king. King Edward had not fought a battle but he had suffered, as an English army always did, from desertions. The army he commanded was a pale shadow of the one he had led north. We passed Stirling where the Scots still defiantly held on to their symbol of independence and when we reached Perth we found another English garrison. From Sir John de Ferrers we learned that supplies had been slow in coming and the king was forced to rely on his ships to supply him. He had edged his way along the coast. This was the heart of Comyn country.

"He has taken Aberdeen and the last message we had was that he was heading for the Moray Firth and Comyn's castle at Lochindorb."

The garrison had little enough to give us in the way of supplies and we tightened our belts as we headed through a land already raided and plundered by our army. We met up with the king in late September at Kinloss Abbey where he made a donation, no doubt from loot plundered in Aberdeen which he had just taken. We waited without as he prayed for victory and to Queen Elanor. I chatted outside, not with the leaders but with Richard of Craven. It had been ever thus. I preferred those with lower rank to those with grand titles.

"How has it gone, Richard?"

The former pursuivant looked around to see that the three of us were not overheard, "The king is not happy and has sent letters to those back in England whom the king feels are tardy in sending money and supplies. Had we not been resupplied in Aberdeen then even more men would have deserted. This has been a long campaign and men want to be paid as they were promised. The money we have taken from the castles is paltry and does not pay either men or for food. The king wants a battle."

"Yet he will not get one," I told him of the skirmish outside Turnberry and Wallace's flight.

He shook his head, "That will annoy him even more."

"And what does he plan now?"

"Now that his son has joined him we will repeat that which worked the last time. He will use two armies and make pincer movements. First, we take Lochindorb. It is Comyn's jewel."

I shook my head, "Comyn is too canny to be within and winter comes soon enough up here."

He lowered his voice, "The king plans to winter in this land. He will let go the ones who live in the north with a promise to return in the spring and muster at Stirling, but we will stay."

Sighing I said, "And therein lies even more expense. Is Scotland worth it?"

Richard said, "The king seems to think it is a prize that he wants."

"No, Richard, the prize is an enemy defeated and the shame of Stirling Bridge expunged. Murray is dead and he wants Wallace's head as a trophy on the walls of London. When we took Wales he wanted not the land, he just wanted the people held in thrall. He ringed it with castles and then gave it to his son. He will do the same here once all the sparks of rebellion are doused."

Hamo nodded, sagely, "At least Jack is out of it."

Richard looked at Hamo, "Is something wrong with Jack? Why is he not here?"

"He broke his arm and I sent him and my sergeants home. He will see his first child born soon enough,"

"He is married?" I nodded. "I am pleased for him and his lady is a lucky one."

We did not talk of family matters outside of the family and even though Richard of Craven was a friend, the only comment Hamo made was, "And he is lucky in her, too, Richard."

The king and his son emerged from the abbey. Prince Edward said, "I will take my men and cut off Lochindorb."

"I will follow with the siege train and the bulk of the men."

It was only then that I saw Piers Gaveston and the lavishly liveried men who followed the prince. They were all mounted on the best of horses and had the looks of men who were well fed. The ordinary spearmen might be hungry but not the elite who followed the prince.

"Well, Warbow?"

There was little point in obfuscation and I came to the point directly, "We have dispersed the rebels in Galloway and the Earl of Pembroke is confident of recovering all within a short time."

"That is good news. Did you manage to bring them to battle?"

"It was a skirmish only but they lost men and will not trouble the Earl of Carrick overmuch," I took a breath, "Wallace escaped us in a Viking ship. I believe he has sought refuge in the isles."

The king's face fell, "Where he is safe. You came close?"

"Close enough for him to shout insults at me. Sadly, I cannot walk on water."

The king gestured over his shoulder, "This is not the place to be blasphemous. You will rejoin my army."

"You wish us to winter here with you?"

He glared at Richard of Craven, "I do. You will be paid."

I did not say that he appeared to have difficulty paying the men he had with him already. I just nodded, "Of course, King Edward."

He sensed my disappointment and smiled, "It will not be so bad. We will use Dunfermline Abbey. No hovels for us and I am confident that by this time next year, we shall have Scotland and all of us can return to England and civilisation."

What was clear to me was that there would need to be garrisons left in place and they would need funding. The king was building up debts that the occupation of Scotland could never repay.

When we reached Lochindorb Castle I hid my smile. Prince Edward had said he would cut off the Comyn stronghold. The castle completely filled a small island in the centre of the loch. The king must have known what he had to do for he did not seem discomfited by the problem. "Get the engineers to build those rafts."

As the camp was set up the recently arrived wagons were emptied of timber, rope, hammers and nails and the engineers began to lay out the wood for the rafts. I looked over to the castle. Its strength lay in its isolation. I doubted that there would be more than a hundred men inside its walls. We had many times that number. It would fall. The reason for our presence was to hurt Comyn. It would eliminate another home in which he could winter.

The rafts and the ladders needed for the escalade were completed quickly for they were simple enough to make and were loaded in the dark of night to be paddled across the still waters of the loch while the garrison could see nothing. They could hear the swish of paddles in the water but they dared not waste either arrows or bolts. We landed and completely surrounded the curtain wall. As soon as we ground up the Scots knew we were there and began to send their missiles and rocks at us. It was like hurling snowballs at a fire for as many sergeants and spearmen stood to protect those landing as defended the castle. Not a man was lost although I did hear that one spearman fell into the loch and had to be dragged to safety by his laughing comrades. The archers we had brought unslung their bows and without the need for a word of command they nocked arrows and sought faces. Even in the darkness of pre-dawn, the faces stood out and as the walls were less than thirty paces from the archers then the defenders soon realised the folly of showing their faces. The ladders slammed against the walls and the sergeants and spearmen climbed. The sun had barely risen when the curtain wall was taken. Even as King Edward and his son were sailed across to join us the Comyn standard was lowered and the Castellan surrendered the sixty survivors. The Comyn stronghold was ours.

The king, his son and the leaders symbolically slept in the castle. Those who had defended it were sent to Perth to be released there. We had neither the food nor the men to guard and feed them. I stayed in the camp by the loch but we kept a good fire burning all night to ward off the midges.

"I do not relish a winter here, Father."

"Then go home, Hamo, I will stay with the archers."

He laughed, "And you know I cannot do that. I am of your blood and just as you did and do, I shall endure the same conditions and food as my men. I was just saying that I am not looking forward to it."

I nodded and tossed another dried piece of kindling onto the fire, "And as we can do nothing about it then it is a waste of air and of words. Grumbling does nothing except encourage others to do the same."

He sighed, "It is hard being a leader for you have to put on a face and pretend that you are stoic."

"Aye, Hamo, it is a hard lesson. I confess that the easy times to endure such conditions are when you are in a small group. When Hamo L'Estrange, Sir John and I rode with our guide into the unknown we had not time to grumble and to whom would we have grumbled? The same when William and Jack and I went to Paris. There was too much danger to worry. Here we have safety in numbers and men like to fill the silence with words. It is better for men like us to fill the silence with words of hope…or remain silent."

The reason for our wintering became clear as soon as we reached the abbey. The king's sister Queen Margaret and her husband King Alexander were both buried there. As we also occupied Perth, from whence we had stolen the sacred Stone of Scone, the king was telling the Scots that he controlled Scotland and its most precious places. Many of the ordinary soldiers were paid off but a sizeable army was kept and we camped in the grounds of the abbey. Every outhouse and building became a sleeping chamber and I persuaded the king to allow my archers to hunt in the woods. It served two purposes, it gave us a source of food but, more importantly, it kept my archers sharp and alert.

It was February when word came to the king that John Comyn wanted to surrender. Our taking of Lochindorb had broken his will to fight. Leaving my archers at Dunfermline and with a suitably attired Hamo carrying my banner, I accompanied the king to St Andrews, on the coast where the Guardian of Scotland and one hundred and thirty landowners waited to swear allegiance to the king. With de Brus an ally and John Balliol still an exile, the only opposition came from those landowners who refused to kneel and… William Wallace.

I could tell, from his face and the way he held his body that the last Guardian of Scotland was unhappy about his submission but de Brus had, effectively, scuppered the rebellion. In joining the king the earl had divided the nobles and the rebellion was fizzling out. I was still of the opinion that the Earl of Carrick was merely biding his time and eliminating his opposition. However, with their word given Comyn and his supporters were allowed to go and we marched to Stirling Castle for that gob of food still lodged in the king's throat. He summoned de Brus and Aymer de Valence. It was like taking a sledgehammer to crack a cobnut. But the king wished vengeance. He had fifty engineers toil, while we waited for spring, to build a giant trebuchet, called Warwolf. It would be a symbol of the power wielded by the King of England. He had also acquired an engineer who knew how to make Greek Fire and he had them work close to the construction of the trebuchet to intimidate the defenders.

The king had smaller war machines that hurled stones and the pots of Greek Fire at the walls but Warwolf, so the chief engineer assured the king, would hurl a stone more than two hundred paces. The king was anxious to see his toy in action. For my archers and me, it was the usual experience of a siege. My men used their bows to keep the walls clear of defenders and watched as the war machine grew. Ten weeks after the siege began a party emerged from the castle to offer surrender. I could not keep the smile from my face. The surrender of Stirling meant the end of Scottish independence.

To my amazement, the king said, "You do not deserve any grace, but must surrender to my will." He sent the deputation back into the castle. He wanted to see Warwolf at work.

A week later the machine was ready and the king watched like an excited child playing with a new toy as the trebuchet systematically destroyed a whole section of curtain wall. Satisfied with the machine and having demonstrated his power he accepted the surrender of the castle and the army prepared to leave.

We were intending to leave the next day for I was anxious to get home. My hopes were dashed when I was summoned to the king. With him were his son, Prince Edward, the earls of Carrick and Pembroke as well as Sir John Menteith, the Sherriff of Lennox. That he was de Brus' man was clear for the two stood close together. I was filled with dread when the king smiled. It did not bode well.

The Hunt

"This war is almost over, Warbow, and I thank you for your service. As a reward, you may have the manor of Lucton which is no longer in the hands of the family who have refused to accept our rule."

The manor of Lucton had been without a lord of the manor in residence for some time and it lay close to my land. I knew not the Scottish family that had received the income but as the manor was run down this was not a great prize. I smiled and bowed, "You are too kind, King Edward."

The frown told me that I had not masked my sarcasm well enough. His tone confirmed it, "When you have performed one last task then I might reward you with a greater prize. Wallace is in Selkirk Forest. I want him taken and delivered to London." I was about to speak but he continued, "This will not be as hard a hunt as before. The Sherriff here has heard that Wallace is to be found close to Kirkhope. That is a smaller place and he has few men with him. Take him and the Sherriff will deliver him to London."

I looked at de Brus and Menteith. They had impassive faces. The Earl of Carrick said, "I will have my men waiting at my manor of Guisborough. Take him hence and then you may head home, Sir Gerald. From there Sir Robert's men will take him to York and thence by ship to London. All will be arranged and all you need to do is catch the elusive rebel."

Wallace was being eliminated so that with Comyn and Balliol effectively out of the battle, the route to the crown lay clear for the earl.

Defeated I bowed, "I shall, as always, obey the king." As I bowed, I caught the eye of Rober de Brus. I wanted him to know that I had seen through his machinations.

We were about to mount our horses, having gathered as many provisions as we could, when Richard of Craven approached, "A word, Sir Gerald."

I knew even before he spoke that he came from the king. We walked a few paces away to stand in the shelter of the house in which we had stayed. It kept us from the icy wind and made it easier to speak without being overheard. Without a word being spoken Hamo and my archers made a defensive wall so that they prevented any, including themselves, from being privy to the king's command.

"The king is anxious that it is Sir John that makes the capture. He said that you were not to seek the glory for yourself even though it is well deserved."

I snorted, "And when have I ever sought glory?"

"Sorry, Sir Gerald, but the king…"

"I understand."

The Hunt

As I mounted Felix I began to work out the king's plan. Sir John was de Brus' man and, by this deception, he was making de Brus an enemy of Wallace's supporters. The nobles all supported one of the three contenders for the crown but the people all adored Wallace and the king was driving a wedge between de Brus and the people. That meant the king saw him as the real threat. I had once been a simple archer but living cheek-by-jowl with the king had given me an insight into the darker motives of men. I would be glad to get back to Yarpole.

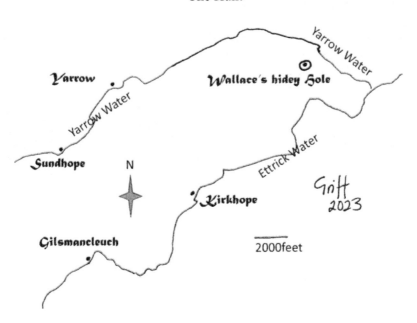

Yarrow

Yarrow Water

Wallace's hidey Hole

Yarrow Water

Sundhope

N

Ettrick Water

Kirkhope

Griff
2023

Gilsmancleuch

2000feet

Chapter 21

Silence was the order of the day as we approached Selkirk Forest. My men and I were not happy about our task. Wallace had done little since the skirmish at Turnberry. If he was a real threat then he would have raised men to make mischief back in Galloway or Selkirk but, despite his popularity, he remained hidden. We had not spoken much on the journey. My men and I were anxious to get home and Sir John seemed to me a solitary man not given to gregarious behaviour. We were men on a mission and the sooner it was completed the better.

We stopped at the trail that led into the forest. We had hunted Wallace here twice as well as seeking the Scottish rebels before Falkirk. My men were familiar with it. Selkirk apart, the places where people lived were hamlets and villages, often with less than ten houses. We could expect no help from the locals, in fact, we could expect the opposite. They would try to put us off the scent. The fawning faces would hide a hateful heart and we would have to use our own skills to find out where he was.

On one of the occasions when Sir John and I had spoken, I had asked how he knew that Wallace was in Kirkhope. "If he was seen then I would doubt the report for Wallace strikes me as a careful man."

The knight shook his head, "It was a priest, one of the earl's men who was returning from a pilgrimage to Jedburgh Abbey. He passed through the village and William Wallace appeared from nowhere and asked him if he would hear confession. The earl's priest would not report the conversation but felt obliged to speak of the encounter."

That made sense. Churches in such out of the way places were as common as hen's teeth. Encountering a priest, a warrior would take advantage and make a confession. Of course, it also told me that William Wallace would not be in Kirkhope but it gave us a place to start. When we had passed through Linlithgow I had sought and secured a map. It was crude but it allowed me to identify other places the fugitive might be using, much as he had done when we had sought him in Galloway. By moving from house to house he had a better chance of evading capture.

I had asked Sir John how many men Wallace had with him but the priest had not known. That, too, was useful information to me. Had there been a large number then the priest would have seen them. It meant he was not putting all his eggs in one basket. A large number of men would attract attention. As in Galloway his men would guard his safe houses and it would be Wallace who moved around.

The Hunt

We stopped, not in Selkirk itself for I knew there would be spies there but in the forests that lay between Ettrick Water and Yarrow Water. We took a circuitous route to get there, by-passing every village and using the forest trails. It took time, but as this would be our only opportunity to take him I wanted to track and hunt him as carefully as I would a wounded boar. There was a distance of just two miles between the two waters and no roads. The only paths were hunter's trails. When a man hunts, especially something as nervous as a creature like Wallace, one used the best hunters he could. That was not me. It might have been in my youth but now I was no longer the lean and hungry greyhound but a large and ungainly bear. Gwillim had the skills as did Hob and Ned. I used them to scout out Kirkhope. We waited in a camp which lacked a fire but afforded the shelter of trees and isolation. There were no game trails close to where we had chosen. I suspected that we might be the first people to set foot on the forest floor for centuries. We did not speak. There was no one close by but it seemed foolish to take the risk and we would only be talking to fill the silence. Until our three men who were moving on foot returned, then there was nothing worth saying.

They returned at dark having waited until then on the remote chance that someone had followed them. The sentries they passed on their way in kept a close watch after our scouts had entered our temporary home.

"Well?"

"We did not see William Wallace, but we did see one of the two men you let go from Lochmaben." That had to be one of the brothers and as they had been with Wallace both in Paris and Turnberry my hopes rose. "There were three others at the house in Kirkhope." Gwillim pointed south-eastwards, "The villagers there were friendly to them."

It was as I had thought, we would have no help in capturing these men from the locals.

"We rise before dawn. Hamo, leave three men to watch our camp and guard Sir John."

The Scotsman bridled, "I want to come with you."

"I want to be home in Yarpole and yet I am here and why? Because I obey the orders of the king. You are under my command. I know that my men and I can move like wraiths but it is not the time to test your skills. Secondly, I want you hidden until we reach Guisborough. If men realise that we are heading to Guisborough with the Earl of Carrick's man then we might have an ambush to contend with. I want Wallace delivered to the king alive."

The Scotsman was not happy but he nodded.

Losing an hour or two of sleep was not a problem when the prospect of catching Wallace loomed so large. We followed Gwillim through the forest for the handful of miles to the hamlet. My archers knew their business and Hamo detailed men to surround the village. I was confident that none would escape us and we had their numbers. Gwillim led Hamo and me to the rear of the house he had told us was used by the men he had recognised. We left Dick and Walter to guard it and then the three of us, with Hob and Ned, went around to the front.

The house was slightly larger than the others but just as mean and humble. It was made of rough stone and was one storey high. There was smoke coming from a chimney on the back wall, but the wind holes were all shuttered. They were too small for any but a child to use for egress. That left the back door and the front door. With two men watching the rear, Hamo tried the latch on the front. The door was barred. There was nothing for it but to demand that they leave.

I nodded to Ned who disappeared to seek an axe. He returned with a wood axe. He stood ready to smash through the ancient timber of the door and I banged on it and said, "Open up in the name of the king!"

My words were greeted by silence. The door of the house next to the one the rebels were using opened and a woman put her head out.

"Who lives here?"

In answer, she slammed shut the door. I would deal with her later on. We could hear movements from within and I said, "Break down the door. Have your bows ready."

I drew my sword and rondel. The other three nocked their arrows and loosely drew them. I heard a shout from the rear and a double cry. Walter and Dick had done their job. Only Ned was close to the door and as his axe finally shattered the door and broke through the bar, three men ran out. Ned was quick thinking and swung his axe hacking into the leg of one man. A second lunged at me with a spear and Hamo's arrow slammed into his chest. The third man was Jack Short and he emerged with a sword and buckler. He looked around, like a frightened deer caught by hunters and he sought an escape. He was confronted with three bows all pointing at him and my sword which was at his neck. He dropped his buckler and sword.

Smiling he said, "I am glad to see you, Sir Gerald."

I snorted, "I doubt that. Hamo, Gwillim, see if the house is empty." The two entered the house. "Ned, stay here with the rest. I want no one to leave their homes until I return."

"Yes, Sir Gerald."

I saw Jack Short look at the man whose leg had been hacked almost clean through by Ned's axe. He had bled out. The one with the arrow in his chest was barely breathing and would soon expire. Wallace's close companion looked up at me, "Aye, Short, your life hangs by a thread. I gave you and your brother your lives once and you repaid me by helping William Wallace to escape. You must have known about the attempt on my life."

He shook his head and babbled, "No, no, my lord. We knew nothing about that."

He was lying and I knew it. The door opened and Hamo emerged. "It is empty. Two tried to flee from the back but they were slain by Walter and Dick."

"Have them and Gwillim join the others and watch the village. You and I will enjoy a private conversation with Jack Short."

The only light in the tiny dwelling came from the fire. Someone had to have been up early to light it for it blazed brightly and made the mean room seem almost cosy. I sheathed my sword but placed my dagger on the table. "Sit."

There were four chairs and I pushed Short onto one of them. Hamo returned and we sat on two others. I took the rondel and placed it in the coals of the fire to heat up the blade. Short licked his lips nervously; he knew what was being threatened.

"Sir Gerald, there is no need for that. I will tell you all that you need to know. I can deliver you William Wallace for I know where he is hiding."

Hamo snorted derisively, "We let you go once, what makes you think we will make the same mistake twice?"

"My son is right, Short. You have used up all the chances that I give a man." I turned the blade in the fire.

Jack Short shook his head, "I am no longer William Wallace's man." I took the dagger from the fire and spat on it. The spit sizzled. "He killed my brother."

I did not return the blade to the fire but held it. "Go on."

"We were playing dice in the house of the Viking after we escaped from Turnberry. He said that Bob was cheating." I cocked an eye. "What if he was? He did not deserve to have his life taken from him. He was butchered and the others laughed." He shook his head, "The man was trying to impress the Vikings. He wanted them to fight with us. He sacrificed my brother and for what? They just delivered us on the shore of the Forth and left."

For some reason, I believed him but I needed to hear more of the story. "Then why did you not leave sooner?"

"The others who surround him are fanatics. They would have slit my throat had I tried to leave." He nodded his head towards the door. "I let them go first."

He was still lying but understandably so, "Then why come out with a drawn sword and shield?"

"The villagers are all Wallace supporters. Give me my life and I will lead you to him but bind me and make me look like a prisoner."

I looked at Hamo who said, "He is a lying little weasel and I would trust an adder more than I would trust him."

"Where is Wallace to be found?"

"There is a house on a high piece of ground close to where Ettrick Water meets Yarrow Water. He is there with eight men."

"Are there any other houses?"

He shook his head. "The house belonged to a man killed at Falkirk. James Bowhill was a friend of William Wallace and died without heirs. We often use the house when we are here in the Selkirk Forest. Few know of its existence. There is water close by and we can hunt."

"And how far away is it?"

"No more than four miles away."

"Are there horses?"

"Three."

I knew that if he was telling me the truth then we had to act fast. If he was lying then the same was true.

"Hamo, bind him."

"You believe him?"

Although the dagger had cooled it was still hot and I placed it close to Jack Short's nose. He tried to pull back. "If he lies then he will die slowly."

"I swear Sir Gerald, I speak the truth."

"We shall see."

I went to the door and waved over Gwillim.

"Yes, my lord?"

"I think we have Wallace. According to Short, he is in a house at the confluence of the two waters. Have Dick and Walter return to the camp. Tell them to bring the others, and Sir John, as well as the horses. They can follow the Yarrow Water downstream. According to our friend in there, it is no more than four or five miles from here. Wallace has men with him and they are fanatics but the house is isolated. We have a chance."

"Yes, my lord."

He hurried to the two men. I looked down at the two bodies. They needed to be covered up but I could use them. The sun had risen and it promised to be a warm day. Soon the bodies would stink. I cupped my hands, "Archers, I want every villager here, now, on their knees before me."

There were less than eight houses in the hamlet and fewer than twenty people were brought forth. Defiance glared in the eyes of some while others looked terrified. Hamo timed the fetching of the prisoner to perfection and the people were all on their knees when he dragged Jack Short out.

"You are all enemies of King Edward. I would be well within my rights to execute you all now and burn your homes to the ground." My words were greeted by hatred but also silence. "I intend to take this man back to my king for punishment. If any attempt is made to follow us then I swear that I will return and make it as though this place never existed. There are bodies to be buried. You shall do that. My men will watch the village and any who disobey me will be punished." I nodded to Hamo who pushed Jack Short towards the path that led north and east, back towards our camp.

I followed and my archers walked backwards. As I passed Ned and Hob I said, quietly, "We will head along the Ettrick beck. Watch the path and if any try to follow discourage them. You can catch up with us."

Ned nodded, "Aye, my lord."

We headed up the path for a couple of hundred paces and then I stopped. "Which way?"

Short nodded towards a barely discernible track that led northeast, "Up there. Will you cut my bonds, my lord?"

"When Wallace is bound and fettered then and only then will I loose you. Until then you will be tethered like a dangerous dog."

The trail was not a wide one and certainly not well used. That made sense. If this was Wallace's refuge then he would not want it widely known. I now knew that his sightings had been deliberate. He had made it seem as though he was staying in places other than his hidey-hole. He had learned from our joint past. I had hunted him in the houses and villages of Galloway when he had moved his men from one to the other. He had known that I would hunt him and this way he had hoped that I would make a mistake and allow him to turn the tables on me and ambush me in his hunting ground.

When Jack Short halted I knew we were close and when I caught the faint smell of woodsmoke then it was confirmed. We were close to the house. I gathered my men. "Dick, I want you to guard this man. If he tries to escape or to warn those in the house, slit his throat."

"With pleasure, my lord." My men had all thought it had been a mistake to let the prisoners go after Lochmaben. Ned and Hob arrived, "Well?"

"Two men tried to follow. Our arrows did not kill them but both will not be walking easily again for some time."

I nodded ahead, "We have one chance to end this hunt. Wallace is in the house we can smell but cannot see. He will be oblivious, for a while, to the fact that we have taken his men at Kirkhope. Gwillim, take half of our men and get to the Yarrow Water and cut off his escape route that way. Hamo, you lead the others on this side. We are hunters and Wallace is our prey. He must be taken alive but the rest can all be slain. According to this man," I almost spat the words out, "they are fanatics. We take no chances. They have three horses. If Wallace mounts one then kill the horse."

Gwillim said, "Do we have a signal?"

"We will give you time to get into position. The wind is from the east and so they will only smell you once you are close to Yarrow Water." They all nodded. "When this is done we deliver the rebel to Guisborough and then we go home. Our work will be done."

They had unstrung their bows in Kirkhope and now they each took a new string and strung their bows. I watched as each one chose the best three arrows from their bag of arrows and, when they were ready Gwillim waved to them to lead them off. Hamo nodded to the others and they spread out in a line. I drew my sword and dagger. We waited. Hamo and I were counting in our heads. When I reached a thousand I looked over to Hamo. He pointed with his bow and the archers began to move through the trees. Each of them stepped carefully. Had Sir John been with us then he would have stepped on a twig or brushed a branch. I followed Hamo and his footsteps.

The land had been cleared close to the house but allowed to run to weeds. It gave the house a derelict look. To any approaching then it would have appeared deserted. The tendril of smoke rising in the air gave that the lie. We paused to look for movement. I studied the house. It had two stories. James Bowhill must have been from a family of means. As I studied it I caught sight of a movement close to the chimney. There was a watcher and in the same instant that I saw him, he saw me and I heard his shout a heartbeat before Hamo's arrow slammed into him and knocked him from his lofty perch. I cursed myself. I should have asked Short about sentries.

We ran.

Jack Short had been right. The men were fanatics and they did not see the overwhelming numbers and surrender but barred the doors and

211

prepared to defend themselves. With Gwillim on the far side, we had them trapped. No matter what happened we would have William Wallace but I needed him alive. We were just twenty paces from the house when the three horses and riders galloped down towards the stream. One of them was Wallace. They had clearly no idea that Gwillim and my men were by the stream for one of the riders was plucked from his saddle by an arrow and William Wallace and the other man jinked their mounts around. The second rider suddenly spread his arm as though he was crucified and fell from his saddle. It was then that the last of Wallace's men ran from the house and raced to save their leader. They were brave but my archers were the best and every one of Wallace's defenders fell. Wallace could not escape. He reined in and looked around but all that he saw was a band of bowmen and their arrows were all aimed at him.

When Sir John Menteith and my mounted archers arrived he shook his head, "So de Brus has betrayed me." No one said anything. He looked at me, "You are persistent, Warbow. My men called you Wallace's Bane, you know?"

"William Wallace, I arrest you in the name of King Edward. Hand over your sword."

He dismounted and patted the horse's neck affectionately. "He is not my king and this is not his country. It is mine. I will not go without a fight."

I shook my head. "My men are the finest of archers. If I so commanded then they could pin your limbs so that you could not walk and we would take you to the king bound and bandaged. He just wants you alive."

He drew his sword, "Warbow, I respect you. You fight well and you keep your word. Fight me now."

"Why? Do you think that if you win and kill me my men will let you go?"

He shrugged, "Perhaps they will end my life here with their arrows which will be a better end than bowing the knee to Longshanks." I found myself admiring the man. He was trapped and he had lost yet there was a dignity in him.

I think Hamo suspected that I would do as the man said for he shook his head, "Father, there is nothing to be gained from this."

I unfastened my cloak and drew my sword, "We have been on a hunt these last years. The longest hunt of my life. If we had hunted a boar and now had it surrounded then we would give it an honourable end. William Wallace is not an animal. He is a man who is noble not through birth but through actions. He deserves to fight his last fight as a warrior." I made the sign of the cross, held up my sword and kissed the crosspiece, "Besides, I believe that God is on my side."

Wallace grinned and then copied me, "And you, too, are the kind of man alongside whom I should have loved to fight. Lay on and may the best man win."

He held his long sword two handed and advanced towards me. I had my sword and rondel dagger. He had the advantage of length. He could sweep his sword in wide arcs and keep me at bay. As I advanced, I studied the ground. The long grass and weeds made our footing treacherous. One slip could result in death. I knew that the king wanted him alive to stand trial but Robert's words rang in my ears. He was not a traitor and, at best, was a prisoner of war. Perhaps the kindest thing would be to kill him. He would no longer be a threat to England, and he deserved the dignity of a warrior's death. God knows I had given enough wounded warriors such an end.

For a big man, he was remarkably light on his feet and when he suddenly took giant steps and swung his sword at my head he almost had me. However, he made the mistake of swinging from his left to right. I brought my sword up and while the blow might have defeated a knight, I was an archer and the oak that was my right arm held. Sparks flew but his sword came no closer to me. I showed him my speed as I rammed my rondel at his right arm. I decided I did not want him dead. The king could be vindictive and I wanted no punishment for my family. I would do all in my power to take him alive. The blade raked through his clothes and tore into the flesh. He nodded and stepped back.

"You are strong, I will give you that."

I nodded and prepared to strike. He wanted to talk and I would lull him with words, "Strong enough to survive the poisoning."

He frowned, "You should know I did not want that. I wanted you dead but by a blade so that you had a chance of life."

I swung my sword backhanded and caught him unawares. He blocked it but the force of my strike knocked his sword back and his own sword scarred his cheek. Blood dripped.

"God, it seems, is turning your own weapon against you."

His eyes narrowed and I had angered him. He lifted his sword as though to bring it down and split me in two but, at the last moment changed to smash the pommel at my head. My quick reactions saved me for I made a cross of my dagger and sword and slowed down the blow. I was still knocked from my feet and as he raised his sword to end my life, I heard yew bows creak.

Rolling to the side I shouted, "Hold your arrows!" I swept my sword at his feet and he danced backward allowing me to rise and advance. The blood seeping from his arm and face were not hurting him yet but they would, and I had endured enough of this. Wallace was not worth making Mary a widow. I swung my sword at his head and when he blocked it I lunged and stabbed him in the thigh with my dagger. He reeled and I swung my sword at his hands. He wore gauntlets but the blow was so hard that he jumped back and winced. I stabbed at his hand with my dagger and the tip entered the leather and drove through to the flesh. He could not hold his sword and it dropped to the ground.

I had my dagger at his throat, "It is over."

His eyes blinked and he said, huskily, "You are the better man and deserve your victory. Give me a warrior's death I beg of you."

Shaking my head I said, "That I cannot do for I am still King Edward's man. Hamo!"

Hamo and Gwillim ran up and took the rebel's sword and bound him.

"See to his hurts." I sheathed my sword. "And now we go home."

Epilogue

I let Jack Short go. My men thought he should have been punished but I think the betrayal of William Wallace and its ignominy would be enough. The journey to Guisborough proved to be more pleasant than I had expected. Wallace and I got on well. It was Sir John who was the outsider. When we left the man we had hunted for years, at Guisborough, our parting was sad. He had done what he had done for his country. I had done the same for mine. There was neither right nor wrong on our part. Those who ruled or aspired to rule were a different matter. The escort to York provided by the Earl of Carrick was a formidable one. He would not be able to escape.

We had been away from Yarpole for so long that Susanna had given birth to John and the bairn was able to giggle and to smile. Mary had grown greyer but was still as beautiful. A month after my return a rider brought me the deeds to Lucton and to the manor of Sadberge. Sadberge lay to the north of the River Tees and I wondered at King Edward's gift. It was Robert who deduced a reason.

"It is a manor that lies within twenty miles of the Earl of Carrick's manors at Herterpol and Guisborough. King Edward is keeping his watchdog close to his enemies."

Mary shook her head, "Surely it is over now. Wallace is in chains and the king has Scotland."

I shook my head, "This is still the Great Cause for King Edward. Until Scotland is in his grip as Wales is he will not cease. The ulcer that is Scotland will continue to cause us pain but, for the moment, I am home and I can enjoy my grandchildren and Yarpole. The warrior is home."

The End

Glossary

An Còrsa Feàrna- Carsphairn in Galloway
Banneret- the rank of knight below that of earl but above a bachelor knight
Bachelor knight- a knight who had his own banner but fought under the banner of another
Centenar- commander of one hundred men (archers)
Familia- Household knights of a great lord
Hogbog- a place on a farm occupied by pigs and fowl
Mainward- the main body of an army (vanguard- mainward- rearguard)
Vintenar- a commander of twenty men (archers)
Wallintun- Warrington

Canonical Hours
- Matins (nighttime)
- Lauds (early morning)
- Prime (first hour of daylight)
- Terce (third hour)
- Sext (noon)
- Nones (ninth hour)
- Vespers (sunset evening)
- Compline (end of the day)

Historical Note

King Edward's war in Flanders did happen. Men were sent to raid northern France but the main attack was on the port of Damme. Gerald Warbow's chevauchée is my fictionalised account of what would have occurred over a wider front. Damme fell to a mixture of English and Flemish. Its success was marred by Stirling Bridge. The Flemish campaign allowed Sir Andrew Murray and William Wallace to trap and defeat the Earl of Surrey. Although many knights died at Stirling Bridge, it was the loss of archers and spearmen that was the greatest cost.

One incident that has me puzzled was Wallace's decision not to attack Durham but to head for Newcastle. I have travelled that road many times and from Bowes to Durham is a relatively short journey. Newcastle is further away. All I can assume is that the snowstorm stopped east of Durham. His route north was determined by the rivers he had to ford. He was held at Newcastle and then took his army north but Wallace had not been beaten and he retired to Selkirk Forest where he used the archers there to defend the camp while he trained men. He was draconian in his recruitment and men were not allowed to refuse service. His army was largely one of the people. The schiltrons fought in huge circles that cavalry could not penetrate. Wallace had few knights with his army.

When the king came north again to punish the Scots, he did bring Welsh mercenaries, ten thousand of them. His supply ships failed to reach him and the hunger of his men caused the Welsh mutiny. Priests were slain by the drunk fuelled Welshmen and they paid little part in the Battle of Falkirk. The incident with the horse and the king's broken ribs did happen. Sir Ralph Basset did insult the Bishop of Durham and caused his men to recklessly charge a schiltron. The account we have of the battle from Guisborough, the monk who recorded the events, notes that the retinue of Basset lost not a horse which suggests he took little part in the actual fighting. The English horsemen did drive the Scottish horse from the field but it was the archers who won the battle. Wallace did flee to France to seek help there. William Wallace was part of one successful battle, Stirling Bridge, but the architect of that battle, Sir Andrew Murray, died of his wounds. Had King Edward not gone to Flanders but completed the work begun at Dunbar then the land of Scotland might have become English far sooner than it did.

The taking of Lochmaben Castle was the trigger for King Edward to head north to punish the perpetrators. It was the Maxwell family who took the castle and then retreated to their fortress. King Edward brought a huge army north and it was like taking a sledgehammer to smash a walnut. Once the trebuchets were constructed the castle fell in just two days. Remarkably the castle was held by just sixty men.

It took a long time for King Edward to defeat the Scots. The campaigns lasted years and he did spend two winters in Scotland. Warwolf existed and his words to the defenders were the actual ones he used. He wanted to see his mighty machine in action and the siege lasted a week longer than it needed to. De Brus was defeated and joined King Edward to fight Comyn. Comyn's ambush is fiction but, as the next book will show, the bad blood between the Earl of Carrick and Comyn involved murder so the ambush is justified. Comyn never faced King Edward in battle. He rarely had more than a thousand men. Robert de Brus also used his castles for defence rather than risking battle. The only man who could have led a Scottish army was William Wallace and Falkirk was his only opportunity to do so.

Wallace's whereabouts after Falkirk are still shrouded in mystery. We know he went to both Paris and Rome but that is all. Comyn, Balliol and de Brus appear to have shunned the enigmatic man adored by the ordinary people. Wallace was betrayed by Jack Short who explained his action by saying Wallace had killed his brother. Sir John did take the rebel to the king. I have used the bones of the story and dressed them with a story of my own invention.

Gerald Warbow's story is not over but it is drawing to a close. The journey is unfinished, yet.

Griff Hosker
July 2023

Other books by Griff Hosker

If you enjoyed reading this book, then why not read another one by the author?

Ancient History

The Sword of Cartimandua Series
(Germania and Britannia 50 A.D. – 128 A.D.)
Ulpius Felix- Roman Warrior (prequel)
The Sword of Cartimandua
The Horse Warriors
Invasion Caledonia
Roman Retreat
Revolt of the Red Witch
Druid's Gold
Trajan's Hunters
The Last Frontier
Hero of Rome
Roman Hawk
Roman Treachery
Roman Wall
Roman Courage

The Wolf Warrior series
(Britain in the late 6th Century)
Saxon Dawn
Saxon Revenge
Saxon England
Saxon Blood
Saxon Slayer
Saxon Slaughter
Saxon Bane
Saxon Fall: Rise of the Warlord
Saxon Throne
Saxon Sword

Medieval History

The Dragon Heart Series
Viking Slave *

The Hunt

Viking Warrior *
Viking Jarl *
Viking Kingdom *
Viking Wolf
Viking War
Viking Sword
Viking Wrath
Viking Raid
Viking Legend
Viking Vengeance
Viking Dragon
Viking Treasure
Viking Enemy
Viking Witch
Viking Blood
Viking Weregeld
Viking Storm
Viking Warband
Viking Shadow
Viking Legacy
Viking Clan
Viking Bravery

The Norman Genesis Series
Hrolf the Viking *
Horseman
The Battle for a Home
Revenge of the Franks
The Land of the Northmen
Ragnvald Hrolfsson
Brothers in Blood
Lord of Rouen
Drekar in the Seine
Duke of Normandy
The Duke and the King

Danelaw
(England and Denmark in the 11th Century)
Dragon Sword *
Oathsword *
Bloodsword *
Danish Sword

The Hunt

New World Series
Blood on the Blade *
Across the Seas *
The Savage Wilderness *
The Bear and the Wolf *
Erik The Navigator *
Erik's Clan
The Last Viking

The Vengeance Trail *

The Conquest Series
(Normandy and England 1050-1100)
Hastings

The Aelfraed Series
(Britain and Byzantium 1050 A.D. - 1085 A.D.)
Housecarl *
Outlaw *
Varangian *

The Reconquista Chronicles
Castilian Knight *
El Campeador
The Lord of Valencia

**The Anarchy Series England
1120-1180**
English Knight *
Knight of the Empress *
Northern Knight *
Baron of the North *
Earl *
King Henry's Champion *
The King is Dead
Warlord of the North
Enemy at the Gate
The Fallen Crown
Warlord's War
Kingmaker
Henry II

The Hunt

Crusader
The Welsh Marches
Irish War
Poisonous Plots
The Princes' Revolt
Earl Marshal
The Perfect Knight

Border Knight
1182-1300
Sword for Hire *
Return of the Knight *
Baron's War *
Magna Carta *
Welsh Wars *
Henry III
The Bloody Border
Baron's Crusade
Sentinel of the North
War in the West
Debt of Honour
The Blood of the Warlord
The Fettered King
de Montfort's Crown

Sir John Hawkwood Series
France and Italy 1339- 1387
Crécy: The Age of the Archer *
Man At Arms *
The White Company *
Leader of Men *
Tuscan Warlord
Condottiere

Lord Edward's Archer
Lord Edward's Archer *
King in Waiting
An Archer's Crusade
Targets of Treachery
The Great Cause
Wallace's War
The Hunt

The Hunt

Struggle for a Crown
1360- 1485
Blood on the Crown *
To Murder a King *
The Throne *
King Henry IV *
The Road to Agincourt *
St Crispin's Day *
The Battle for France *
The Last Knight *
Queen's Knight *

Tales from the Sword I
(Short stories from the Medieval period)

Tudor Warrior series
England and Scotland in the late 15th and early 16th century
Tudor Warrior *
Tudor Spy
Flodden

Conquistador
England and America in the 16th Century
Conquistador *
The English Adventurer

Modern History

The Napoleonic Horseman Series
Chasseur à Cheval
Napoleon's Guard
British Light Dragoon
Soldier Spy
1808: The Road to Coruña
Talavera
The Lines of Torres Vedras
Bloody Badajoz
The Road to France
Waterloo

The Lucky Jack American Civil War series

The Hunt

Rebel Raiders
Confederate Rangers
The Road to Gettysburg

Soldier of the Queen series
Soldier of the Queen
Redcoat's Rifle

The British Ace Series
1914
1915 Fokker Scourge
1916 Angels over the Somme
1917 Eagles Fall
1918 We will remember them
From Arctic Snow to Desert Sand
Wings over Persia

Combined Operations series
1940-1945
Commando *
Raider
Behind Enemy Lines
Dieppe
Toehold in Europe
Sword Beach
Breakout
The Battle for Antwerp
King Tiger
Beyond the Rhine
Korea
Korean Winter

Tales from the Sword II
(Short stories from the Modern period)

Books marked thus *, are also available in the audio format.
For more information on all of the books then please visit the
author's website at www.griffhosker.com where there is a link to
contact him or visit his Facebook page: GriffHosker at Sword Books or
follow him on Twitter: @HoskerGriff

Printed in Great Britain
by Amazon

41433075R00126